Nasty
Business

Gillian Godden

BOOKS BY
GILLIAN GODDEN

Francesca
Dangerous Games
Nasty Business

ISBN: 9781075399657

ACKNOWLEDGEMENTS

Thank you to Deryl Easton and the NotRights Book Club on Facebook for their help, encouragement and support.

Sincere thanks to my neighbour, Avril, for reading drafts, supporting me, and encouraging me to keep going.

Many thanks to my editor, Julie Lewthwaite, whose patience and guidance turned a writer into an author.

And finally, special thanks to my son, Robert; the best son any mother could have.

AUTHOR'S NOTE

No character in this book is based on any person, alive or dead.

CONTENTS

1

OPENING NIGHT

At long last, the club was ready. It seemed to have taken forever to gut and fully renovate the bossman's old club in the West End of London, but now the wait was over. Lambrianu's was no longer just a dream – it had become a reality.

Tony Lambrianu, the manager, had walked round it with Jake Sinclair – his business partner and the man he thought of as his brother – Jake's wife, Sharon, and Elle, who had fostered both boys from a young age. They looked at the furnishings and took in the whole ambience, and they were astonished by the transformation.

The building works had been watched by the public, as they passed by on their way to work each day. Buses full of passengers and black cabs driving through the West End all seemed to be waiting for the finished result. It seemed the large building – now no longer surrounded by scaffolding and covered by long dust sheets – had attracting a lot of public interest.

Tony's request that the sign, outside, should be pink neon had initially seemed shocking, but there was no denying it worked. The designers had continued the pink theme inside, to create an intimate atmosphere.

The bar was circular, the black top resting on a chrome base, and chrome stools with pink leather seats surrounded it. The dance floor looked like it was made of large glass tiles. Multi-coloured lights flashed and flared beneath it, lighting up the whole area, making it the centrepiece of the club. The theme continued with round black tables, surrounded by horseshoe-shaped pink leather sofas. There were private booths for those who wanted to sit away from the crowds, in the company of their own party. High up, near the ceiling, was a large glass DJ's booth, and there was a stage, should they want to put on live entertainment. It all looked amazing.

CCTV had been installed both inside and outside of the club. Tony and Jake had their own office, and the CCTV monitors lined the walls, so they could watch everything that was going on. Tony had felt that this kept their finger on the pulse of the place. No one was going to creep up on him and walk in without warning, the way he had done to the South London mob boss, Marlon, and the hapless – now deceased – Eddie Rawlings.

All they needed, now, after all this hard work and waiting, were customers.

Sharon had suggested flyers advertising opening night and a notification in the local newspaper. Local tearaway, Dan, and his gang, had been given the job of posting the flyers everywhere and anywhere they could. Sharon had interviewed and hired bar staff, while Tony and Jake had sorted out security.

And now was the moment of truth; would anyone actually turn up?

Everything was in place. Two of the bouncers, smartly dressed in black suits and ties, were in charge of the doors, supposedly keeping the crowds safe – if there were any crowds. The bar staff and waitresses stood ready, dressed in black trousers, white shirts and pink bow ties.

Tony stood at the bar on opening night, having a drink with Sharon and Jake, impatiently waiting for the clock to strike nine. That was opening time. This project would either take off and be a success, or turn out to have been a money pit and a waste of time.

The club felt like an empty ghost town and suddenly twice the size. Even though there was excitement in the air, there was also nervous tension, and none of them had much to say to each other.

The bar staff were polishing the glasses and making themselves busy, to pass the time. The waitresses stood at the side of the bar, waiting patiently for some customers. It felt like time had stopped. Everyone seemed bored and restless; even when the music started up, it didn't seem to make much difference.

'I can't stand this anymore,' said Jake, 'I feel sick. I'm going to take a look outside to see if there's anyone around.' No matter what happened, both Jake and Tony knew they had to put on a brave face and look confident. At this stage there was nothing else they could do.

Moments later, Jake came running back over, nearly tripping up in his haste. His eyes were wide and his face wore a shocked expression. 'Tony! Tony!' he shouted.

Tony was still standing at the bar with Sharon. He was drinking a large whisky for Dutch courage. They turned to Jake on hearing him shout and, even in the dimly lit club, they could see the colour had drained from his face.

Jake was out of breath, he was panting and trying to speak at the same time.

'There's a queue around the block, loads of people are waiting to come in! Come and see.'

Jake led the way, almost running the full length of the club to get back to the doors. Tony and Sharon followed. Looking past the bouncers on the doors, Tony saw a long line of people patiently waiting for the doors to open. He looked at the bouncers and then back at the queue, then turned to go back inside. 'Let them in,' he said.

The three of them went and stood at the far side of the bar, almost in the shadows, and watched as people came flooding through the doors.

A blonde woman wearing a very expensive-looking pink gown walked in first, with a party of similarly dressed men and women hot on her heels. 'Champagne!' she shouted at the bar staff. Silver champagne buckets were filled with ice and corks were popped. The staff, recently idle, were now rushed off their feet, trying to keep up with orders.

More and more people came through the doors. Many followed the blonde woman's lead and ordered champagne. She was adorned in diamonds that Sharon assured Tony and Jake had to be the real thing. She sat in the middle of one of the private booths, men and women seated each side of her, as though holding court.

The three of them watched as an older man walked up to her, kissed her on the cheek and sat at her side. He was dressed in a tuxedo, and had an air of authority. Everyone seemed to know him. One of the waitresses walked up to Jake.

'Mr Sinclair,' she said, 'that woman over there keeps ordering champagne, but she isn't paying for it. She keeps telling the bar staff to put it on her account. Do you know her? Does she have an account?' She looked worried.

Tony and Jake looked over at the woman, and the man that had joined her. They were now circling the room, stopping to talk to people and shaking hands with them. Tony and Jake's curiosity was roused. The woman got louder and louder as she drank more champagne, then she started moving in time to the music.

Jake was just about to call the bouncers to escort her out when her male companion was suddenly in the shadows at their side. He held out his hand towards them. 'Ralph Gold,' he said, 'and that lady over there, encouraging your customers to buy champagne and have a good time, is my wife, Julie.'

Ralph Gold? Tony looked at Jake, and then back at the man. This was his club. He owned it. Tony, for the time being, was only the manager. This was the man he was hoping to buy it off, in a year's time. Tony's heart sank. They had both obviously come to see what he had done with the place, and to keep an eye on him. He felt almost embarrassed; this man and that woman were, effectively, his bosses!

Tony held out his hand to shake Ralph's. 'Tony Lambrianu, and this is my brother, Jake Sinclair,' he said.

The man was smiling and, in between talking to them, kept looking over at his wife, who was now encouraging everyone on to the dance floor.

'It seems to me that you two gentlemen are shirking your hosting duties,' Ralph said. 'People want to know who the man is whose name is in pink neon above the door, and to meet the owner.'

Tony nodded and he and Jake walked towards the centre of the bar with Ralph Gold. People instantly recognized Ralph and walked up to him.

'This is Tony Lambrianu and this is Jake Sinclair,' said Ralph, introducing them to the people gathered around him. A sea of hands came out to shake theirs.

Julie walked up to them. 'Come on, we need to show them how to dance.' She pulled Tony forward, and into the midst of people.

Sharon nudged Jake with her elbow. 'Isn't he the owner?' she said.

Jake nodded, but he also found it strange that Ralph was not introducing himself as such.

The Golds were telling the party of people they were with that they had seen the club being renovated and, being a 'family friend' of Tony Lambrianu, just had to dance the night away at his new club.

'More champagne,' shouted Tony, trying to fight his way back to the bar and away from the crowds. For the moment, he just wanted to stand and watch all the people that were in his club. What only a few hours ago had been a ghost town was now a thriving, noisy nightclub, crammed to the rafters with people enjoying themselves.

Tony felt a tap on his shoulder and was pleased to see Marlon, the South London mob boss. As a gesture of goodwill, he had made a point of sending him a personal invitation.

'Nice club, Tony, business must be good.' Marlon smiled and shook hands with Tony and Jake, like they were old friends. 'Your DJ isn't so hot, though. Tell you what … I know a young guy, freelancing, he's good, gets the people going. If you like him, you do and if you don't, no skin off my nose, he doesn't work for me.'

Tony felt this was Marlon's reciprocal gesture of goodwill; he was trying to help him. He knew he had a lot to learn about the nightclub business and was prepared to listen to friendly advice.

Sharon was mingling with the women and showing them the ladies' room, which was large and full of mirrors, and even had a sofa inside it. Everyone seemed to be having a good time. It was a great success. Then Jake walked over. 'Have you seen who just walked in, Tony?'

Tony looked across the room and again, his heart sank. He took a deep breath, expecting trouble. Walking towards him was the detective from Scotland Yard who had been involved in the diamond heist investigation. He didn't walk up to Tony and Jake; instead, he walked up to Ralph Gold and shook his hand like they were old friends. They were talking and drinking, and even Ralph's wife, Julie, was joking with him and trying to encourage him to dance.

'Friends in high places, eh?' said Tony, looking at Jake and then back to the three of them, laughing and joking together. As the night went on, Tony began to relax. He had made a point of drinking with Marlon until Marlon had been swept away by some young woman who wanted to dance. He began to mingle, and to enjoy himself. He introduced himself, and everyone seemed pleased to meet him. It felt like a parallel world. Not that long ago, these people would have passed by him in the street, without giving him a second look. Now he was Tony Lambrianu, the club owner and their new best friend!

'Evening, Mr Lambrianu.'

Tony looked up to see the detective reaching out his hand to shake his. *Mr Lambrianu*? Tony couldn't believe his ears. Tony shook his hand, and for the sake of something to say, asked him if he was enjoying himself.

The detective nodded, and took a large gulp of his whisky. Seeing that his glass was nearly empty, Tony raised his hand to a member of the bar staff to fetch a fresh one, then stopped the detective when he saw he was going to take out his wallet.

'This one's on the house,' he said.

'Thanks.' The detective looked around. 'Nice club, Mr Lambrianu, it looks very different to the last time I was here.' He looked directly at Tony. They both knew that the last time the detective was there was after he had been anonymously tipped off that the diamonds were in the bossman's safe. 'You have a very distinctive voice, I'd recognise those dulcet tones of yours anywhere.'

Tony had made a point of disguising his voice, so that the detective wouldn't recognize him, but it seemed his plan had failed.

He raised his glass to Tony and winked, even though he had let Tony know that he knew it was him that had made the call that day.

Thankfully, Julie Gold, now very tipsy, interrupted. 'Time for photos, boys,' she said. Julie Gold had got the local newspapers to come and take photos of the opening of this new West End club, with its elite customers. Tony and Jake stood side by side with Julie and Ralph, and smiled. Tony noticed the detective shied away from the photo shoot and stood off to one side.

'What's wrong with you, Jake?' asked Tony, when he noticed Jake just staring into the crowd. He was trying to follow his eyeline, but couldn't understand what was mesmerizing him.

'Look, Tony,' said Jake, not turning his eyes away. 'That

lot, over there, are some of the actors and singers from the West End shows, I've seen them on the television. Over there, those are models I've seen in Sharon's magazines. I can't take my eyes off them. Do you think I would look stupid if I asked them for an autograph?' Jake was star-struck, he couldn't help watching the crowd and spotting some celebrity or other.

'Don't you dare! If anyone's giving out autographs tonight, it's going to be you and me. Don't even think about it,' said Tony. The last thing he wanted was Jake looking like an amateur.

'Sorry, Tony, I can't help it. I've never seen so many famous people.'

'I must say, though, I think I might just go over there and introduce myself to some of those models. Very nice indeed.' Tony put on his most charming smile, straightened his tie and went over to join a group of young women. Their long hair was flowing and their make-up was immaculate. Their designer dresses had the labels on the outside, so that people would know whose clothes they wore. They posed for photos, and Jake could see they were very impressed by this handsome, blonde club owner, who oozed charm.

The night, or rather the early hours of the morning, was coming to an end. The music became slower and people were starting to leave. Everyone seemed to have had a good night, and many made a point of walking up to Tony and Jake and saying goodnight.

The detective from earlier walked up to Tony. 'Nice club, this,' he said again. 'The police usually have a yearly ball, with their wives, but it's always so hard to find a venue. Do you know what I mean?'

Tony knew exactly what he meant; he wanted the club to host this annual ball, and Tony had no choice but to offer Lambrianu's as this year's venue. After all, if word got out that it had been Tony who had tipped off the police about the bossman's diamonds, people would think he was a police informer and his reputation would be in shreds. It was friendly blackmail, but blackmail nonetheless.

'Why don't you hold it here? We don't have a restaurant, but we could do a buffet.' Tony toned down the invitation, he didn't want to look overzealous.

'That would be very nice of you, Mr Lambrianu, I'm sure we could come up with some form of catering. Thank you, I'll be in touch.' He shook Tony's hand and walked away towards Ralph to say his goodbyes to him and Julie.

Ralph made a point of walking over to Tony, afterwards. 'I take it, by the look on your face, that he's asked you to host their annual ball?'

Tony gave Ralph a weak smile and nodded.

'Keep your friends close and your enemies closer, Tony, whoever they are. It's no skin off your nose.'

Again, Tony nodded. Than he realised he'd heard that saying before. He had once heard Don Carlos say that.

'Maybe we could talk business, sometime, Mr Gold.'

Instantly, Ralph shook his head. 'No business to talk about, Tony, and definitely not while I'm having an evening out with my wife. I talk business by appointment only.'

That was final. Ralph hadn't snubbed him; he had just made his point. Tony was not in his league; don't run before you can walk.

Tony waved Ralph and Julie off and walked over to Jake. 'I'm shattered,' he said. 'That Ralph Gold is a hard guy to get to know. How much money have we made, do you know?'

Sharon was behind the bar, checking the till receipts, and she handed them both a final tally of the night's takings. They both stared at it, then at each other. Tony picked up the receipt and walked into the light behind the bar. They had taken a fortune, it was unbelievable.

Sharon handed each of them a money bag, and they all walked towards their newly refurbished office. They filled the safe with the takings, and then turned to each other, giving out an enormous squeal of laughter and excitement, dancing around and hugging each other.

The staff were leaving, and Sharon noticed one of the young models Tony had been talking to earlier was still hanging around. 'Goodness sake, Jake, doesn't she want to go home? Show her out, will you.'

Tony walked towards Sharon. 'She is home, Sharon, for tonight, anyway. I've invited her to see my new apartment.' He gave her a wink and a smile, and walked towards the young woman with the blonde flowing hair, waiting at the bar.

'That, Jake, my love, is our cue to leave. Let the cleaners do the rest in the morning. Come on, let's go home.'

෨◊ർ

The following morning brought proof of just how successful the night had been. There they all were, in the local newspapers with Julie and Ralph Gold. The headlines were saying that this new place in town was the place to be – if you wanted a great night out, go to Lambrianu's.

Tony and Jake read the various newspapers, all giving great reviews.

The next night at the club was just the same, except the Golds weren't there. But, they all had to admit, the promotion from the Golds was definitely worth its weight in gold!

Tony noticed more leggy models came to the club, as it was the place to be. They brought their group of friends and their latest sugar daddies. Everyone knew that beautiful women attracted men, and so they would come flooding in, looking for the girl of their dreams.

After a couple of weeks, two accountants came to see Tony and Jake. They spoke in the office and informed them both that they were in charge of the money laundering that Don Carlos had spoken about.

These two men were to take charge of the money side of things, for the time being. They would make sure that all the money was accounted for, and that not a single pound laundered there could be traced back to them.

Tony and Jake felt that they were way out of their league, they had never been involved in anything like it. They both knew they were taking a big risk with their new business venture, but they had no choice, this was all part of the deal.

The accountants would have the laundered money picked up daily, by security guards. They sat in Tony's office, going through receipts and auditing the accounts. Neither Jake or Tony knew exactly what they did; it was all very confusing.

Two detectives came to see them. When they showed their ID badges, both Tony and Jake took a deep breath and swallowed hard, fearing their cover had been blown. They took the detectives into the office and Tony calmly asked what he could do for them. What they said caught him off guard.

They had been sent by the detective from Scotland Yard to discuss using the club for their annual ball. This wasn't what he'd expected, and to be fair, with everything going on at the moment, he had actually forgotten about agreeing to it.

They told Tony and Jake the provisional date for the ball, and the numbers they were expecting. The detectives seemed relaxed and friendly. They were thanking Tony for his hospitality; he couldn't believe his ears. For once, he was sitting in the same room as the police and he wasn't being accused of anything!

Once preliminary arrangements were made, they all shook hands and the detectives thanked Tony and Jake again. Of course, there had been no mention of paying for the venue, and as they were looking at a Saturday night for this forthcoming event, Tony felt sick inside.

It was the busiest night of the week; he would lose a fortune, having a private party. The small consolation was the bar takings but, they both agreed, they would be expected to play host and provide free bottles of wine.

Sharon's logic came to the rescue and made them feel better. She had a way of putting things in perspective.

'It's better to be on the right side of the devil, than have him breathing down your neck and raiding the place. If the police are here, no gangs are going to turn up and customers will feel it's a safe haven,' she said, after the police had left.

She had a fair point; the business and the money were a lot to lose, but in the long run, it could be to their advantage.

They all agreed it was for the best; yet again, Sharon was right – it could make or break them.

During the coming weeks, there were more photos in the newspapers and now word about the club was spreading to the glossy magazines. Tony enjoyed being the centre of attention; it seemed to come naturally to him. He ordered well-tailored suits, and made a point of being immaculately dressed at all times. The journalists revelled in it. What they particularly liked was writing about Tony's love life in all the gossip columns.

The women who visited the club seemed to flock towards Tony. He discovered power, money and authority attracted women, and he was more than prepared to take advantage of it. When Jake arrived at Tony's apartment in the mornings, there would be the usual scene of Tony saying goodbye to some woman he had met the night before. On occasion, Jake saw the same one twice, but it was always the same routine – Tony more or less threw them out in the morning, telling them they'd had their fun, now it was time to leave.

The hurt, disappointed looks on their faces as they left, wearing last night's clothes, were quickly followed by a sarcastic remark.

ഔ ◊ ഌ

For the evening of the long-awaited policemen's ball, the tables in the club were all arranged differently and half of the club was roped off for the catering. There was to be a large buffet delivered by a local restaurant.

'You know,' said Sharon, again stating the obvious, 'if we had a restaurant area, we could have made money on the food. In fact, that's not a bad idea, Tony. Get the customers in early. They all go out first, possibly for a meal or something, then they come here. If we provided both, they wouldn't have to go anywhere else.'

It was a good idea, but one to be shelved for the moment; they were still getting the hang of the club business, always being the showman, playing host and making sure everyone was having a good time. It sounded easy, but it was actually hard work, not to mention all the very late nights took their toll.

All the detectives of the police force and their wives seemed to be having a good time. Tony had laid on complimentary champagne, and went from table to table, introducing himself. He even took the liberty of dancing with the police commissioner's wife. Everyone was in high spirits.

One chief superintendent went and stood by Tony at the bar, and thanked him again for his hospitality – then the real reason for him standing with Tony came out.

'It's a shame this place is just a nightclub, Mr Lambrianu. I remember the old days, when it used to have the odd "exotic dancer" here. Bit of light relief after a long day, if you know what I mean.' He laughed at his own joke.

Tony remembered those days only too well, days when the bossman had some back-street prostitutes hanging around the place, laying on all kinds of entertainment. He didn't want that reputation for his club. He had tried too hard and come too far.

'Sorry, sir, this isn't that type of establishment.' Tony tried to be as respectful as he could to the man. He was wearing his uniform and there were all kinds of special buttons and honours on it. He saw the man's face drop. He was in his late fifties, and had obviously hoped to see some bare flesh before going home. 'It's not the kind of club I'm aiming for. Anyway, don't you need a special licence for that?' Tony tried to hide behind the legal requirements, rather than just flatly refuse to consider the idea. It was making him cringe inside.

'Laws are meant to be broken, Tony, my friend,' said the policeman; again, he laughed at his own joke.

Tony gave him a weak smile, he could feel himself blushing, and he felt cornered. Another high-ranking officer came to join them both, and for once Tony was relieved to see a policeman – until he spoke.

'He's right, you know, Mr Lambrianu. Dare I say it, but we are all men of the world. Some of the gentlemen here still pop around to the East End pubs for some light entertainment. You're a businessman, and a ladies man, I've read.'

Now Tony felt angry. He didn't want to cause a scene, but he felt he had to get his point across. 'I do understand what you're saying, gentlemen, and I also understand that the man who had this place before me had quite the knocking shop.' Tony used that term to make his point. 'Brothel' didn't seem to have the same impact. 'I'm trying to run a respectable nightclub, and I don't feel that's the way forward.' He gave his most charming smile, and made his excuses to leave, stating that he was needed elsewhere.

He walked into his office and found there was an accountant there, sitting at his desk, working out figures and having a drink with Jake. He seemed like a very professional man. His suit jacket hung over the back of the chair, his glasses were perched on the end of his nose, and he was constantly tapping away at his calculator.

'What's wrong with you, Tony?' Jake saw Tony's red, angry face, and watched him storm around the office. He was pacing and gritting his teeth.

'Those bloody high-ranking detectives out there only want me to start running some back-street strip club. Bloody hell, Jake, let the perverts find their own fun.'

'What, you mean all those respectable men out there want to stand toe to toe with some of the men they arrest, while ogling strippers?' Jake found it funny, but he could see Tony didn't.

'Not necessarily,' said the accountant. He was continuing with his work, but obviously paying attention to the conversation.

'What do you mean?' Tony gave him an icy glare.

The accountant took off his glasses; he wasn't shaken by Tony's response. After all, his bosses were much bigger fish in larger ponds. Tony was just a beginner, and he had been put there to guide him, whether he wanted to listen or not.

'What I mean, Tony,' said the accountant, 'is look at the Las Vegas showgirls. There's nothing cheap or tacky about them, and yet they wear the same skimpy underwear, it's just done with style and elegance. Anyway, your busiest nights are Thursday, Friday and Saturday; how much money are you wasting on electricity and staff wages the rest of the week? Even if you closed on those nights, it wouldn't be profitable.'

Tony couldn't believe what he was hearing. Now he really was angry. 'Are you saying we're running at a loss and making no money? Or is it because you keep fiddling around with the books!' He ran his hands through his hair and loosened his tie.

'No, I'm not saying that – and for the record, I don't touch your personal accounts, only the accounts I need to adjust, if you like. You knew I would be here when you accepted the job.'

The job? Tony felt his world was crumbling. The job? Is that all he was, some bar manager? 'Tell you what, you can shove your job up your arse, I'm out of here. Come on, Jake.'

Tony was about to walk out when Jake stopped him. 'Calm down,' he said. He tried reasoning with Tony. 'The place is crawling with police, don't make a scene. We both know it's a job we're doing for now. It gives us time to build a reputation. Nobody is saying this place isn't yours. Come on, your name's on the sign. Lambrianu's – it's your club.' He felt Tony had got carried away with everything and had forgotten he didn't own the place – yet.

Tony knew Jake was right; tonight was not the night to lose his cool. There were a lot of high-ranking officers out there. He didn't want to attract any attention or raise any suspicions.

He sat down and Jake handed him a drink. He was breathing heavily, and clearly upset.

'I didn't mean to undermine you, Tony.' The accountant looked apologetic. 'We both know who owns this place and we both know who he does business with. That's why he came to promote your club – to help you, the way you're helping him, with me. Capisce?'

Tony had his head in his hands. When he heard the accountant speak Italian, he looked up at him. 'You're Italian?'

The accountant nodded at him and smiled. 'As I was saying, done properly, the striptease idea isn't a bad one. It could be done earlier in the week, and then the place could revert to use as a nightclub the latter end of the week, with certain conditions.'

'Such as?' asked Jake. Even he was surprised that this man was Italian. There had been occasions he and Tony had spoken in Italian, so the other staff wouldn't understand what they were saying. Thank God they hadn't said anything bad about Ralph Gold or Don Carlos!

'Personally, now you're up and running, I think you should start charging people to come in. That would make the club more exclusive, and not just a "walk-in" joint. People like that, to be able to afford to come in, it makes them feel special. If you did have exotic dancers here, and it was all in good taste, again, they would have to pay to come in, they'd tip the girls, and you could pass off lower quality champagne at top prices. All these rich men want to impress the ladies.' The accountant smiled at Tony.

Now Tony was calming down, even he had to admit this man made sense. Paying to come in would make it more exclusive. It would seem like a treat and people would look forward to rubbing shoulders with the people who could afford it on a regular basis. Even the rich and famous liked to see pretty women taking their clothes off. Plus, if it was done exclusively for the wealthy, it wouldn't be the dirty mac brigade walking in off the streets. He looked at Jake and then at the accountant.

'How much do you think we should charge for the clubbers to come in and dance the night away, then?' Tony really didn't have a figure in mind. How much would people pay for a good night out? Surely, charging an entry fee would lose them custom.

'Considering everything they've read about you in the papers and magazines, a lot of people will want to come to see the man behind the stories, and then dance the night away. You would be their number one entertainment. I would say a hundred pounds, with discounts for parties, and so on.'

The accountant was all very nonchalant about charging a hundred pounds to enter a club, but he knew for a fact he wouldn't pay it himself.

Tony looked surprised. 'Are you saying I'm like some animal at the zoo that they all come to see, or something?' He was disgusted at the thought.

'You've made that reputation for yourself. You always have a lady on your arm. Gossip is circulating that your bed is never empty. The models love you, because there's no such thing as bad publicity. They have their photos taken with you, and before long their agents are ringing them with offers of a photo shoot. Let them pay for the pleasure.'

Tony blushed; he hadn't seen it like that. He was just having a little fun, but now he was in the public eye, he supposed everything was news. 'Okay, you're the accountant, let's try it,' he said.

'Go and see to your guests, we'll talk about this in the morning.' The accountant put his glasses back on, hunched over again and started tapping away at his calculator. Jake stood up and opened the door, indicating to Tony that they should both leave the man in peace.

Tony made a point of walking over to the superintendent he had spoken to earlier. 'Excuse me, sir. If I were to consider putting dancers on during the week, what licence would I need?' Tony showed him full respect, even though his stomach was churning.

The superintendent broke into a large smile. 'Don't you worry about that, Tony, I have friends in that department.' Tony looked at him; he didn't doubt this man had friends in high places. Everyone wanted something. It was all a case of 'you scratch my back and I scratch yours. The police were more corrupt than the mobsters he knew.

At the end of the night, everyone shook hands with Tony and thanked him for a wonderful evening. His hands were aching and so was his face, from keeping that famous smile of his in place. When they had all left, Tony, Jake and Sharon surveyed the room. What a mess. Food had been dropped on the floor, party poppers had been pulled and streamers were scattered everywhere. As quick as the waitresses could clear the glasses, another round of drinks had been brought to the tables.

'Why don't we all have a drink? We can let the staff go home and clean up in the morning,' said Sharon. It had been like walking on eggshells all night. No one had dared say anything out of place. Everyone knew the police were never off duty, and having an accountant in the back office, laundering money, had set their teeth on edge.

'No lady tonight, Tony?' Sharon laughed at him; she could see he was tired. He worked hard, he was passionate about everything he did. This club was his baby. Jake had already half-told her about what the accountant had said. 'I hope you're not losing your touch.' She poured them all a drink, took her shoes off, and sat on a chair. The last of the bar staff had gone, and the bouncers were saying their goodbyes.

Tony put his glass to hers. 'I will never lose my touch, Sharon, but sometimes business has to come first. Don't worry, I'll make up for it tomorrow.' He felt better, now. He was already thinking seriously about what the accountant and Jake had said. He intended to try charging at the door, to see if it worked. The dancers, however, were a different matter.

2

CELEBRITY STATUS

It felt like a backward turn. Nevertheless, while Tony still wasn't overjoyed at the prospect of having exotic dancers in the club, he was prepared to listen to new ideas. The accountant, Jake and Sharon were all waiting in the office for him. He'd had a sleepless night, tossing and turning. Would this be a downward slope, the beginning of the end?

When he walked in, the three of them looked up; it was obvious to him that they had started the discussion already. 'Well, what have I missed?' he said, sitting down and picking up the mug of coffee Sharon had made for him.

Sharon spoke first to ease the way. 'It could be a good idea, Tony, having dancers here at the beginning of the week. Are you concerned it would make the place seem cheap and cheerful, the way it used to be?' She had hit the nail on the head, and they all knew it.

'It won't,' said the accountant, 'not if it's handled right.'

'Well, that sounds like a load of crap to me. How on earth are we going to make this a classy and interesting club, somewhere people will want to come for their hen nights and an evening out, if it gets a reputation as a strip club?' snapped Tony, trying to make his point.

'Why do people flock to Vegas, Tony? Because it's a den

of iniquity – gambling, girls, music – but still, they all go there for a good time. As I said last night, make it exclusive – a celebrity night out. Even the richest men like to look at pretty women, they just don't want to do it with reporters around, or with some scruff off the streets standing next to them. Exclusivity – that's where the money is,' said the accountant, rubbing his fingers and thumb together. He'd spent some time the previous evening looking at the options and had an idea of how much he thought they could make. 'Let the girls pay you to work here; a commission, if you like.'

'What about Ralph Gold? We all know his interest in the place, would he want it turned into a strip club?'

'All Mr Gold requires is profit, not loss. As far as he's concerned, it's up to you what you do with the place; after all, it's your reputation at stake, not his.'

Tony kept throwing out the arguments, but felt he was fighting a losing battle.

At last, Jake spoke up. 'Why not try it?' he said. 'The options look pretty bleak, otherwise. We're paying more for staff on a Monday and Tuesday night than we're making. The other option would be to close, which means no money at all.'

'Where are you going to get these exotic women from, then? The usual ratholes? Women the punters have all seen before, who are only interested in doing extras with them … is that what you really want, Jake?' Tony sighed. He ran his hands through his hair and sat back in his chair. He knew Jake was right, it was costing more to open on the quiet nights. Nobody went clubbing on a Monday, most of them had work in the morning. 'Okay,' he said, 'but you had all better have some good ideas, to make this work.'

Tony wasn't happy, this wasn't his dream, but he could see everyone's point of view. He was beginning to wish he hadn't mentioned the policeman's suggestion, the night before. Still, he had, and now, finally, he was prepared to listen.

'I've had some ideas,' the accountant said. He seemed to have it all worked out. He had taken into consideration both Tony's feelings and the money-making opportunities the idea held. After all, he was an accountant; money was all he knew. 'We're going "Vegas", Tony, pole dancers, all the same height and all the same size. Diamante costumes, and house rules. Firstly, no messing around with the customers, and secondly, you have nothing to do with it.' He pointed a finger at Tony, in what seemed a threatening way. 'You are the weekend showman, the playboy host. Sharon and Jake will run the strip club. Sharon will do the hiring and firing.'

Sharon nearly fell off her chair; she hadn't expected this. What did she know about strip clubs? She interrupted the accountant, saying, 'I'm really not the right person to do that, I don't know anything about it.' She blushed at the thought.

'Then do your research, Sharon, go and see some of the pubs and clubs and then put a different slant on it. A woman running things would make it harder for the strippers to influence with their feminine ways. They couldn't flatter you or tempt you in the way they could tempt a man, if you know what I mean.' The accountant moved his glasses to the end of his nose and looked over them at Sharon.

She looked around the room. The three of them were looking at her and waiting for some kind of reaction.

'Can I think about it?' she said. She was beginning to feel pressured. They all nodded in agreement.

During the course of the day, Jake kept talking about it, and for each argument Tony put up, Jake had an answer. Tony even complained about the expense of having chrome poles put on the stage, safe enough for the dancers to use.

'You're complaining about money?' That made Jake laugh out loud. They were raking in the money. Life had never been so good. They were taking thousands from the protection racket. The security firm that Tony had suddenly plucked out of the air and put in Jake's name had taken off considerably. It operated as an agency, and people were ringing for security guards to go to festivals, and even warehouses. It was crazy, but they were employing more people to do the job and earning a lot of money in the process. The money-lending, or loan sharking, as Tony's side business was known, was also making a lot of money in interest payments. No, money definitely wasn't the problem. Tony's attitude was the problem. They were chauffeur-driven now, which made it easier for them to talk business in the back of the car. 'Come on, Tony, let's try it. Let Sharon do the interviews, and take control of that side of things. Let's show the world "Lambrianu's" not only is a great nightclub, but is also the place to see beautiful women.' Jake raised an eyebrow and smiled at Tony.

'Okay, mate, it's all Sharon's decision now, I want nothing to do with it. I'll pay for the alterations to the club, but that's it. I'm not the bossman, using the club for my own recreation.'

Jake knew he could get Sharon onside. He had already seen that she liked the idea and was drawn to the position of power it would give her, rather than just being the bar manager. Since she had given up her job to work with them both, he knew she felt that she had lost some of her independence and status. It was all about Jake and Tony; Sharon was just another member of their workforce and Jake's wife. This was her opportunity to be someone in her own right.

Jake had spoken to the accountant, and everything he had said made sense. Taking a commission off the dancers would pay their wages; charging an entry fee on the door would pay towards the cost of the bills. This was an opportunity to go forward, but he could sense Tony's reluctance, for obvious reasons.

Sharon started looking into things. She found out where some of the pubs were that had dancers, and visited them. She had never been in that kind of atmosphere before, and although some thought it was strange, a woman going in and keeping her clothes on, some men just presumed she would be auditioning.

Sharon could see why Tony was reluctant to turn his new glamorous club into a dive, like some of the ones she had seen up to now. That said, the atmosphere was good, and the men seemed to be having a good time, laughing and joking with the girls, so she could see what the accountant meant, too. There was serious money to be made.

She had looked towards Soho, known by everyone and arguably London's premier red-light district. The main thing she noticed was there was nowhere like the accountant had suggested. Nowhere with style and class, like the famous Playboy Club in Mayfair, with its world-renowned bunny girls.

'I'll do it,' she announced to Tony and Jake, 'on the condition that it's my baby and I call the shots. I know I can do this, I have the vision and the sight to see it through. You two only see it from a man's point of view; I see it from a woman's. Is that a deal?' Like Jake, she was a bookkeeper and accountant, so she could look at things from a business perspective. She felt she could prove herself to them and make this work.

Tony and Jake looked at each other and smiled, this was going to be a sight to behold. What would Sharon come up with?

'Deal,' they both said in unison. The curiosity alone made Tony want to try it, and after all, if it didn't work, it would be down to Sharon and the accountant. As he'd been told, he was the showman in charge of the club.

3

STRIPTEASE

A few months had passed. The club nights were doing well and, even though it had been announced that there was an entry fee of a hundred pounds, a lot of people still came in. There were a few that couldn't afford it and stopped coming, but the accountant had been right. Those who moved in the right circles, the people with the money, felt it was nothing to pay to have some fun, rub shoulders with this famous gangland boss, and pursue the beautiful models that Tony still let in for free, as long as they brought their champagne-buying sugar daddies.

The stage and its spotlights gave the place a different look. Six large poles were installed, and there were long pink curtains at either side. Over the last couple of months, Tony had handed the budget for that part of the business over to Sharon.

Already, on the club nights, some of the wealthy gentlemen looked at the closed curtains hiding the long poles that stretched from floor to ceiling on the stage, and asked what was happening. On hearing they were putting on events with Las Vegas-style showgirls, Tony saw their eyes light up, and a big grin spread across their faces.

Sharon advertised for pole dancers to come and audition. She had emphasized 'pole dancers', and not strippers. She was surprised when so many turned up to her group audition. Some were even out of work models, hoping this would give their career a boost. After all, who knew who would be having a drink in the club? A photographer, a journalist?

Immediately Sharon saw anyone over thirty, they were dismissed. Anyone who had a stretch mark, or weighed more than nine stone, was also out, and anyone who didn't have the style and grace to be able to climb up the poles and dance around them was also out. The pool of applicants went from around fifty women to twenty in less than half an hour.

Sharon could see they all seemed rather shocked and upset that it was a woman interviewing them and making the choice, and not the blonde playboy they had seen in the newspapers. It was crazy and funny because, all the time, Jake, Tony and the accountant were watching on the monitors in the office.

Once the girls had been chosen, Sharon hired a choreographer, and rehearsals began. She also hooked up with a seamstress who made costumes for dancers in some of the West End shows, and she made sure everyone looked the part. Jake, Tony and the accountant were all present for the full dress rehearsal, prior to the launch of the business, and even Tony had to admit the show was spectacular – and there was nothing tacky about it.

Finally, opening night arrived. Mondays were usually dead, so the change of focus was no great risk. And, as Dan and his friends had been dropping off leaflets at local offices where there were more men than women, they were hopeful of a decent crowd.

Jake and Tony stood at the bar. The disco lights were on and the dancefloor was lit up; all they needed now was custom. One by one, a few well-dressed men in suits started trickling in to the club. They looked a little pensive, because it still looked like a nightclub, but they were reassured when they saw the stage and the dance poles.

Then a group of men came in that included some Tony and Jake recognized from television and magazines. They were all eagerly awaiting the main event. Jake went to the doormen and asked them if they had paid – they nodded, and they could prove it. Each man was given a card when his entry fee had been paid, and it also got them their first drink at the bar.

Sharon was backstage, in the newly decorated changing rooms, with her clipboard. She was making sure everyone was present, properly dressed and made up, and ready for the show. At last, the music started up and, one by one, in their spangled, tasselled costumes, the girls walked out, took hold of a pole each and started to climb up them, swing around them, and teasingly wrap their legs around them.

The atmosphere was relaxed, the men were shouting to the girls and some were even throwing money at their favourite. The girls were like gymnasts, and it was all in good taste and good fun. Each one dropped a strap of her specially designed costume, and when they took off their bikini bottoms, there was an even smaller G-string underneath. There was applause and laughter from the men. Sharon had done well.

Each dancer, in turn, had her own spot, and at the end of the evening, they all came on in different costumes and took a bow to the audience.

The cash register was ringing away and the credit cards were in the machines. *Yes*, thought Tony to himself, *no matter who they are, all men like to see a pretty woman, scantily clad*. He admitted he had been wrong.

'What you need, Sharon,' said the accountant, 'is a star attraction, a full stripper for the end of the evening, to finish off. These girls tease and show as much as possible, but they're not completely naked or just wearing their stockings, are they?'

Sharon agreed, the show did need a finale. One of these women would do it, she was sure, especially if the money was right.

Tony had been concerned about the club nights and how it would affect them, but again, he was wrong to worry. The curtains at the stage were pulled together, almost looking like a pink wall, and the party people came in – after they had paid their entry fee, of course.

So, now they had their nightclub, for the couples, singles and hen parties, and their revue bar, for men who liked to see showgirls dance around poles, and the show finished off with a stripper. There was no such thing as a quiet night at Lambrianu's. The money on the door, alone, paid the girls wages.

Tony was invited to movie premiers and theatre nights, and spent his time dating his choice of pretty women that hung on his every word. Jake felt it was good promotion for Tony and the club, but it was also promotion for the young starlets who wanted to be photographed with Mr Clubland, the notorious racketeer. It worked both ways, and Tony constantly had his photo in some glossy magazine or other, standing on the red carpet with a wannabe model or would-be actress. He revelled in it. This was living!

His own party nights, in his apartment, caused the odd scandal, but it only served to make him more popular, to the point where the newspapers called him 'the Italian stud'. Jake and Sharon laughed when they saw him disappearing at the end of the night with some glamorous woman – or even a couple of them, to make the party go with a swing.

Eventually, though, these models decided to make extra money by selling their 'kiss and tell' stories. It seemed everyone wanted to know about Tony's sex life and the women he entertained, which made the club even more popular, because people then came to see the man himself.

Time passed and the year was nearly up; Tony and Jake were soon going to find out how much Ralph Gold would want for the club, which was now very much a going concern.

Sharon had hired more strippers, not just one for a finale, and had the pole dancers on in their break times. She held stag parties, and got the dancers to encourage the customers to buy cheap champagne at top prices. These were all well-known wealthy men and each paid their fees, then made a point of going to Tony's office to meet him.

This was the part that Tony enjoyed the most; they came to his office to shake his hand and meet the man behind the myth. No one knew anything about him, other than he was Italian and came from a wealthy background. *If only they knew*, he thought to himself, *if only they knew I lived on the streets, and went through dustbins for food.*

Tony and Jake still visited the local pubs and kept in touch with the landlords, as Tony didn't want to appear as though he had taken his eye off the ball for one second. When he felt someone was taking advantage he reverted back to his old ways, showing his short temper and using his fists. He might be 'Mr Lambrianu' to his wealthy customers, but he was also still Tony who ran the protection racket and didn't suffer fools gladly.

The strippers at the club were exclusive and signed a contract; while working at Tony's club, they weren't allowed to work anywhere else. This way, if the customers wanted to see their favourite stripper, they had to come to Lambrianu's to see her. The strippers were happy; they were well-rewarded, everything was above board and they paid their taxes. Plus, they also got money tips from the men and commission on the champagne they sold.

Sharon discovered some men didn't like to share their favourite girls with the other punters and, despite the fact they were all married, seemed to get a little jealous when their favourite stripper was showing attention to someone else. Sharon had a word with the accountant about this, omitting Tony and Jake from the conversation, and he suggested installing VIP booths. That way, a man could have the woman he wanted to see dance exclusively for him.

CCTV cameras were installed in these booths, so there was no reason for the strippers to feel unsafe or opportunity to offer anything more. Of course, exclusive exotic dances came with an exclusive exotic price. Tony and Jake were surprised these men were prepared to pay it, but pay it they did, and the revue bar nights became even more popular.

4

THE KING OF SIN

That was what the newspapers called Tony Lambrianu – the 'king of sin', in every aspect of his life. No stone was left unturned when it came to his private and his business world.

There is no such thing as bad publicity, so this reputation only made the women love him and the men envy him. Tony made a point of having a woman of model status on his arm, every night. And yet, as much as the money poured in and Tony and Jake's lives took on celebrity status, Jake was worried. He felt there was something lacking, but he couldn't talk to Tony about it, he would just laugh it off.

Jake often went to see Elle. He felt Tony had reached his goal, but lacked an intimate personal life. Jake had Sharon, but Tony had no one special, and this bothered Jake; it was as though Tony was afraid of getting too close.

Tony liked to be in control; that way, he felt secure. The more he reached for the stars, he seemed to get the moon as well. Over the months, things had kept on getting better and better for Tony, but now it was crunch time. The year was finally up: it was time to find out if he could keep his empire. Today was the day.

The meeting was set for noon at the solicitor's office.

This was one meeting that made Tony sweat. He hadn't slept, he had even spent the evening before alone, which was unusual for him. Jake felt the same fear; today was judgement day.

The solicitor was Mr Mathews, who Tony had met when he was in Italy, visiting his grandmother. The man had turned up with Don Carlos. Tony had learned that Eddie Rawlings had betrayed him, and had undertaken to kill him for it. He had also shared his dream of owning the club. Both he and Don Carlos had signed their names over the sealed flap of an envelope that contained Ralph Gold's asking price; he had no idea what that was, but he was about to find out. Tony and Jake had banked all their funds together. All in all, they had two and a half million pounds. They were hoping, if nothing else, this showed willing and could maybe be used as a deposit.

Tony went dressed in a well-tailored grey suit from Savile Row. His gold cufflinks were engraved with his initials. As it seemed the newspapers and the glossy magazines wanted to know everything about him, he made sure that he was always dressed to perfection, just in case a photographer or journalist turned up out of the blue.

It was Jake who knocked on the solicitor's door. They had already passed by the very efficient secretary, who was expecting them. She had telephoned through to the solicitor and informed him they had arrived.

The door opened and the solicitor welcomed Tony and Jake and shook hands with them both. He showed them to seats in front of his desk and offered them a drink. Tony shook his head; he thought this was a test from Don Carlos, who had told him never to drink alcohol when doing business.

'Well, gentlemen, we all know why we're here, so to save you any more waiting, I'll get straight to the point.'

Mr Mathews walked over to a safe in the wall, dialled in the combination and opened it up. He took out an envelope. Tony recognised it as the one he and Don Carlos had signed.

Tony swallowed hard and ran his hands through his hair. He could hardly speak, his throat was so dry. He really could have done with a drink.

The solicitor seemed to wave the envelope in front of their faces, teasing them, then he said, 'Here you are, then, Antonias.' He handed the envelope to Tony. 'You know your own signature, yes? Can confirm this is the same envelope you signed when you were at your grandmother's vineyard?'

Tony nodded and Mr Mathews sat watching him, a smug expression on his face. Tony and Jake weren't sure whether he was familiar with the contents, but they both thought he probably was.

With his heart in his mouth, Tony started opening the envelope. He looked at Jake, then back at the envelope, as he tore it open. The letter inside confused him. His brows furrowed; again he looked at Jake and then at the solicitor, who nodded and smiled at him. The silence was deafening.

Tony handed the letter over to Jake to read.

'What does it say, Jake?' Tony wanted Jake to confirm what he had read, just in case he had missed anything. His heart was pounding, and his breathing seemed to get faster. He wiped the sweat from his brow and waited for Jake, whose face paled as he read it.

'It says Ralph Gold is willing to sell the club to you for one pound, provided you make one million pounds while acting as manager. Also, he would like to come to some kind of arrangement to allow the money laundering to continue, with you on a commission,' said Jake. He handed the letter back over to Tony.

Inside the envelope were the deeds to the club, all in Tony's name. There was a sharp intake of breath, then he looked at the solicitor and said, 'Is this for real? Does he only want a pound for the club?'

'Well, let's be honest, Antonias, when you took it over, it was only the land that was worth anything,' said Mr

Mathews. 'The club itself wasn't worth a pound, was it? You have to prove you've made the million, though. Can you?'

Tony showed the solicitor the bank statements that he had taken with him. It showed he had more than was required.

The solicitor shook hands with Tony, then with Jake. 'Well, gentlemen, it seems you own a club, lock, stock and barrel. Congratulations.'

Tony and Jake were still stunned. It felt like they were glued to their chairs, they didn't know what to do next. 'This money laundering, what about it?' asked Tony.

'If you decide to proceed with that, speak to the accountant. He'll sort it out.'

Tony looked down at the letter again. He felt as though at any moment someone might jump out of the cupboard and tell them it was all a joke. He stood up.

'Aren't you forgetting something, gentlemen?' The solicitor raised an eyebrow and looked at them. Tony and Jake looked at each other; they weren't sure what he meant.

The solicitor beckoned to them. 'You owe Mr Gold a pound.'

Tony nodded; of course, that was the price he was asking. Tony reached into his pocket, took out a pound coin and put it on the desk. 'What happens now?' he asked.

'Well, first, I give you a receipt for your payment, then I hand the money over to Mr Gold, like any business arrangement. The deeds are already in your name, so there's no need for me to draw up any paperwork, and you carry on just as you are. Good luck.'

That was it; in less than an hour, it was all over and done with, how crazy was that?

Tony wanted to leave as quickly as possible, just in case there was another condition or something he had missed in the letter. He thanked the solicitor and almost yanked Jake out of the office.

෪ ◊ ඏ

Even when they were standing in the street outside of the solicitor's office, neither of them spoke; they were dumbfounded. They had saved every penny, and been seriously stressed out about today's meeting. They'd even tried to gauge what the price of the club would be, based on the cost of other properties in the area. They had been tested, Tony knew that. Were they serious businessmen or not? They had proved themselves, and that was the main thing.

Tony felt a little disappointed that Ralph Gold hadn't been there. He would like to meet him in a professional manner, even do business with him, but for Ralph Gold, the time was obviously not yet right.

It had been months since Tony and Jake had met Ralph and his wife Julie, when they had come to the opening of the club. Since then, they had heard nothing. What would it take to get an appointment with Ralph Gold and his business associates? Still, if Tony carried on laundering the money and earned a commission, too, that would be a start.

Tony and Jake got into the back of their chauffeur-driven Jaguar. 'For God's sake, Tony, say something,' said Jake. He was waiting, even though his own brain was spinning.

'I don't really know what to say, Jake, really I don't. The club is actually ours, can you believe that? We own the club, it's ours, it's all bloody ours!' For the first time since the meeting Tony burst into laughter and his face beamed. He grabbed hold of Jake and hugged him. He felt like crying. There was a lump in his throat as he hugged Jake even tighter.

When they got back, it seemed to Tony the club looked different; suddenly, it all seemed different. This was his club, for real, and that seemed to make it take on a whole new aspect. Sitting in his office with Jake, explaining to Sharon everything that had happened, Tony at last felt like lord of the manor.

He had come a long way since sleeping out on the dark,

cold streets of London. Suddenly, he felt charitable. One of the first things he was going to do was fulfil the crazy idea that Jake had had, a long time ago.

The two of them had needed to get cleaned up and Tony had taken Jake to the twenty-four-hour toilets he and his mother had once used. They were a place where a lot of the homeless went to wash – or even sleep, when the weather was bad. He was going to have them refurbished. He'd have new basins put in, and new toilets, and properly tiled walls, to get rid of all the mould and the cockroaches. Yes, that would be a good place to begin.

Then he would set up some kind of fund for the soup kitchens that provided a meal for the homeless. It was all self-funded, with donations from anyone who wished to contribute. With a regular donation from Tony, they would be able to stay open and continue their work.

Of course, once he'd contacted the local council to ask their permission to refurbish the toilets at his own expense, the story soon got into the newspapers. Although he was still the well-known and feared gangland boss and club owner, he was now also a charitable man with a heart. This made even the most sceptical of decent people have at least one good word to say about him.

Tony and Jake both agreed that this was the kind of good publicity they needed. Again, this was a far cry from the seedy underworld they usually operated in. This was decent businessmen doing charitable acts. Tony always had fond memories of listening to the Salvation Army when he was a child, and of the caravans they used to set up around Christmastime, for the homeless. Their brass brand would play Christmas carols and it would seem like time had stopped and only the moment mattered.

As a result of this fond childhood memory, Tony gave money to the Salvation Army so they could carry on with their good works. Again, this got into the newspapers. As much as it must have stuck in the throats of the journalists who had to report good deeds done by this feared gangland boss, rather than details of his outlandish lifestyle, they had no option but to do so.

It was the accountant that pointed out they could claim some form of tax relief on charitable gifts, and so not only were they attracting the right publicity and encouraging respectable people to enjoy their club, it was also a major tax benefit.

The striptease acts Sharon organized were very well thought out. All the women who worked there felt it was a privilege to do so, and gladly paid their commission fees. It worked both ways, because the wages they received for being exclusive to the club were more than they would have ever earnt, working in the local pubs. They also knew much they were going to earn, which gave them security.

5

A WINK OF AN EYE

The years rolled on and the money rolled in. Tony and Jake were now in their early thirties, and known as the 'kings of the underworld'. It seemed as though, as time had passed, they had taken over everything. The club, which was now run by Sharon almost entirely, was known as the most famous nightclub in the West End of London. The weekly striptease revues were known as very stylish and classy.

Sharon thought it was quite funny, in a way, because some of the businessmen who came regularly to see the strippers and chat them up and buy them cheap champagne at top prices were also the same respectable men that would come on the weekend club nights, with their wives or girlfriends, and pretend not to know her.

Discretion was everything; under no circumstances were the bar staff to be familiar in any way to these men, or act as though they knew them. Everything was dealt with in a professional manner. Famous male celebrities would make a point of coming in, and felt safe in the knowledge that everyone there was under the strict code of silence. They could be at their ease and have some fun, bringing their mistresses one week and their wives or girlfriends the next.

The private VIP booths seemed to have developed their own rules, although there was a grey area no one knew quite what to do about. Everyone knew the booths had CCTV cameras in them. The girls who were providing this more intimate striptease on a one-to-one basis would stand on a small stage and dance more provocatively. Although the golden rule was that there were to be no sexual exchanges between the stripper and the customer, Sharon couldn't dispute that there were times when the customer would be touching himself! When she spoke to Tony and Jake about it, none of them were sure how to handle it.

The girls were not breaking the rules and neither were the men – they were masturbating themselves. It was a very grey area, but Tony felt that since they knew they were on CCTV, they obviously trusted him. On the other hand, he also felt that they had been fairly warned about the cameras by the notices on the doors and so their behaviour might just represent a golden opportunity. Some of these men were high-ranking police inspectors and MPs, and one day he might need a favour in exchange for the recording they would so badly want to destroy. Blackmail, Tony felt, was an ugly word; it would be more an exchange of gifts. They would each have something that the other wanted, and there was no better way to get around that than to sit, discuss and exchange.

Tony couldn't believe how time had passed so quickly. He had paid Miriam back every penny she had given him. In recent years, he had been a regular visitor to Italy and the vineyard. It felt like a good place to relax and be himself. There were no reporters there.

They had all moved on. Sharon and Jake had put their adoption plans on hold, claiming that life was too hectic at the moment. Their life was so busy, they wouldn't be able to give a child the time it would need. Their working schedule was changing on a weekly basis. There were late nights involved, and sometimes running the club meant working seven nights a week, especially around Christmas and New Year, with all the festive parties they had to deal with.

Jake felt a little disappointed about this, as he had looked forward to having a child, but Sharon was adamant; it wouldn't be fair on the child. She was going to wait till things calmed down before committing herself. Poor Elle yearned for grandchildren, but she knew there was nothing on the horizon, especially if Tony had anything to do with it.

Tony had girlfriend after girlfriend – and sometimes more than one. Then there were the private parties he held in his apartment with a few of the more well-known models he had become acquainted with. There were many and yet there were none. As the years had passed, he had met just one woman anyone might say was Tony's girlfriend.

They were both cut from the same cloth, it seemed. Roxy was a well-known model who was now hoping to start a television acting career. She had sugar daddies coming out of her ears and they all adored her. You could see that, by all the expensive diamonds and furs she wore.

They had met at the club, and Roxy had invited Tony to a photo shoot she was doing for a magazine. He had gone along out of curiosity, not expecting much, but when the photographer realised who Tony was, he instantly started taking photos of him.

The photographer said Tony had 'natural beauty', and seemed more engrossed with taking photos of Tony. In the end, Tony and Roxy were in the photos together. They made a very handsome couple. Roxy was just over six foot tall, with very long legs. Her blonde hair hung all the way down her back, the ends touching her backside. She, like a lot of models, had had a boob job, making her waist look even slimmer. She loved life, she loved the nightlife.

She enjoyed going to the club, sitting on a bar stool at the end of the bar near where Tony stood. She liked this glamorous lifestyle. She drank champagne, and waited for Tony to ask her to dance or make conversation, in between his business deals.

Sometimes it seemed she had waited in vain and wasted her time, because there were nights when some other woman caught Tony's eye and flirted with him, and it would be this other woman Tony would stand and drink champagne with, and then take more bottles up to his apartment with.

Roxy would leave with her girlfriends, feeling disheartened and hurt, but Tony had never made any promises, nor had he ever called her his girlfriend.

Roxy would then play her own game and take one of her many sugar daddies or would-be television producers to the club. Sharon would raise one eyebrow at Jake and smile. She thought it was quite funny that Roxy was playing the jealousy game.

Roxy would laugh loudly and flirt with the man on her arm, hoping that Tony would notice or, even better, care about it. He never did. He liked the fact that their relationship, if you could call it that, was more of a 'friends with benefits' arrangement. He told her he liked her because she wasn't clingy or needy, and wasn't after commitment; just having a good time was all she cared about.

Sharon and Jake both knew that wasn't the case. They both saw the way Roxy hung on Tony's every word. She was trying to play the waiting game, and lived in hope that he would wake up one day and suddenly realise he loved her. Roxy had hated the fact that, on occasion, Tony slept with some of her friends. She had felt humiliated by this and even started an argument with Tony about it.

Roxy stormed into the office, full of anger, ready to give Tony a piece of her mind and possibly an ultimatum. Sharon and Jake had been listening down the corridor and heard it all.

Tony had just sat at his desk and listened to her complaints, then leaned back in his chair and let her have his very calm response.

'Who I sleep with, Roxy, and who is my flavour of the

month, has nothing to do with you. We have fun, and we're good in bed together, but I'm not exclusive. Do I complain when some television producer comes in here on the pretence of you doing some audition for him on his casting couch? You were a famous model when I met you and you're even more famous now, because you hang around here and with me. I have made you famous, Roxy, you've had your money's worth. No; either accept it or move on. I don't care either way, my diary's full.'

Tony had been very cold to her, heartless, even, but he had firmly put her in her place. There was nothing else for her to do but leave in tears; it seemed all her dreams had come to an abrupt halt.

Then, a week or so later, she came in one evening and, at the end of the night, went up to Tony's apartment. It was as though nothing had changed, although everyone knew it had. Roxy was the one making a fool of herself, because Tony had made it abundantly clear they were not an item, yet she was still prepared to go to the club, drink with him and sleep with him. She had no cause for complaint, because it was now her choice.

Tony had never tried to hide the fact that he dated other women, he didn't feel the need to. He was a single man, women liked him, and he liked women. As far as he was concerned, that was it. He didn't force them to have sex with him, nor did he force them to participate in the little orgies that he had in his apartment. It seemed his heart was made of stone.

'One day,' Sharon used to joke with Tony, 'Miss Right will come along, and that will knock you off your high horse.' She used to laugh about it with Jake, but they both agreed it would have to be one hell of a woman to maintain Tony's interest. Did she even exist?

Tony never let his private life interfere with business, however many women had stayed over the night before. He always seemed to be showered and ready to get to work first thing in the morning. He'd had a good night's entertainment, but now it was over, it was back to business.

Tony would discard the women as quickly as possible, and try his hardest to get them to leave. He would hand over some money for a taxi or get his driver to drop them off at home. If they were especially stubborn, he would more or less throw them out of the door. Already, while waving them off, he would have Jake in the kitchen, talking about the day's business.

It did make Jake laugh to himself, because sometimes these women were hardly given the chance to dress. One even left in Tony's dressing gown. Sharon used to shrug her shoulders when Jake told her. 'They know what he is, Jake, they're adults, and if they're prepared to come back for more and be thrown out in the morning, well, that's their problem.'

Jake knew she was right, of course, but he felt something was missing from Tony's life. He was always striving to do better and better, and not let anyone or anything get in his way. As much as he liked the ladies, he had even laughed about them one night while having a drink with Jake. 'They're all the same, Jake, each and every one of them wants her hands on my club and my bank balance. No one wants Antonias, they all want Tony, club owner, millionaire. They're all gold-diggers, so why shouldn't I take advantage of it? I like sex, and I would be a fool to turn it down.'

Meanwhile, there was always business to take care of. There were other pub bosses and up-and-coming guys who fancied themselves as gangsters, and they all had to be dealt with in Tony's own professional, psychopathic manner.

At one point, having heard that some of these would-be gangsters had been mouthing off about Tony only being interested in the women and taking his eye off the ball when it came to business, he had gone into a pub he knew they drank in, one lunchtime, with Jake and a machine gun. When they got there, only the landlord and the would-be gangsters were in the place. He opened fire, waving the gun around, and shot the place to pieces. While firing at the walls and the furniture, and blowing the pub to bits, he watched these men cowering behind the bar and under tables.

Tony had walked behind the bar and stared at the three men hiding there. One fumbled around in his pocket and took out a knife. Tony's eyes had darkened and his charming smile became a grim sardonic smirk. He knelt down beside the man and ripped his own shirt open.

'Go on then, do it,' he said.

Jake and the other men watched as Tony knelt there with his shirt open, displaying his chest and stomach to the man with the knife. He was daring the man to thrust the knife into him.

'You haven't got the guts,' Tony sneered, his eyes wild and blazing.

Jake saw the man with the knife look at Tony, then he took the knife and thrust it forward towards Tony's chest. In the nick of time Tony moved, but he was slashed across the arm. Tony burst out laughing. 'My turn,' he said, and he took a handgun from the waistband of his trousers and shot the man through the right hand, then he picked up his left hand and shot him through that, too. Blood poured out everywhere.

Jake and the others watched the injured man writhing on the floor; he was screaming and shouting. Tony stood up and put his gun back in his waistband. He picked up the machine gun and put it on top of the bar, then promptly started doing up the buttons on his jacket. The knees of his trousers were stained with blood. He looked at his watch. 'Time to go, Jake,' he said.

'What about him, you crazy bastard?' said one of the other men cowering behind the bar; he was pointing at the man with the ruined hands. 'They all say you're crazy but I never believed them how much till now.'

'He's your problem, call an ambulance or something, but whatever you do, always remember that you've just witnessed how crazy I am first-hand, okay?' With that, Tony took the machine gun off the bar and bent down to the man writing in pain on the floor. He took hold of the man's hands and pressed his fingers on the body and the trigger of the gun. It was only then that the other men saw that Tony was wearing leather gloves. The only fingerprints on that gun belonged to the man writhing on the floor.

Tony walked towards the door. The landlord popped his head around the side door to see if the coast was clear.

'You,' Tony said to the landlord, 'need to watch the kind of custom you let through the door. Here.' He took a bundle of money – a thousand pounds – from his inside jacket pocket and threw it at the landlord. The money went flying through the air and hit the floor. The publican bent down and began hurriedly picking it up.

'Thank you, Mr Lambrianu, thank you, sir,' he said, as he shoved the notes down his T-shirt.

Tony got back into his car and told John, his driver, to get his other suit out of the boot. 'For God's sake, Jake, this suit cost me nearly three thousand pounds and now it's trash. I hate blood, it gets everywhere.'

He got changed in the back of the car, then sat back in the seat and straightened his tie.

'Did you really need to shoot him in both hands, Tony?' asked Jake. He had witnessed Tony's anger many times, and always thanked God he had never been on the receiving end of it.

'Not really, I just felt like it. Don't worry, he'll soon get patched up. And, in future, he'll think twice about calling me names, and so will his friends.' That was the end of that, just another day's work in the life of Tony Lambrianu, another problem solved.

6

TOP DOG

'Lambrianu, Lambrianu, that's all I'm fucking hearing! I've had it up to here!' Marlon raised his hand to head height to make his point.

The room was stifling; there was no air, and they couldn't put any fans on because it would blow the very expensive cocaine around. Marlon was hot, sweaty and bad-tempered. He was sitting at his cocaine-encrusted table, surrounded by his bodyguards and, yet again, they were telling him about that fucking madman.

'What's wrong, boss?' Errol, one of Marlon's most trusted men, stepped forward. His feet sounded heavy on the floorboards – left bare, as it made it easier to mop up spillages. 'Everything's nice and easy, has been for the last two years since you and him became friends. It's good, easy money – better than when we were dealing with that other guy.'

Marlon jumped up and grabbed Errol by the throat. He was beyond angry. Cords stood out in his neck as he throttled his bodyguard. Damp sweat patches were visible in the armpits of his bright red shirt. 'Whose fucking side are you on, bounty bar?' Bounty bar was an insult – black on the outside and white on the inside. Marlon's large, black, heavily ringed hand squeezed tighter around Errol's neck. Errol was trying to push him away. The other men in the room froze and cast each other sideways glances. This was not the time to interfere.

Marlon's hand gripped tighter. Errol's eyes were bulging as he tried to breathe. His face was so close to Marlon's, they were almost touching noses. Spit flew out of Marlon's mouth as he rasped into Errol's face, 'I'm the fucking boss, do you hear me? That fucking half-breed is nobody. I let him work the other side of the water because it suited me, that's all.'

Marlon had made his point and so loosened his grip, leaving Errol to gasp for air and stagger towards a wooden chair. Errol sat down heavily. He held his neck, trying to breathe, his head drooping down toward the floor. Marlon was a big man and could easily have choked him or, worse, broken his neck.

'What you gonna do about him, boss?' Marcus sat at the far side of the room on an old sofa. He felt nervous breaking the tension, but felt it was the right thing to say.

Marlon was breathing heavily from the exertion, and his chest heaved as he slowly got his breath back. He turned to Marcus and smiled, then flexed his hands and rubbed his nails on his shirt, as though polishing them. 'Get fucking rid of him, boy, what else? It's time that nancy boy remembered who I am.' He straightened the black leather hat he was wearing. 'I deserve respect, I've been around a lot longer than him and yet all I can hear on the streets is his name, not mine.'

Marlon went and sat back in his chair. He had been thinking about this for a while. He wanted rid of the cocky blonde upstart, but to cause gangland warfare and shoot that club up wasn't worth it. This was between himself and Lambrianu … only one boss could rule.

Marcus decided to try a different approach. 'You're right, boss, he's a loose cannon. He not so businesslike as yourself.' Marcus's thick accent dominated the room. He was more African than Jamaican. His rubbed his flat, squashed nose. 'You hear what he done de other week?'

Marlon ran a hand over his face. When he saw how sweaty it became, he wiped it on his trousers. 'What?' He sounded bored with it all, but he waited.

'It done seem some wise guys thinking he don't care about anything anymore but clubbing and the women. Say he taking his eye off the ball and losing his touch, but that loco white boy totally lost it when he heard what they been saying.' Marcus related the incident in the pub, then said, 'That the kind of guy he is, boss. Waving machine guns in the air. That what I heard, anyways.'

Marlon had listened intently; this, indeed, was interesting. He'd heard that something had gone down in the pub, but no one ever saw or heard anything in the East End, so the details had been sketchy at best.

Marlon nodded. He was beginning to think more clearly, now. 'There has to be more than one way to skin a cat,' he said. 'That white boy leaves a bad taste in my mouth.' Suddenly Marlon's eyes lit up and he smiled, displaying a mouth full of gold teeth. He leaned back on his chair and pushed his leather cap forward over his brow.

He looked over to where Errol was sitting. 'Errol, stop snivelling,' he shouted. 'You got your breath back now. Go to my special first aid box and see what in it. Maybe we pay him a friendly visit tonight at that posh club of his, see those strippers of his.' Marlon rubbed his crotch. 'Some of them sure do look like they could do with some black tail, eh, guys?' Now Marlon sat there laughing to himself. Only he knew the joke he was going to play on Tony and he was going to have some fun in the process.

☙◊❧

When Marlon turned up at the club, with three of his bodyguards in tow, he made a huge show of walking up to Tony and putting his arms around him.

'Good to see you, Tony, mate,' he said. 'Just thought I'd

pay you a visit and have some fun with your girls.' He smiled and looked towards the strippers and then back at Tony.

Tony smiled as he greeted Marlon and his men, but inside, he felt uneasy; Marlon generally stayed to his side of the river. They had their meetings, but he never just turned up out of the blue. Tony liked Marlon well enough, and they were business associates, but he wasn't so foolish as to trust him. He had suspected for a while that something like this might be on the cards. He had expected it and, true to form, Marlon hadn't let him down. So, tonight was the night, was it?

'Give him the parcel, Marcus, for fuck's sake.' Marlon looked impatient as Marcus held out a Tupperware box for Tony to take. 'That from my mama,' he said, 'she makes the best jerk chicken around. Thought you might like some. You can warm that up and eat it later. Now, pour me some rum.'

Tony took the box from Marcus. He could already smell the garlic, chilli and onions in the spicy food, even though it had a lid on. Phew! He was hoping to get laid tonight, but it wouldn't happen if he was stinking of that stuff.

With all the enthusiasm he could muster, he said, 'Thanks, Marlon, I bet it tastes great. I'll have it later, thank you.' He put the Tupperware box on the bar and told the bar staff to bring a bottle of rum over.

'Fancy some of this, Tony?' Marlon tapped the breast pocket of his jacket. 'Can I use your office?'

Tony nodded and led the way, and Marlon followed along behind. He had brought his little packets of cocaine with him and Tony didn't like it. He didn't want that stuff on the premises, just in case.

Marlon sat at Tony's desk and chopped the white powder into lines, then began snorting it up his nose. He laughed as he wiped away the dust. 'It's a shame that girlfriend of yours isn't here, she would be licking that stuff up.' He laughed at his own joke.

Tony looked confused, then the penny dropped and he

realized what Marlon was talking about. A few weeks earlier, Tony had seen Roxy with some powder on her top lip and nose. When he had pointed it out, she had told him it was special face powder the models used to hide blemishes. *The lying cow*! he thought to himself. She was a cocaine sniffer, and he hadn't realised it.

Marlon seemed to know her well, so she had obviously been to him or one of his dealers for her supply. Now, it all made sense. She always seemed to be full of life and never tired. Her sexual fantasies were a little off the wall, sometimes, and she quite liked a threesome, with one of her friends and Tony. *This*, he thought to himself, *is because she's completely off her head*. No, she definitely wasn't girlfriend material.

Tony and Marlon smiled at each other like old friends, but they both knew there was a lot of resentment behind those smiles.

𝕊◊ℂℝ

They went out to the bar and Tony gritted his teeth as he watched Marlon wander off back to his men and his bottle of rum. No doubt he had a stash of fifty-pound notes to tip the strippers with. He didn't like anyone fooling around with the strippers, but he felt tonight he had to make an exception.

'What's he doing here, and what the fuck is that?' said Jake as he eyed up the plastic box on the bar top.

'That,' said Tony, nodding at the box, 'is shit. He seems to think I'm going to eat it.'

'It stinks,' said Jake.

'We'll give it to the dogs, out the back. As for him, well, he's come to put me in my place.'

'Do you think he's going to cause trouble in here? Really?' Jake looked at Tony, shocked.

'He's not going to get the chance. Do you still remember how to sort the cars out, if needed? If not, John does. Go and sort it while I keep him busy.'

'You sure? That's a bloody expensive car to waste.'

'That, Jake, is why I pay insurance.' Tony smiled back at him and chinked his glass against Jake's.

❧ ◊ ☙

As the evening drew to an end, Tony went and sat with Marlon and his men. 'Found one you like, Marlon?' Tony indicated the stage, where the strippers were.

'Bit skinny for me, Tony. Nothing like a nice Jamaican woman's arse to make the blood hot. Believe me, white marble can be cold but amber is warm to the touch, eh?'

Ignoring the comment, Tony said, 'How you getting home? Do you want to stay here?' Tony was silently praying that he would refuse and, thank God, he did!

'Gonna get my driver to come.' Marlon took out his mobile.

'No, that'll take ages. Why not take my car and bring it back tomorrow? I've given my chauffeur the night off, but do you think one of your guys can drive you? You can take it, if one of them can.'

Marlon's eyes lit up. The very thought of sitting in that fancy Rolls Royce of Tony's, with the 'Lamb 1' number plate, made him grin. 'My boy, here, had nothing to drink. He can drive,' said Marlon pointing at one of his men.

'Wait here; I'll just get you the keys.' Tony stood up and walked to his office, where Jake was waiting for him.

'Is the car ready, Jake?' Tony's face was set like stone.

'Are you sure about this, Tony? Maybe the guy just came to see you for a drink. Think about what you're doing.'

'This is no hunch, Jake. It's make or break time. Come on, let's wave our friends and allies off.'

Tony passed the keys to Marlon's driver, then walked Marlon to the door and said his goodbyes. The driver got into the front seat and Marlon got into the back, with his other two men. Tony stepped back inside the club. The driver turned on the ignition.

The explosion from the car was enormous. The walls of

the club seemed to sway and there was the sound of breaking glass as the impact of the blast shattered windows in its wake. The street was lit up by the flames from the car. Another explosion sounded just after the first. It was deafening.

Knowing what was going to happen, Jake and Tony had run to the far end of the club. Fortunately, there were only a few stragglers left inside, plus the staff. People were in shock; they knelt down behind the bar and the tables to protect themselves from the glass and dust flying through the air.

When the blast was over, Tony ran to the entrance and peered out. He saw his pride and joy, his beautiful Rolls Royce, in flames. People in the street were screaming and running, scared out of their wits. Some had been hit by flying glass and were bleeding. Others had been thrown across the street by the force of the blast.

Jake was shaking. 'Shit, Tony, look at the mayhem. Look at those people, they're hurt.'

'Collateral, Jake. They're not dead. It's two in the morning, there aren't that many people around. Call the fire brigade.'

Jake took out his mobile, but it wasn't needed; he could already hear the sirens. 'That second explosion must have been the petrol tank blowing,' he said. Tony had explained all that to him when he had worked as a mechanic and said just how easy it was to put a load of explosives in a car and wire it to the ignition.

Once the firemen started putting the flames out, and the police and the ambulance arrived, things seemed to calm down.

A crowd had gathered from nearby streets and restaurants, and the police moved them back. A detective saw Tony standing outside the club and he started asking him about what had happened. Happily, Tony told the truth: his friend, Marlon, was using his car and it had blown up.

Tony had the sense to look distraught and shocked, and feigned dizziness, which meant he had to sit down. The detective told him they would be back tomorrow to discuss things further, and left. The whole building was taped off for the time being and outside stood the charcoal shell of his car.

'Bye, Marlon, rest in peace,' said Tony. He looked at the doors, which had been blown in, then turned to Jake. 'Right, let's call someone to sort these doors out. We'll have to redecorate, as well – the walls are black with smoke. Time to get down to business.'

'You're a cold bastard at times, Tony. What about those other people going about their business in the street? Some got hurt.'

Tony smiled and shrugged his shoulders. 'What about them? I never put the explosives in the car, you did.' He walked away, leaving Jake standing there, feeling guilty.

7

THE SWEET SMELL OF SUCCESS

When the police arrived the following morning and stated the obvious – that they thought the explosion was meant for Tony – he went into full acting mode, looking distressed and worried.

'Do you have any enemies that might have wanted to do this?' The detectives looked at each other and then down at the floor. They both knew who and what Tony was, and what the answer was, too, but they had to ask.

'No, officers, but a man in my position has many enemies, I suppose.'

'We want no repercussions from this, Mr Lambrianu. Leave the investigating to us. Do you understand? Let's face it, we'll know whose door to come knocking on if people start dropping like flies.'

Tony put on an innocent expression and shrugged.

'Good day, Mr Lambrianu.'

'Tony! Tony!' Jake had waited until the police had left but couldn't hold it in any longer. 'Come out the back, you were right!'

Outside, in the back yard, an Alsatian dog was convulsing and foaming at the mouth. It had spewed everywhere. Suddenly, it gave one last howl and collapsed.

The dog lay still; it was dead.

'What happened, Jake?' Tony stared at the dog lying dead on the ground; he was at a loss for words.

'I gave it that jerk chicken Marlon brought you last night. It ate it, then it just started spewing and foaming at the mouth. What the fuck was in it?'

'Marlon was going to poison me and make me look like that?' Tony looked at the dog, bewildered. 'Well, Jake, he got a nicer death than the one he planned for me, didn't he?' He turned round and walked back into the club, where a team of workmen were sorting out the mess.

'Sorry, Tony, you were right,' was all Jake could say.

'Get someone to sort the dog out, then we have some work to do. The South London Mob boss is dead. We need to sort things out before someone else steps in and it gets out of hand.'

ଐ◊ଈ

Once Tony arrived at Marlon's place, he saw that the bodyguards were still there. A little mournful and at a loss, but they were there. They seemed pleased to see him; it was time to talk.

'Will you be taking over, Tony?' one of them asked. They didn't know what to do. It was pretty obvious they were at a loss and needed a leader.

'I don't deal drugs, lads, you know that.' He was adamant he wouldn't get drawn into that game.

One of the men spoke up. 'Bennie knows all the drug dealers around here and he's getting a little too old to be standing at his usual street corner,' he said. 'Maybe we could leave things in his hands. After all, he's known and they all trust him.'

It seemed to Tony and Jake that they had already thought this through. Bennie was a good and trusted friend. They knew him well.

Scratching his chin and leaving them in suspense, Tony made a big pretence of thinking about things. There was money on that side, to be sure, and he could offer protection and possibly even do some money-lending.

Tony felt sick to the stomach about how things had ended up. He had liked Marlon in the beginning. They both worked their own turf in their own way, without any gang wars. It was now up to Tony to put the South London mob in order and make sure the drug dealing was done as far away from him as possible. He knew people took drugs; he wasn't stupid. He just felt that, if he was going to spend twenty years behind bars, it wasn't going to be for drug dealing, plus it brought back all those horrible memories of his mother and her 'medicine'.

'If that's what you want fellas,' he said, 'but I'll be putting my own manager over this side, just to take care of things. If you don't like it, well, remember it is you who asked me.'

Nodding in unison, they all agreed to Tony's terms. Better the devil you know – plus, this way, they were still on a wage. Without this, they had nothing.

❧ ◈ ☙

Tony knew Marlon had an ex-wife. There would be no legal issues, because he had left her secure. The house and plenty of money were in her name. Marlon had spoken of her fondly. There was no ill feeling, she had just got fed up with her house being permanently turned upside down by the police, and asked for a divorce.

Tony also knew Marlon had a girlfriend, which he kept quiet about. All this had come spilling out one evening when they'd had a drink together.

'Tony, man, will you do me a favour?' Marlon had handed him a piece of paper with an address on it. 'That my girlfriend. If anything was ever to happen to me, like taking too much of this stuff, give her ten thousand from me.' Marlon had handed over a brown envelope containing the money and Tony had taken it and promised. Now was the time to keep that promise.

ℬ◊ℭℛ

Tony didn't know how young she was until he got there. She was just seventeen, and he didn't know how long Marlon had been seeing her for. It made him feel uneasy.

She was living in a shared house with some friends. When Tony told her he had something from Marlon for her, she simply held out her hand. He didn't like the idea of turning over that kind of money to her, but he had promised and, after all, it was Marlon's money. Tony handed over the brown envelope containing the notes, and she shut the door in his face. He was pleased about that, because he had done his duty and didn't want to get into conversation.

When Tony told Jake, and John, his driver, about Marlon's girlfriend, they seemed to already know how much he liked very, very young women, bordering on schoolgirls.

'I thought you knew Marlon liked them young,' said Jake. 'Everyone else does.' He was nodding his head to emphasize his point.

Tony was amazed. No wonder people thought he was taking his eye off the ball. All this had been going on around him and he knew nothing about it.

'Well, why didn't you tell me? Bloody hell, Jake, she's just a kid.'

'Not really. Besides, they were all looked after, none of them suffered any hardship. I think his youngest was sixteen, nothing lower than that. All consenting age.'

Tony shrugged. 'Yeah, I suppose.'

'Anyway, do you know that drunk doctor, the one who got struck off?' said Jake.

'No.'

'Yes, you do. He lives in some shitty bedsit down Camberwell. I got Dan to have a quiet word with him. He tested that Tupperware box and it had cyanide in it.'

'It had to be something like that to work as quick, but I wish you hadn't involved Dan and this doctor bloke.'

'I just wanted to find out what it was. How the hell did

Marlon get his hands on that kind of shit?'

'He was a drug dealer, Jake. They can get anything. I've heard that he sometimes mixed cocaine up with rat poison to get rid of his enemies. With me not taking any of that shit, he had to come up with something else.'

Jake felt deflated. For once he thought he had come up with a good idea and now it had backfired.

'Dan will keep his mouth shut, Jake, but this drunken doctor needs taking care of. Make sure he has a nasty drunken fall and breaks his neck, eh? That Angus will do it. Keep it nice and quiet, and then only you, me and Dan know about what Marlon had in mind.'

'What makes you sure we can trust Dan?' Jake was now kicking himself. He had involved too many people. If people thought Tony and Marlon were at each other's throats, the police would be suspicious.

'Dan's a good boy, he reminds me of myself as a kid. He's streetwise and knows what side his bread is buttered. He likes the money and he likes his friends knowing he works for Tony Lambrianu.'

A few days later Tony heard that some drunken doctor who always sat in the pubs hoping someone would buy him a drink had been buying more drinks than he could usually afford. He was on his way home when suddenly he slipped or fell while crossing the road and fell in front of a London bus.

No one was surprised or cared.

Now was a good time to toast Marlon, Tony thought. He had been a good associate, in many ways, but he couldn't be trusted. Now Tony was the undisputed gangland boss of London, and that was how he liked it.

8

THE SOUTH LONDON MOB

After a lot of discussion, both Tony and Jake decided it would be best to keep the reputation of the South London mob going. It would be good for business. After all, a lot of the pubs who paid them both were frightened of the idea that the South London mob would try and take over their pubs and demand they paid their protection money to them. If there was no South London mob boss, who would they fear? They needed Tony and Jake to keep the drug dealers and the trouble away from their front doors.

It seemed like a good idea, but they needed a front man, someone they could trust. They would also go and see Bennie and his associates and give them their own patch to do their dealings on. Neither of them wanted to be associated with drugs, or the low life they attracted.

There was a local pub not far from where Bennie did his dealing that they thought would be perfect. It would keep him away from the street corners, which was only right, at his age, and keep the other dealers and users in one place. It would be like some drug ghetto, all in one place.

One of the men that worked for Tony, and had for a while now, seemed like a safe bet to front the South London mob and act as boss. Obviously, he was an ex-con. They had turned out to be as reliable as Tony had said they would. Each and every one of them was glad of a second chance and having someone show some faith in them. It gave them self-respect.

Scottish Angus, or 'Angry Angus', as he had been known in prison, was a typical Scottish guy, with bright red hair. He was as tall as he was wide. His arms, neck and God only knew where else were covered in gruesome tattoos. Even the guys he worked with, whom he actually liked, were afraid of him. What was worst was, when he had a few whiskies too many, on his night off, they weren't sure if his red face meant he was just drunk or if it was anger. Yes, he would be a good safe bet.

The side none of the men he worked on the doors with as security knew about was that he was a happily married man with a family, but the way he looked and the image he presented meant he had never been given the opportunity to be anything other than a petty thief and a fighter.

Angus was invited into Tony's office, and Tony explained that he was a very busy man, and was thinking of hiring a foreman or some kind of overseer to look after things in the south of London. As much as Angus was large and scary, he was also as thick as a plank, and Tony and Jake squirmed as they watched Angus stroke his ginger beard, as though trying to think of someone to recommend.

Dear God, couldn't this guy take a hint? They weren't asking his advice, they both wanted him to ask for the job, or at least show some interest in it.

He shook his head, and said, 'Dunno, boss, have to be someone you could trust, though.' He was still stroking his beard, as though trying to think.

In the end Jake had had enough. 'What about you, Angus? You're well respected around here, no one would mess with you and we both trust you a lot. After all, we're all friends.' Jake felt that was the simplest way of putting it, and hoped the suggestion might just seep into the man's brain.

The surprised look on Angus's face made Tony realise he had picked the right man for the job. As big and as scary as he looked, he was a modest, good man at heart who only wanted the best for his family. He looked even more surprised when Tony mentioned how much more money he would be earning. That seemed to be the icing on the cake.

'I can't do maths that well, boss, and I'm not so good at writing things down, the wife deals with all that kind of thing, but I would make damn sure your collections were made and no one would make any trouble, that's for sure.' Angus waved a tattooed fist in the air.

'Don't worry about that side of things, Angus, we'll take care of all that. But here's the thing; no one must ever know that you're working for us. Even when you have more than just a wee dram.' Tony mimicked Angus's Scottish accent, when he said the last bit. 'If you ever mention Jake and I are your bosses, I don't care how big you are, I, personally, will see to it that you never see daylight again.'

Angus knew Tony meant it. He'd seen Tony lose his temper, on occasion, and as much as he was a fighting man with a temper of his own, and even feared by his friends, he knew Tony was far worse. Angus got a little drunk and caused chaos, but Tony did it when he was stone cold sober and he seemed to enjoy it. That was the scary part, he hurt people with that charming smile on his face.

'I'll give it a try, boss, but all I am is muscle. I'm not clever, like you two, and as for telling anyone, why would I cut my nose off to spite my face? The wages you're offering me would pay for a nice holiday for the wife and the wee ones. Aye, boss, I'll give it a go. You do all the clever stuff and I'll handle the rest.' His face seemed to go even redder with embarrassment at having to admit he could hardly read or write. And yet, despite that, Tony was giving him a good wage, respect, and now a promotion as a boss, answerable only to Tony.

'All I want you to do is the same as you do here, but

you'll be in charge of the other men, you'll make sure they do their collections and come back with the money. If there's any trouble in the area that needs to be sorted, you speak to Jake or me and we'll tell you what to do. There are drug dealers in the area, it's a popular place for it, as you know, and I don't want to hear that you're doing it as well. I want a clear head at all times, or they'll think you're weak and a pushover, not the kind of man I want as a boss for the South London mob.'

Angus suddenly forgot himself, and forgot he was talking to Tony. He was quickly on the defensive. 'Hold on, laddie, I don't do anything like that. I like a little drink, but you know I've never been drunk on duty. The wife would kill me, and believe me, laddie, I'm more scared of her than I am of you.'

Tony and Jake both burst out laughing at that one. The thought of this big man being frightened of his wife was, indeed, funny.

'Maybe I should let her take things over in the south, then, she sounds like she keeps you in order,' said Tony. Suddenly, a thought occurred to him. This was his angle. The upstairs accommodation that Marlon had used as his office was now clean, decorated, and set up as normal living quarters. He knew Angus and his family were living with his wife's mother. She had always lived there, because Angus was always in and out of prison. If she had her own home, and all she had to do to keep it was keep Angus in good order, Tony was sure she damn well would.

'Of course,' he said, 'there's a large flat above one of the pubs. It's a good size and has a few bedrooms. Maybe you and your family could live there? That is, if you want to.' Tony knew this was a great big carrot to dangle before Angus's eyes. A home of their own, without his interfering mother-in-law bad-mouthing him. It would be sheer paradise.

'You mean we get our own place as well, boss, just for looking after things for you and making sure no one tries to swindle you? Boss, you just got yourself a deal. Hell, my wife in her curlers and dressing gown, shouting and screaming, is a bloody scary sight. Aye laddie, I'll do it, and I'll make sure I do a good job for you. You just tell me what you want me to do, okay.'

Tony held out his hand to shake Angus's. 'Well, leader of the South London mob, you had better go home and tell your wife to start packing.' He smiled, oozing charm. Tony felt this show of flattery and trust would make Angus the loyal puppet he wanted.

After Angus had left, all fired up and excited to tell his wife the good news, Jake burst out laughing. 'I think you've made a mistake there, Tony, sounds like we should let his wife take over, instead. Can you believe it? A guy that size is frightened of his wife! I bet she's only five foot.' They were both laughing at the irony of it.

'Make sure Angus gets some extra cash, Jake, for gadgets or furniture or something that will make his life a little harder.'

'Make his life harder?' Jake echoed.

Tony grinned. 'There's no way on God's earth will his bossy wife let him make mistakes and lose her home and livelihood. The more nice things she has, the more she'll want to keep them.'

The deal was sealed, and what was more, Tony knew there would be no hiccups. Mrs Angus, or whatever her name was, would make sure of that.

As well as sorting Angus out, Tony and Jake spoke to Bennie. He was more than happy to take over his little quarter, so that he could carry on dealing with his friends. Apart from keeping it all together, it also put everyone on the same side. Now, that was good business.

ᏚᎧ◊ᏟᎡ

'What time does the auction start, Tony?' Jake was looking at his watch. Today was a day they had been waiting for, for some time. A large well-known casino, situated only a few streets away from the club, was being auctioned off. It had been losing money, though God knew how or why, and in the end the bank had taken it and was now auctioning off the building.

It was a huge place, and after looking at the accounts and weighing things up, they had all come to the conclusion that it had been badly run, and some of the staff had been embezzling, and things had gone wrong from there. Considering it was a casino, there were hardly any roulette tables. It mainly focused on slot machines. This didn't attract the right custom, as far as Tony was concerned.

On occasion, a few of the high-ranking police detectives liked to play poker, and needed somewhere to play it. They had asked Tony if they could use one of the booths that were used for the strippers. He had let them. He wasn't too happy about it, because he didn't have a gambling licence, but this was the police, after all. He liked to play cards, himself, so he thought why not open a casino, with poker tables, roulette wheels, and even the slot machines?

The accountant who had been sorting out the money laundering liked the idea. A casino was a fantastic place to launder money. There would be so much of it going in and out, it would be extremely hard to trace.

Today was the auction. They all knew the price would be high, because of the West End location. The accounts had been checked and double-checked, everything had been looked into, and everyone agreed this would be a good buy. Tony had dropped the idea of buying the casino building into a conversation he'd had with the detectives, while losing to them at poker one night.

Tony was losing a lot of money, and was prepared to. So, each time he had a winning hand, he folded his cards and dropped them on the table, and let the chief inspectors win. They had all had a good drink together and a thoroughly enjoyable evening.

Naturally, after such a good night, and with goodwill between friends, Tony was assured he would be granted a gambling licence. This was what he wanted. A licence like that was hard to get, and Tony knew it. Even after all these years, his prison record would go against him.

He was already making plans for the casino, and mentally decorating it in the famous Lambrianu pink. He would also make it exclusive, and not just let anyone walk in off the streets. That was one reason the place had gone bankrupt in the first place. Gamblers with real money were what he wanted.

Rich men liked 'exclusive'. They liked their own men's club. Tony had realised that early on, with the strippers, and to get that, they were prepared to pay.

9

A GAMBLERS' PARADISE

The auction room was packed to the hilt when Tony and Jake walked in. They recognized some of the other businessmen that wanted to buy the casino. There were other properties up for sale, as well, including a small men-only drinking club, not far from Tony's own club. It had always been a gentlemen's club; when the owner died, there was no one to take over, and so his widow was putting it up for auction. Tony liked the look of it. It was a quirky place on the high street corner, almost triangle-shaped, and better still, it was to be a quick, cheap sale.

People had taken notice when they saw Tony and Jake arrive; they hadn't known he was interested in the casino. They didn't want to offend him, and so approached him in a businesslike manner that they hoped would be acceptable.

'I didn't realise you were interested in the old casino, Mr Lambrianu. If you wish, I'll gladly step down and leave,' a couple of them had said to him. He had assured them all was fair in love and war, and may the best man win. After all, even if he didn't get to buy it, they would still have to pay him to protect it. As far as Tony was concerned it was a win-win situation, but he wanted to do things fair and square. There were some real estate businessmen there that wanted to transform the building into separate apartments, not keep it as a casino at all. Everyone had their own dream about the place. The trick was not to look too eager.

Before the big sale of the casino, while the auctioneer had everyone's attention, he offered up the men's drinking club. There were a few bids on the property, including telephone bids, but most people were too interested in the main prize – the casino – to pay much attention to the club. They were itching for the sale to be over, so they could get on with the main matter in hand.

Tony was still thinking and deliberating as he saw and heard the bids for the club come in. Then, as the auctioneer was about to bring down his gavel, Tony shouted out a much larger bid than was currently being offered.

Jake looked at him oddly; he hadn't expected this. Tony hadn't discussed it with him, it was obviously something done on a whim. He didn't ask any questions while being watched by the other men in the room, but it did set the cat amongst the pigeons. All the other businessmen were now curious. What did Tony Lambrianu have planned, and what had he seen in the place that they had missed? They had been too interested in the casino to pay any attention to the club. Was that all Mr Lambrianu had come for?

Everyone breathed a sigh of relief when the auctioneer eventually started the bidding on the casino. The auction was a little like a poker game of its own. None of the other bidders wanted to discuss how much their spending limit was. No one wanted to show their cards, as it were.

Tony and Jake didn't place a bid straight off, they waited to see how eager everyone else was. Tony wanted to see how quickly they would exhaust their spending limit. Obviously, this drove the price higher and higher, and then the room went silent. The auctioneer was giving everyone a chance to think and calculate. Tony and Jake looked around at the crowd. There were only, maybe, half a dozen serious bidders left. Some were consortiums that had put their money together and were going to have shares in the place.

At last, Jake made the first bid, and everyone turned to look at him and Tony. They had presumed that Tony and Jake weren't going to bid, because up until now they had been silent. The auctioneer seemed to sigh with relief and carried on. The final bid was ten million pounds. The auctioneer looked around, waiting. 'Fourteen,' shouted Tony. He knew this was more than expected. The more serious bidders might have gone to twelve, but Tony had gone over that, and that was pushing it too far. He was trying to look cool and nonchalant about it. He didn't want to look flustered or nervous, though deep inside, his heart was pounding.

Someone on the telephone made another bid. Tony felt angry and frustrated, but he tried remaining calm. 'Plus one more million, auctioneer,' he said. At last, the gavel went down; the casino was Tony's. He had paid sixteen million pounds for a casino that had gone bust. He hadn't expected that much would be necessary but, hopefully, in time, he would make his money back. He felt like strangling whoever had been on the other end of the telephone. Whoever it was, they weren't going to steal his thunder.

Suddenly, the auctioneer interrupted the proceedings. It seemed everyone at the auction had had to prove they could afford to bid on this property, to stop time-wasters. It was a closed auction. Everyone who had shown interest in the casino had been shown around the property, and put on the 'approved' list after verification.

The auctioneer announced that the telephone bid had been from someone who was not on their list. He then offered the casino to Tony at the original price. Tony's smile lit the place up; he was in his element. But who the hell had been messing around on the end of the telephone? He would make it his business to find out. He wouldn't be made a fool of.

'Don't worry about it, Tony, whoever it was drove the price up high against the other bidders, and then withdrew it, once they knew they were only bidding against you.' Jake laughed. 'They did you a favour; none of these guys were going to pay that, and now they're seriously pissed off that you didn't have to pay it, either.'

Tony nodded, it made sense, but he was still curious.

Once the auction room had cleared, it was time to go to the auctioneer's office and pay his debts. Everything was finalized, and papers were to be drawn up in the name of the new owners. At last, the auctioneer handed Tony the keys to both the gentlemen's club and the casino.

Tony looked at Jake and then back at the keys; he had won, it had definitely been a gamble, going for the casino, and he had held the winning hand. 'Who was the telephone bidder for the casino, do you know?' he said to the auctioneer.

The auctioneer looked awkward and flustered, and didn't seem to want to say, but said he would check with the staff who were on the telephones. He disappeared out of the office.

'Leave it, Tony, what does it matter?' Jake couldn't understand why Tony was so interested, he thought it was better left alone. Whoever it was had done no harm. If anything, they had turned the bidding events around and it had cost Tony no more than he had been prepared to spend. Was it really worth fighting over?

'Just interested, Jake, that's all.'

The auctioneer returned. 'It seems we didn't get the bidder's full details,' he said.

'Was it a man or a woman? What name did they give?' said Tony.

'Erm … it was a woman.'

'Called?'

'The only name we got was "Julie".'

'And is this how you usually do business?' demanded Tony.

'No, sir,' said the auctioneer. His cheeks were pink. 'It seems our systems came up short this time.'

෨◊ର

They left the auction room and got into the car, and Tony told John, his driver, to take them to the casino. John was full of congratulations; he knew Tony had wanted this, and had heard him making plans for it on many occasions.

'Why do you want that men's club, Tony? You never mentioned it before,' said Jake. He was still surprised Tony had bought that place, as well.

'A well-known men's club, in the heart of the West End? It just appealed to me. It would be a good place for another strip club, don't you think? It's already got the reputation as "gentlemen only".'

Jake nodded his head. The place was small, although the auctioneer had called it 'intimate', but it had a good reputation and wasn't run-down; it was simply being sold off following the death of the owner.

'Fair point, I see that now. I presume it'll stay a men's club, full of beautiful women to make it even more exclusive.' Jake smiled. Tony had foresight. He had seen this opportunity and got the place relatively cheaply, because it had been overlooked by the other bidders.

John pulled up at the casino and the men got out of the car. Tony took the keys out of his pocket and opened the doors. The place was still in good condition, and it wouldn't take a lot of work to make it more to his own taste. He would need croupiers he could trust, and knew a casino not too far away that trained them. He liked the idea of new fresh faces, people who would only ever know him as their boss.

The roulette tables were a little worn, but that was easily rectified; in any case, he wanted more tables brought in. He thought they helped to create the authentic casino atmosphere.

Although Tony liked a gamble himself, neither he nor Jake knew anything about running a casino. They would have to learn fast. There were all kinds of strict rules and regulations in force, something a good lawyer would be able to handle.

A lot of the equipment needed updating, but again, there was nothing that would cause too much of a problem. Firstly, the place needed a good overhaul, and then a manager would be needed, someone they could trust who could show them both how things were run.

It was a huge project, Tony knew that he really was out of his depth, but other people had learnt how to run a casino, so why couldn't he?

Jake was standing at a table in the empty casino, spinning one of the roulette wheels. 'Do you think we've bitten off more than we can chew?' he said. Even he was starting to wonder, now. It had seemed like such a good idea, but hindsight is a wonderful thing.

'Yes and no,' said Tony. He ran his hands through his hair and looked around the huge room; it was truly a gamblers' paradise – in the right hands, of course. 'It's going to take time and a lot of money, but I like a challenge, you know that.' Tony gave Jake a weak smile.

'Come on,' said Jake trying to lighten the mood, 'let's go and see the rest of this place. It's like a TARDIS, it just gets bigger and bigger on the inside.'

At the very back of the main room of the casino was a large bar, and behind that was a large kitchen area, which had provided mediocre food for the small restaurant. The casino had two more floors. The top one contained a room fitted out with safes, for the cash, and an apartment.

The amount of money that would be handled through the casino would be vast, which meant the very best security would be needed, and the money would have to be collected on a regular basis. Tony and Jake had both seen guards with their metal helmets and steel boxes carrying cash to their vans, which would be what they would need. Thinking again, the accountant would know all about that side of things, and so would the croupier training centre. All the tutors there had been working in casinos for most of their lives, and that would possibly be where he would find a manager, too.

'I want to set up my main office here,' said Tony. 'I'll leave the strip clubs to Sharon. Each one of us needs to be based somewhere, to keep an eye on things. I'll go to the club when the strippers aren't there, and I'll host the club nights.' Tony thought it was for the best that he gave the strip clubs a wide berth, and not be forever looking over Sharon's shoulder.

Jake burst out laughing. 'What you mean, Tony, is that you would rather be known as the casino king, than the king of sin. No, you're right. Anyway, it'll add a bit of mystery to the place – all those beautiful exotic dancers in your club and not one of them meets the boss.' Jake nodded.

It gave the place a little more style and class. Tony had never wanted to appear to be interested in his employees. He had never made any attempt to charm the dancers or even go out of his way to meet them, he had left all of that to Sharon. He was strictly hands-off, and didn't want to mix business with pleasure.

'Right, well, I've seen enough for now. Next, I want to go and see this men's club.' They both walked out of the casino, locked it up and got back in the car. Jake was surprised; this men's club seemed to intrigue Tony more than the casino. There was obviously something about it that appealed to him.

Although Tony hadn't been to the viewing of the place, he had imagined what it would look like inside, and he wasn't disappointed when he saw it. Apart from the long, marbled hallway, which led into lounge rooms furnished with wingback Chesterfield armchairs, club chairs and sofas, it had a large reception and bar area. *This is what a men's club should look like*, he thought. Somewhere the elite would come, relax, read their newspapers and be at their ease. They had always had to pay a membership fee, and so that wouldn't come as a surprise. Tony knew it'd had some form of maître d' or butler to see to the men's needs. Most of the waiters and bar staff were also men, and that was something Tony aimed to change.

He knew he couldn't have a Playboy-style 'bunny girl' club, that had already been done, but he would come as close as possible. There were a couple of lounges, so the girls could be in one room and the men who just wanted to relax with their newspapers and talk over the day's business would have a whole lounge space to themselves – although Tony had a feeling they wouldn't be reading their newspapers for too long. All men liked to see a pretty woman, unless they were dead! This way, it could be discreetly run, without any kind of advertising.

The members that would come here would be businessmen whom Tony could get acquainted with and, you never knew, he might even earn a few favours by ingratiating himself, and so make some business deals of his own. This was another reason he wanted to be more than just a strip-club owner. He wanted these members to take him seriously.

Upstairs were a few bedrooms. *It's basically a posh bed and breakfast place*, Tony thought to himself. Apparently, when some of the members had a few drinks too many, they were known to 'stay at their club' for the night. Tony liked it, it all seemed very cloak and dagger. Like some secret society.

All of this was included in the price of their membership. Tony and Jake both agreed, one of the first things they needed to do was gain access to all of the old member's names, so they could invite them back to their club. The men were probably devastated to no longer have somewhere private to call their own. The staff who had worked there previously were hoping that maybe the new owners would employ them. That had been one of the requests of the widow of the former owner, and Tony thought it was a good idea, as well.

Why spoil a good thing? Tony thought. This butler, or whatever, already knew the members and would have a good rapport with them. He would also know all their little quirky ways and how they liked things done. He would be a real asset.

As he walked out of the club and into the sunshine again, Tony felt happy. Things seemed to be going well, business was on the up, his money-lending business was flourishing, and all of his collectors had turned out to be good, decent guys, just waiting for a second chance. Not once had their collections been short, although how they achieved that was their business.

As he sat in the back of the car being driven back to the club, Tony was mentally making a list of things that needed to take priority. 'It's going to be a busy week, Jake, we've got a lot to do.'

Jake nodded, he knew this, and hopefully so did Sharon. It seemed they both led their own lives these days. At some point things would calm down and maybe, just maybe, they could get their own life on track – although it seemed whenever he had thought that in the past, Tony had come up with yet another scheme.

'We need the accountant to sort out the money side of things, and I presume he'll want to use the casino for his laundering activities, too. Well, he's got away with it so far, so let's see. Those licences need sorting properly and, of course, the decorators need to go in and put our own stamp on both places.'

'I presume at some point we will eat?' Jake was smiling to himself; he knew full well when Tony was all fired up like this, nothing else mattered.

'I want to go and see the widow of the previous men's club owner; maybe she could contact some of the staff for us, including this butler guy. He'll be able to put us in the full picture of the place.'

'Let's go and see the accountant first, and let him know we've bought them, then he can work his magic. Then let's sort out the lawyers, and they can work theirs. We also need to go to that croupier training school, and see what they have on offer, but firstly, I need a bacon sandwich and a coffee. No arguments.'

John heard Jake and pulled the car into the side of the road, near a well-known greasy spoon – one of those cafés where cholesterol is never mentioned and fried breakfasts are all they have to offer.

Even while Jake was trying to enjoy his extra-large fried meal, Tony was still making lists and trying to work out their plan of action.

'Tony, give it a rest, will you?' said Jake. 'At least until I've finished eating.' With that, he reached over to Tony's untouched plate, picked up a sausage and put it in Tony's mouth.

10

TONY'S EMPIRE

I t was a month later, and things were well underway. The accountant had sorted out all the necessary paperwork and the lawyers had been able to obtain the licences that were required. Tony had been promised that the licensing wouldn't be a problem, and it wasn't. He liked having friends with influence.

Tony and Jake had both been to visit the croupier training school. The main tutor was a man who seemed to have worked everywhere, in his day – Las Vegas, cruise ships, you name, it this guy had done it. Considering the glamorous world he had chosen as an occupation, he didn't seem fazed by it. He was now around fifty years old, and had wanted to settle down in London. He said that, even though he had travelled the globe, there was no place like home.

He had a lot of salt and pepper hair, making him look like some mad scientist. He was tall and slim, but he had an air of authority about him. He came across as very friendly, and told Tony and Jake all they wanted to know, and even advised them on the best croupiers he was training. They all had their licences, and were drilled every day on their mathematical skills and how to 'kiss up' when they needed a supervisor.

'Kiss up' is a gambling term especially for croupiers. All the supervisors walk around the tables regularly, checking on things. To get their attention, instead of shouting or waving, the croupiers make a kissing sound. That's the code that means the supervisor is needed. It was all these little tricks of the trade that Tony wanted to know about.

Graham, the croupier trainer, was worth more than his weight in gold, and Tony couldn't help himself – he offered him the manager's job there and then. He didn't want to wait; this man knew his stuff. He also knew the croupiers he had trained, and he was already their boss.

Graham was taken aback; he hadn't expected this. He had been flattered when he had heard Mr Lambrianu wanted to meet him, at his own convenience, and even more flattered when Tony asked his advice.

'Have you ever managed a casino before, Graham? You seem to have done a lot.' Tony was eyeing him up. He reckoned Graham was just what he was looking for – a well-known, well-respected croupier trainer, without a blemish on his record.

'I have, Mr Lambrianu, but the hours are long and stressful. Keeping people happy enough to want to spend their money can be very hard work, at times. It's nice to go home, for a change, at the end of the day, and not worry that there's something you may have forgotten.'

Tony nodded his head, he knew exactly what Graham meant. He felt like he was always on call. On the odd occasion, he disappeared to Elle's house. There, he could be himself. Jake was around, if needed, but sometimes Tony just wanted to escape the limelight and eat Elle's sausages and mashed potato, and lounge on her sofa, watching nothing in particular on the television while Elle was at bingo.

There were no journalists there, no photographers to catch him out when he wasn't wearing one of his famous

Savile Row suits. This was home, somewhere he could be himself. There were times when, after all these years, Tony felt the women in his life were becoming boring. Everyone wanted the 'showman'. He knew he had only himself to blame for this, he had wanted the publicity and played up to the cameras for it, but sometimes having no privacy made life hard.

That was another reason he had liked the idea of the men's club. All of the rich, elite men had used it as an escape from the public eye. Maybe he should take a leaf out of their book. Everyone needed their own space. Jake went home with Sharon, back to their home and their own little nest. That was where they could relax and be themselves. Of course, Jake and Sharon had a much bigger house now, much nearer the West End for convenience, but it was their much-needed space to be alone.

'Can I think about it, Mr Lambrianu? I mean no disrespect, but it would be a lot to take on.' Graham knew who Tony was, and he had heard of his gangland reputation, so by no means did he want to upset this man. Even though not in the circle, he knew by the gossip it wouldn't be good for his health.

'I respect that, Graham. Bear in mind you'd be free to hire your own assistant manager, someone as trustworthy as yourself. After all, whoever you hired, you and you alone would be responsible for.' Even though Tony was turning on the charm and being friendly, the fleeting thought that passed through Graham's mind was how threatening that sounded. Any hiccups his assistant might make would put his head on the chopping block.

'You'll need four or five managers, Mr Lambrianu, and then they would answer to one main manager, who would answer to you. That's how it works. You need managers for the roulette tables, blackjack tables and so on.' Graham actually started feeling sorry for Tony; he realised now that Tony hadn't realised how much work he had taken on. This wasn't a nightclub.

Tony smiled at him, his cheeks beginning to colour. He had shown how naïve he was in the casino game. He looked towards Jake for backup.

'Well, Graham, it sounds like we need you more than you need us,' said Jake, trying to make light of the situation. 'If nothing else, why don't you come on the payroll as an adviser. We need you, that's pretty obvious.' Jake's free and easy way seemed to do the trick.

Graham nodded. 'I'd be happy to help in any way I can. What plans do you have for the casino? Don't get me wrong, it's a nice place, but it's dated. That's why it lost money; it didn't attract new custom.'

Now Tony felt he was on firmer ground. 'If it's updated glamour you want, I'm your man. Jake's right, we're going back to school and you're going to be our teacher.' Tony held out his hand to shake Graham's. He felt he had fallen on his feet with this man.

৪০◊ൠ

Tony was in his apartment above the club, discussing the day's proceedings with Jake, when Sharon rang to say there was someone here to meet them. She didn't say anything else; she just put the intercom phone down.

'What the hell is it now,' Tony muttered. He pushed back his hair, put on his jacket and went downstairs to his office. They were both surprised to see a gentleman in his late fifties, possibly sixties, waiting for them.

The man was extremely well dressed, his suit impeccable, his tie knotted with a perfect full-Windsor, and he didn't have a hair out of place. He was stocky, but held himself upright and proud. He was definitely old school. He held out his hand and introduced himself. 'I'm Bernard Mathers, I believe you wanted to see me.'

Tony shook his hand out of habit, then he and Jake looked at each other and then back at this overpowering man, with his British public-school accent. His tone of voice, and the way he pronounced each syllable, with a kind of inherent snobbery, reminded them both of a headmaster. Thankfully Sharon was on hand to solve the mystery.

'Mr Mathers, has come at your request, Tony. He was the maître d' at the men's club,' she said. She didn't want to use the word 'butler', in case it caused offence.

'Of course. My apologies, do come in, Mr Mathers.' Tony unlocked the office door and held out his hand to usher Mr Mathers in first. 'Please, take a seat. Would you like some tea, coffee or maybe something stronger?'

'Not just now, thank you.' His curt reply caused an awkward silence in the room. Even the way he sat upright on the chair seemed to make Tony want to sit up straighter. Jake broke the ice first. 'I'm sure you are aware, Mr Mathers, that we have bought the men's club. The widow of the previous owner has requested that we keep on some of the staff that have worked there loyally for many years. I'm sure we don't need to tell you all of this, because I am fairly sure you have been kept up to speed on things. So, what about you? Are you still willing to work there?' Jake felt it was the quickest and easiest way to put it. If this man wasn't interested, he wouldn't have come. On the other hand, seeing that he was a typical British gentleman, he had probably come to tell them he didn't want their job. Now was the time to find out.

'You should wear a Windsor knot in your tie, Mr Lambrianu, it shows style.' Mr Mathers reached over the desk, took hold of Tony's tie and started adjusting it.

'That's better,' he said, and he sat back in the chair again. He looked across at Jake, who wasn't wearing a tie, because he had left it upstairs, and gave him a look of disdain.

Who's interviewing who here? Tony thought. His face turned pink. Tony cleared his throat and tried to compose himself; he felt about five years old in front of this man. 'So, as Jake, my brother, has asked, are you interested in working at the men's club?'

Mathers paused before answering, then said, 'That

would depend, Mr Lambrianu. I was in charge of the club, and the staff where answerable to me. There is a housekeeper, Mrs Gibbins; she instructed the cleaners and made sure the rooms were aired. My gentlemen relied on me and how I ran things.'

Tony liked the way this man called the members his 'gentlemen', he thought that showed real style. No wonder they depended on him. He was like one of those butlers you knew about from old movies or posh television dramas. This man was looking for a job, but he had given his terms and put Tony and Jake firmly in their place.

'Nothing in that department would particularly change, although I do have a few changes of my own that I wish to make.' Tony was trying to pronounce his words as accurately as Mr Mathers was doing. He had always made a point of speaking properly, but this man made him want to improve himself further. It wasn't just clothes that made the man.

'Such as?' Mr Mathers got straight to the point, he wanted to know what kind of changes Tony was thinking about making before agreeing to anything. He waited patiently. Tony tried diverting his eyes from Mr Mathers, he really didn't want to tell him he was thinking of having scantily dressed women in 'his' club. He felt embarrassed saying it.

Jake came to the rescue. 'We think a better kitchen, offering a broader menu would be in order, Mr Mathers.' He waited and watched Mr Mathers nod his approval. Now for the big one. 'We, well, I, also thought it might be a nice idea for your gentlemen to have the opportunity to appreciate some female entertainment, or at least waitresses. We anticipate they'd be dressed in sexier clothing than waitresses traditionally wear, although it would still be very classy.' Jake was trying to find the right words and realised he had failed miserably.

Thank God Sharon walked in with a tray of coffee. 'Here you are, gentlemen, I thought you might like this.' She had organized a tray with a jug of milk and a bowl of sugar. Rather than their usual mugs, there were proper coffee cups and saucers. She knew how to appeal to Mr Mathers.

Jake explained to Mr Mathers that Sharon was his wife, and gained an approving nod. This was hard work. Sharon could see Tony and Jake were at a loss for words and thankfully intervened. 'Would you like to pour, Mr Mathers, or shall I be mother?' She put her hand out towards the coffee pot and instantly, Mr Mathers took over.

Sharon had read and seen all of those Jane Austen novels, and remembered how the butlers behaved.

'We would like to leave the club as it was, Mr Mathers,' she said, 'but as it is a members-only club, we also felt that we should provide everything for the members. There would be you, of course, overseeing all of the arrangements. We want a good chef who can offer whatever takes the gentlemen's fancy and, as there are a few large lounges, we think one of them could be an entertainments room. All the rest would stay exactly the same. However, we thought that maybe some of the younger gentlemen might appreciate that feminine touch.' Sharon had cracked it. She had said just what Jake and Tony were thinking, but couldn't find the words to express.

They could all see Mr Mathers was deep in thought. He obviously didn't like the thought of women invading his club. 'Of course, it's your club, Mr Lambrianu, and it's no secret you hire exotic dancers, that's your business. Personally, I wouldn't like to think of the club as some sort of brothel, with all due respect.'

'Neither would I,' said Tony. 'We're just offering entertainment, Mr Mathers. That way, if they wanted, the members could be entertained in their own private space, without having to rub shoulders with … well, just anyone.' Tony didn't want to say 'commoners', because he felt that Mr Mathers thought he was common. Brothel, indeed!

'Well, that sort of thing would have to be left in the capable hands of Ashley, he would be good at that sort of thing. Personally, I would like to distance myself from it and tend to my gentlemen in the other lounges.'

'Ashley? Who is Ashley?' asked Tony. Now they were getting way ahead of themselves. This bloody butler was already organizing the staff.

'Ashley is a young gentleman, fully trained as a butler, who was an under butler at one of the large estate houses. He was always on hand to cheer the gentlemen up and see to their needs. Looking after the entertainment side of things would be his dream come true. Yes, Ashley is definitely the man for the job.'

It seemed Tony that Mathers had already made up his mind, and now he was beginning to lose his patience with this pompous old butler. Sharon saw the look in Tony's eye and knew she had to step in again.

'He sounds excellent, Mr Mathers. And, of course, with that kind of recommendation from you, how could we refuse? So, do you wish to continue as butler of the club, or are you going to leave us to find a poor substitute for you?' Sharon smiled at him, and cast a sly glance over at Tony.

Then Mr Mathers took them all by surprise; he reached into his coat pocket and took out a notebook, which he handed to Tony. 'I have contacted most of the gentlemen in the book, who were members. Some are away at the moment, many have houses abroad, you know.'

Jake looked at Tony, amazed; his jaw nearly dropped. That crafty old sod had always intended on taking the job, he had already informed all the old members that the club had a new owner, and would be re-opening soon. This Ashley guy, whoever he was, was going to be in charge of entertainment? No way, Sharon did that.

'You seem to have thought of everything, Mr Mathers, what would we do without you? Of course, we're planning to get the decorators in and to spruce the club up, a little. As you know, the kitchen area will have to be sorted out. Would your housekeeper be willing to carry on with her good work, do you think?' Sharon knew how to appeal to this man; although she was acting like the lady of the manor, she was still entrusting the butler to make all of the necessary arrangements. That was the way he liked it. 'Maybe I could meet Ashley, and we could discuss the entertainment?' Sharon left it as an open question, and waited.

'I think that would be acceptable. I'll contact him immediately, and let him know you wish to meet him.'

Suddenly, Tony and Jake realised they were not included in the conversation. All these arrangements were between Mr Mathers and Sharon. Tony and Jake just looked on, like sleeping partners of the club. Or spare parts.

'So, Mr Mathers, do we have a deal? Are you going to carry on doing your good work and look after "our gentlemen"?' Sharon smiled at him. She didn't want it to sound cold, like a job interview. It was obvious Mr Mathers knew his stuff and had been around the block many times and seen it all. On the surface, he was the typical English butler; underneath, he knew everyone's secrets.

All the men in that club had confided in him at some point or another, and he knew everything about them. They trusted him, and it would be hard going to find someone else they would trust in the same way. Of course he was going to carry on with his old job, he had always intended to, he just wanted to make his presence known. He was nobody's fool, and he wanted the great Mr Lambrianu to know it.

'Of course,' interrupted Tony, trying to think of something to say, so that he wouldn't be totally forgotten, 'there would be a wage increase, and if there was anything that you weren't happy with, you should let us know.'

Mr Mathers shook his finger at Tony. 'Let's not talk of vulgarities like money and wages just now, Mr Lambrianu. And it's "were not", not "weren't". People notice these things.' Now Mathers was correcting Tony's speech. In an odd kind of way, Tony liked him. He came across as a little pompous and scary, but he was more like a father figure. He stood up; the meeting was over.

'You are right, of course, Mr Mathers. Give me time and I will learn, I promise.' Tony stood, too. He smiled at him and shook his hand. Then Sharon linked her arm through Mr Mathers' arm and showed him out. It was all a little familiar, and he showed surprise at Sharon's intimacy, but he smiled back at her.

'Bloody hell, Tony, are you sure you can handle him? He acts like he's royalty; he scares me. You had better learn to dress and speak properly, and fast!' Although Jake was laughing, he meant it.

Sitting at his desk, listening intently to Jake's ramblings about the scary butler, Tony felt satisfied. Normally, people were scared of both him and Jake, and the men that worked for them. This butler was scary without using a threatening fist; just his authority was sufficient. Now, that was clever.

Having Mr Mathers' loyalty would indeed be a prize. There would be no question that he would keep the men's club in good order and the members satisfied. He had interviewed Tony and Jake without them even realising he was doing it. He had heard of Tony's reputation and so had come to assess him and assert his own authority – and he had done both.

'So, Jake, let him use his skills. I always thought I dressed stylishly, but he seems to think there's more to learn. Let's use his experience and knowledge. More to the point, let's use his reputation. If some of the old members think he is prepared to work for us, it's like a seal of approval. The old members will join again, and feel safe knowing they have their old friend back.'

'Well, Sharon seems to like him, I suppose that's something. What about this Ashley guy?'

'Again, Jake, he's one of the old staff members with the butler's approval; that will do for me.'

As far as Tony was concerned that was the end of the subject. He could easily leave the supervision of the refurbishment and workmen under the eagle eye of Mr

Mathers. If anything, he doubted Mr Mathers would want him interfering. That was fair enough; if it wasn't broken, why fix it? The man was more than capable.

11

MISSION IMPOSSIBLE

J ake ran into Tony's office, where Tony was at his desk,
deep in conversation with the accountant. 'That's it,' he
said, 'I've had enough.'

Tony and the accountant both looked up at the doorway
and gawped at Jake, who was red-faced, angry and swearing.

It was early in the morning, the club wasn't open, the
only people around were the cleaners, so what could have
upset Jake so much?

'What's wrong, what's happened?' said Tony.

Jake was still shouting threats about how he was going
to 'kill him', and that he'd 'absolutely had enough'. This
wasn't like him at all. He was always the calmer of the two.

'Calm down and sit down, will you, and tell me what you
are going on about.' Tony was losing his patience. Over the
last couple of weeks he had hardly slept. His brain was
constantly thinking over his plans, trying to spot anything
he might have forgotten. Right at that moment he hadn't
shaved, he was dressed in jeans and a T-shirt, and he was
stressed to the max. No one but the people closest to him
ever saw him like that, he made sure of it. Now he had Jake
in his office, shouting and raving like a lunatic, dressed in a
tracksuit. This wasn't the image he liked to present;

thankfully, there was no one around but the accountant and the cleaners.

'That bloody Ashley bloke, he's having an affair with my Sharon. She didn't come home last night. Just because I was working late and didn't go home till the early hours, she decided to stay at Ashley's. She left a bloody sticky note on the fridge. It's been like this for weeks, all I can hear is his name, and her laughing on the telephone with him. Where's your gun? I'm going to kill him.' Jake walked towards Tony's desk and held his hand out for the gun.

'No married person having an affair, Jake, leaves a sticky note on the fridge, telling their partner they are staying with someone else,' said the accountant. He sat back in his chair and adjusted his glasses.

Jake stopped shouting and looked at them both. What the accountant had said seemed to be seeping into his angry brain. 'So, why is she with him all the time, then?'

'They do have business to discuss about the men's club,' said Tony, trying to appease him. Personally, with everything that was going on, he hadn't noticed Sharon's absence.

'Right, and that takes all night at his house, does it?' Jake looked at them both with a steely glare. He knew he was right. It was all Sharon had been talking about lately, 'Ashley this' and Ashley that'. He was sick of hearing the guy's name.

'Have either of you met him?' The accountant waited for an answer. He saw Tony and Jake look at each other. Neither of them had bothered to meet him, they had left it all to Mr Mathers and Sharon.

'No, but I want to meet him, because I'm going to fucking kill him!' Jake was just about to start shouting again, when the accountant held up his hand to stop him.

'Go and face the enemy, Jake. Find out what Sharon finds so appealing about this man. My advice is to go and meet him for yourself, before you do anything stupid.' He was frowning, and his brow was furrowed. 'We're a few days from finishing all the refurbishments, the last thing we need before opening the casino and the club is a murder on our hands.' The accountant spoke calmly and reasonably.

'Right, I will then. Are you coming, Tony? Let's get to the club and see this boy wonder, shall we? We're his bosses, we can sack him!' Jake stood with his hands on his hips and waited for Tony.

'Before either of us goes anywhere, we're going to shave and put our suits on. We do not go anywhere looking like this. As you say, we're his bosses, so we go there looking like bosses.'

Jake nodded his head. He was beginning to calm down a little, but when it came to Sharon, he lost all sense of reason. He loved her, she was everything to him, and the thought that some other guy was sniffing around her like a dog on heat fired him up.

After showering and shaving, and putting on their suits, they looked like respectable businessmen. They got into the back of the car and John drove them to the gentlemen's club. All the time, Tony was telling Jake to keep calm. 'We know nothing about this guy, Jake, he could be married with ten kids, for all we know. Sharon could have stayed at his house with his wife.'

Jake looked down at his feet, like a spoilt child being reprimanded by their parent. He hadn't thought of that. It was true, though, and now it was time to meet him and find out. They had taken Mr Mathers' word about Ashley. They should at least know their staff.

The door of the men's club was open, as there were delivery drivers dropping off new furniture for the club. Tony froze; he could hear Sharon laughing. Why on earth had he come unannounced? What if Sharon was having an affair with this guy? What were they going to find when they went in? Tony wished he had telephoned ahead, to warn her.

Jake stormed ahead of him and followed the chatter and the laughter; he was ready for an argument. In his mind, he could see Sharon all over this guy, doing whatever. He stopped short at the door to one of the lounges. Surveying the scene before him, he gave a weak smile.

Tony was hot on his heels; if he had seen something wrong, Jake would have been going crazy by now, so why the sudden silence?

Sharon, Mr Mathers, and a couple of women, obviously the cleaners, were sitting having a pot of tea.

Sharon looked up at Jake; although surprised to see him, she beamed a smile at him.

'Jake, love, what are you doing here? Hi, Tony.' She stood up and walked towards Jake and kissed his cheek. 'Why didn't you say you were coming? Do you want some tea?' She was being loving and friendly, the same as always.

Tony looked on and took a breath, trying to assess the situation. He felt the need to assert his authority, so he walked up to Mr Mathers, who stood up to greet him, and shook his hand. 'How is everything going Mr Mathers? Everything running to schedule?' He knew that was a stupid question, because this guy was like an army major.

Mr Mathers offered Tony his seat and stood at the side of it. 'If I may be so bold, Mr Lambrianu, a gentleman always wears a silk handkerchief in his breast pocket, and carries a linen one for personal use. I will show you around, if you would be so kind as to follow me.' He started towards the door to show Tony and Jake all the decorations and the new furniture that had been delivered.

Yet again, Tony felt like a schoolboy and blushed at Mr Mathers' reprimand. He would have to take more care, next time, when getting dressed.

Each room had been redecorated, and smelt fresh and clean. The new wooden coffee tables by the side of the replacement chesterfield suites made the place look exactly the same, just updated. The kitchen area, and its huge ovens surrounded by stainless steel worktops, looked amazing. They had already hired a good chef to run it. Tony had been to see the chef at the Italian restaurant he used most frequently and asked if he could recommend someone.

The bar was fully stocked, and the upstairs bedrooms had been refurbished and redecorated. Everything looked spick and span. It looked exactly the same, but more modern, and offered more comfort. Mr Mathers had suggested a log burner fire, which he felt would give the place a warmer, friendlier feel, but the insurance for that had been silly. They had compromised and got one that looked real, but was, in fact, electric. It sat in the white marble fireplace and gave off the same cosy glow. Jake hadn't understood why he wanted a fire, because the whole place had central heating, but Tony had gone along with Mr Mathers' suggestions.

Mr Mathers then opened a huge black book that was on a table stand in the reception area.

'This is the list of the members that have rejoined, plus some new ones they have recommended us to.'

Tony looked down at the huge book and the list of names. He couldn't believe it; the list was long, and some of the names on it were famous celebrities, MPs and very respectable stockbrokers.

'There is a list, here, of reserves. These are the people that wish to join us, when we have the capacity.'

Tony looked up at Mr Mathers, who looked very pleased with himself, although he didn't crack a smile. Tony had known this man would be worth his weight in gold. He had already done his job, and done it very well indeed, contacting all these men personally. Looking back at the list of members, he saw Ralph Gold's name.

'Do you know Ralph Gold?' He looked at Mr Mathers, and waited. Now he was curious. He had wanted a meeting with Ralph Gold to discuss business and hopefully do some business dealings with him, but Ralph had been aloof, and never available.

'I do, a very nice gentleman indeed.' With that, Mr Mathers closed the book. He gave no more information about Ralph Gold. Tony might have been the boss but Mr Mathers was in charge; he felt this man enjoyed pulling him down a peg or two.

'That lounge, over there,' Mr Mathers pointed to a closed door at the bottom of the corridor, 'is Ashley's domain. I believe Mrs Sinclair has been dealing with him.'

Ashley! Christ, Tony had almost forgotten why he was there. Ashley was the very man they were there to meet. Jake had come to check out the competition.

'Is Ashley here?' Tony said, as naturally as possible. 'Maybe it's time I met him.'

Jake had obviously heard the name, and he came out of the lounge into the hallway. He looked at Tony, stuck out his chin and pouted.

Mr Mathers walked towards the closed door and knocked. 'I'll leave you to it, Mr Lambrianu. By the way. You do not have to call me "Mr Mathers". "Mathers" will do; all my gentlemen call me "Mathers".'

Tony sighed again and looked at Jake; of course, he was the butler, they were all called by their last names, and there was no 'mister' attached to it. He gave 'Mathers' a nod and a smile.

Sharon came down the corridor and stood with them. Mathers walked away, having informed them he would be upstairs, checking the housekeeper had everything in order.

'Don't worry, you two, he never comes into this den of iniquity.' Sharon laughed at them both and opened the door. What a difference they saw. It looked like a small nightclub. In one corner of the dimly lit room was a triangular stage, with a silver tasselled curtain behind it. There were stage lights, and tables and chairs, and in the very far corner was a small bar.

A handsome young man emerged from behind the bar and walked towards them. He had a full head of black hair, cut and layered to perfection. He looked to be in his late twenties, and stood six feet tall. His white shirt seemed to glow in the fluorescent lighting, making it appear even whiter than it was. He made a beeline for Sharon, his smile displaying a perfect line of white, bleached teeth, his eyes topped by well-defined, expertly waxed and shaped eyebrows, his arms open to embrace her. Tony and Jake looked at this very handsome young man, then at each other.

'This,' said Sharon holding her hand out towards him, 'is my Ashley.' She was smiling broadly and didn't notice what Tony saw; Jake's hand, slowly turning into a fist at his side. Tony knew there was going to be trouble, he could see Jake's anger rising.

'This one, Ashley,' Sharon took hold of Jake's arm, 'is my lovely husband, who I've told you all about. He's beautiful, isn't he?' Sharon was smiling and giggling at the young man, while holding on to Jake like a schoolgirl showing off her first boyfriend.

Ashley looked Jake up and down, then put his hands on his hips. 'Well, hello, handsome. You're right, Sharon, love, he is a beauty.' He drummed the fingers of one hand on his mouth, as though thinking, the other hand left provocatively on his hip. 'You remind me of a handsome movie star, but I can't think of his name,' he said, then he smiled at Jake.

At this point, the penny finally dropped, and Jake turned to look at Tony. This handsome young man was undoubtedly gay. Jake held out his hand to shake Ashley's. Thankfully, the dimly lit room, with only the stage lights and bar area lit up, concealed Jake's embarrassment. He wasn't embarrassed about Ashley being gay, but about the fact that he had been ranting and raving earlier, that he had doubted Sharon and made a fool of himself with his jealousy.

Tony clenched his fist and dug his fingers into his palm to stop himself from laughing. This was Jake's competition? This was who Jake was so jealous of? He was doing his best to stifle his laughter. He walked forward to introduce himself and Ashley beamed a cheeky smile at him, overacting his part completely and giving him a wink.

'I know all about you, Mr Lambrianu, I've got magazines at home full of pictures of you.' Again, Ashley put his hands on his hips, and he looked Tony up and down, as though surveying a masterpiece in a museum. He nodded. 'May I say, you are just as beautiful in person.' Now it was Tony's turn to blush.

Ashley oozed personality and charm. His friendly attitude put people instantly at ease. Mathers had been right, yet again. Ashley was, indeed, the man to be in charge of hosting the entertainment area. He was entertaining on his own.

'Well,' said Ashley, opening his arms wide and doing a twirl, 'what do you think of the entertainment room?' He went and stood at Sharon's side and put his arm around her waist, and watched Tony and Jake as they surveyed the room.

'You've both done a fantastic job,' said Jake. He was smiling at Ashley. He was one of those people that just made you smile. The flair and the energy he gave off just made you feel good about yourself. 'It's great, isn't it, Tony?' Jake turned to look at Tony, who was looking around properly, checking things out.

Tony walked up and down the laminate flooring, which had different coloured lights reflecting on it from the ceiling. 'This is absolutely great, and you, Ashley,' Tony pointed at him and put one hand on his hip to mimic Ashley's stance, 'are going to be one great host.' They all burst out laughing.

Tony and Jake had seen enough. They stayed and had some coffee and talked through some of the entertainment plans with Ashley. One of his suggestions had never crossed their minds, it was alien to them both, but they were prepared to listen.

'Do I call you "Mr Lambrianu" or "boss"?' Ashley had said, waiting for an answer from Tony.

'Whatever you're comfortable with, it makes no difference to me.' He liked Ashley, he was funny and genuine. Tony respected the fact that he was gay and proud of it. He made no attempt at hiding it. Tony felt the only people who felt uncomfortable around gay men were those men who were insecure about their own sexuality. Just because they were gay, it didn't mean they fancied you, did it?

'Well, then, "boss" it is. Mm, I like that, it sounds so dominant.' Again, he was smiling at Tony and Jake. 'What about a drag artist night and maybe a couple of male strippers?' He paused and waited for Tony to speak.

'I don't understand, Ashley, it's a men's club, why would I employ male strippers?' Tony said. He felt that was an odd question to ask. He was frowning at Ashley.

'Well, I'm a man in a "men's club", but I don't want to watch your women. I know some of the members from here, and believe me, they don't want to, either, if you know what I mean.' Ashley nodded at Tony and Jake, trying to make his point.

The thought had never crossed Tony's mind. He really didn't know what to say, it took the wind out of his sails. 'Are you telling me, you want to put on a gay night, or something, because some of these respectable men want to see handsome young men like yourself?'

Ashley nodded his head; he had made his point and he knew it. He didn't want to overstep the mark, so soon, but he'd thought he would ask while it seemed Tony was in a good mood.

Tony was out of his depth; he shook his head. 'That is all another world to me,' he said. 'Ashley, you have my permission to organize one night of this, but if it all goes wrong, it's your head on the block, okay?' He was still a little shocked by what Ashley had said. It was a big risk, it could cause a lot of bad feeling, he really wasn't sure about it.

'I'll play it low key and see what some of the members think, first, then, if they like the idea, I can go ahead with it. A trial, to see if it works. Although, believe me, I know it will.'

Ashley had lost his smile and his flamboyant ways, and was now deadly serious. He was giving away some members' secrets, and he would only do that to the boss. Mathers, of course, knew everything about everyone.

'Okay. Let's start with the girls, while you sound out the members about the other thing. You know them, I don't, and I don't pretend to. If they are okay with it, I'll leave it to you to set things up. But listen, nothing underhand, no rent boys or anything like that. Do you understand?' Now Tony was serious. His voice changed and so did his mannerisms. He had done his best to keep his strip clubs in order, without a bad reputation. He didn't want the men's club known as some kind of male brothel.

Ashley held out his hand to shake Tony's. Behind the façade of this camp young man was a businessman that wanted to do the best for Tony and for the members. Tony shook it; the deal was sealed. With that, Tony and Jake said their goodbyes and left.

'He's already been approached by these so-called members,' Tony said to Jake when they were both back in the car.

'Do you think so?' Jake looked at Tony. It was a fair point; once Ashley had flattered them and got them onside, as it were, he had thrown out the subject instantly. 'So, why haven't they done it before?'

'Because, Jake, the previous owner was not into the entertainment business, and wasn't interested. Now they all know we own it and that is what we do, they are obviously asking Ashley. By the way, what do you think of him?'

'What? You mean Sharon's new sister? I think he's a bit over the top, but he's okay. In fact, I like him.' Jake was nodding approval and smiling.

The smile crept back on Tony's face. 'Sharon's new sister? No, he's much better looking than Sharon's sister.' With that he nudged Jake with his elbow and they both burst out laughing.

12

PLACE YOUR BETS

I t turned out that Graham, the croupier trainer, had a brother and a wife also in the gaming business. He had discussed Tony's options with them and they had all agreed to work at the casino. It was a good opportunity, as they had all heard of Tony's reputation and generosity. Each croupier went through even more vigorous training under Graham's watchful eye and Tony was over the moon with his decision. Tailored uniforms had been ordered for all of the one hundred staff, with their pink bow ties, black trousers, white shirts and pink waistcoats. It sounded garish, but looked very appealing and flamboyant. It was the Lambrianu style, it was expected.

The casino was only a week away from opening, and it looked stunning. Graham had everything in order and was drilling the staff, not only with regard to their specific duties, but also their 'meet and greet' mannerisms. Tony had given him a free hand, and he was as proud and excited about it as if it were his own place.

Magazines and newspapers were full of gossip about the opening of the Lambrianu casino, people were already curious and waiting just to get a glimpse of the inside. The 'Lambrianu Casino' sign was high in the air, in now traditional pink neon. It looked amazing.

Huge glass chandeliers hung from the ceilings. Alarmed glass-fronted banking areas, where people either bought or cashed in their chips, stood out and provided easy access for people to exchange their money.

Even though everything was alarmed and secure, and had been handled by a security company that specialised in that kind of thing, including banking systems, Tony still had his own men on hand. He had them discreetly patrolling the area, with guns carefully hidden, in case they were searched.

Sharon had laughed at the idea. 'Who the hell is going to burgle or raid the casino, knowing who owns it, and what would happen to them if they did?' she had said.

Tony took her point but didn't care; he wasn't taking any chances. There was a lot of money involved, this could make or break him. Security monitors had been placed everywhere, on the insurance company's instructions, and he was leaving no stone unturned.

Opening day finally arrived; Tony was nervous and his palms were sweaty. He and Jake had decided to go to the casino early, to make sure everything was ready for the customers. They were surprised to see that Graham had all the staff lined up like soldiers on parade, awaiting their inspection. It was a long process and, thankfully, they all wore name badges. Graham walked with them, introducing the staff and explaining what area they would be working in. Tony and Jake remained poker-faced, as though it was all matter of fact and they had done this numerous times, even though inside their hearts were pounding.

After the inspection, they walked upstairs to the main office and both gave a sigh of relief, once they were out of sight. 'Bloody hell, Tony, my arm is aching with all that hand-shaking, I didn't realise how many employees there were.' Jake was rubbing his arm, and shaking it.

Tony ignored him and went and sat down on the huge leather swivel chair at his desk. Jake's desk was at the other side of the room.

'We've made it, Jake. Did you see all those people? They looked at us like we were gods.'

They both sat in silence, deep in thought, taking in everything that was going on around them. They had come a long way from the old days, leg-breaking for the protection money the bossman had demanded from the local publicans.

An hour later, Graham came up to inform them it was time to open the doors to the public. They were ready for business. Tony stood up, straightened his tie and swept his hair back. 'Graham, just a minute please.' His voice was genuine and sincere; he had a lump in his throat and fought to contain his feelings. 'It might be our casino, but this is your opening night. Thank you, we couldn't have done it without you.'

Tony and Jake both walked up to him and shook his hand. They could see how much Graham appreciated their acknowledgement of all his hard work.

'Thank you, Mr Lambrianu, fingers crossed all goes well.' He also felt a little humble that these well-known, much-feared men had graciously taken the time to thank him.

'Call me "Tony", and this, of course, is Jake. You're the manager of this empire, this is your baby. Good luck, Graham.' Again, Graham nodded at them both, then he left.

Jake poured two glasses of whisky and handed one to Tony. He felt they both needed it. 'To us, boss,' he said, and raised his glass in the air for a toast.

It was time for them to go down to the casino and watch the proceedings. After all, this was opening night, people would expect them to be there – including the journalists and photographers who wanted to be the first to spread the gossip.

They couldn't hear much activity below and that bothered them. Had no one turned up? They looked at each other, before pushing the door to the casino open. They were hit by a burst of noise. *Of course*, Tony thought, *the room is soundproofed! No wonder we couldn't hear anything!* To their surprise and delight, people were swarming in. Customers were at the tables and the staff were all busy. Waitresses walked the floor with large silver trays of drinks, tending to all the gamblers desperate to win a fortune.

Jake pushed Tony forward. 'Time to wander around and play host, Tony, work your magic.'

Tony felt proud and nodded. After all their hard work and planning, it had finally come together. He felt a lump in his throat, and stuck out his chest with pride, as he surveyed the room, bustling with customers. He walked forward in between them all, wishing them good luck and shaking hands with some of the people he knew and recognized from the club.

Newspaper photographers took photo after photo of Tony and the casino, journalists interviewed him and Jake about how they felt on their grand opening. They were both very nonchalant about it, and played it very matter of fact. They were businessmen, this was just another project.

'Lambrianu Casino a roaring success', read the reviews in the newspapers the next morning. Each and every one of them told the story of the night's proceedings and there, in the middle of it all, were photos of Tony smiling and posing for their cameras. Everything had gone brilliantly and, under Graham's watchful eye, very smoothly.

13

GENTLEMEN ONLY

The opening of the men's club was a much more low-key affair. The waitresses were dressed in black satin bustier corsets, which looked like tight-fitting bathing costumes, sleek and figure-hugging and, of course, they had on the trademark pink bow ties.

Members of the club wandered in and out at their own pace, spoke to Mathers, and acknowledged Tony as the owner, but not as an equal. In fact, Tony felt snubbed by some of them. He knew that most of them were high-class gentlemen with breeding, born into money. Sometimes, that alone made him feel inadequate. He had never felt like this since he was a child, wanting acceptance and not knowing how to get it.

Even though he now had plenty of money and lots of businesses that were flourishing, these 'gentlemen' still saw him as a protection racket boss with an eye for the ladies, and a bad reputation.

'You and they are wrong, Tony. You were born into money, for God's sake. You're Lambrianu wines. You own half of Italy. Remember?' Jake was doing his best to make Tony feel better, though he could see his efforts were wasted. He knew Tony wanted some form of respect from these men. Approval, if you like.

Mathers noticed Tony didn't spend a lot of time at the club, and that even when he was there, he kept himself to himself and let his maître d' run things. He also gave the entertainments room a wide berth, not wanting to be associated with the strippers.

It seemed even when everything appeared to be going right in Tony's life, there was always something to bring him back down to earth.

'Problem, Mr Lambrianu?' Mathers said, raising his eyebrows at Tony on one of his rare visits.

Tony pushed back his hair with his hands. 'No, Mathers, you have everything in hand. You don't need me here, time for me to leave.' Tony walked towards the door.

'You have no need to stay in the shade just because you're not a respectable married man, Mr Lambrianu,' Mathers said. He looked Tony up and down. 'If I may make an observation, I believe a double-breasted suit jacket would suit you more than the one you are wearing.'

Tony looked at Mathers and grinned, which took some of the stress away. 'I tell you what, Mathers, why don't you come clothes shopping with me and give me the benefit of your experience.'

'Good idea, sir, that is just what I have been thinking,' was all he said.

Tony felt it was blatantly obvious that this was what Mathers had wanted all along. At least if he chose the clothing, he couldn't constantly find fault with it.

Tony backtracked a little; he was curious about what Mathers had just said. 'What do you mean, Mathers, about being a married man? Is that why some of the members feel more comfortable with Jake in the room, because he's married?' He looked at Mathers and waited for a response.

Mathers put his fist to his mouth and gave a cough. 'All the members here are married, sir. You and your colourful reputation, if I may say, seems to set the cat amongst the pigeons. To be a gentleman, you first have to dress like one.

But remember, Mr Lambrianu, even the most respectable of men have skeletons in their cupboards; you just have to know which cupboard to look in.'

Tony wasn't quite sure what Mathers was talking about, but he would find out. He couldn't believe his single status seemed like some kind of threat to these men. Were they afraid that just because he played the field a little, their wives would think they were following his lead?

It was time to go back to the nightclub, but Mathers had certainly given Tony something to think about.

Somehow, he felt safer there, on home ground as it were. Maybe he would have a drink with Roxy and some of her friends and live up to his tarnished reputation as a 'good time guy'. But he vowed to himself he would make these holier-than-thou members accept him, one way or another.

ဆာ◊ର

'How come your butler never tells me how to dress?' said Jake, while having a drink with Tony. 'Or does he think I always get it right.' Jake was curious, Mathers never mentioned how Jake was dressed.

Tony took another sip of his drink and glanced at Jake. 'Because, even dressed in the best Savile Row suits, Jake, you still look like a scruffy bugger. There is no help he could offer you.'

They were both smiling, it was an 'in' joke, the way Mathers always went out of his way to reprimand Tony. Even when Tony and Jake were alone, in their boxer shorts and T-shirts, Jake would scold Tony and say, 'Whatever would Mathers think?'

'If I had Ralph Gold's seal of approval, those members would be eating out of my hand. He's as thick as thieves with them.' It was still playing on Tony's mind.

'Forget it, Tony, it'll all sort itself out in the end. Ralph Gold knows we want a meeting with him, and he's forever dangling the carrot in front of our noses. "Yes, boys, I'll let you know when I have an appointment free." That's all he ever says,' said Jake. They were both exasperated. Considering all the money laundering they were involved in together, and the deals they had done, without actually discussing things with each other, Tony felt it was about time they talked properly.

'Maybe I'm just stressed, with one thing and another. I think I'll go and see what the ladies are doing, I could do with a spot of light entertainment of my own. Let's see, over there, to the right, is the lovely Roxy, waiting for her prince charming, and on the left is Bernice, waiting for a decent quickie before she goes home to her boring husband.' Tony took a coin out of his pocket. 'What do you reckon; heads for Roxie, tails for Bernice?' He was grinning broadly, and waiting for Jake's answer.

'I'd say why not both, unless you're not up to it anymore.'

Tony picked up his glass and grinned, showing a perfect set of white teeth.

'Now that is a bloody good idea, Jake, why didn't I think of that. One warm up quickie, and the rest of the night's my own.' He picked up his glass and walked away to where Bernice was waiting for him.

'You're worse than he is.' Sharon was standing behind the bar collecting the cash register receipts. She leaned over and gave Jake a peck on the cheek. 'By the way, tomorrow night is Ashley's men's night, if you know what I mean. Why don't you come along?'

Jake nearly choked on his drink. 'Not bloody likely! If I want to see a guy stripped down to his bare arse, I only have to go to Tony's apartment early in the mornings, when some woman has stayed over. Not a pretty sight.' Suddenly Jake had a fleeting thought. 'So, has there been a lot of interest in the idea, then? Is Ashley sure the members would like that sort of thing in the club?'

Innocently, Sharon looked up from the bar where she was looking at the till rolls and putting them into a bag for the accountant to check. 'Oh, yes. Apparently, once Ashley threw out the idea, some of the members were asking what night he had it planned for.'

Sharon hadn't realised what she had said, but it certainly got Jake's mind working. He looked over to where Tony had been standing with Bernice. He had gone, and no prizes for guessing where. Jake wanted to talk to Tony about some of these respectable members. Mathers was right; some of these respectable married men had skeletons in their cupboards, alright. They liked looking at men! No wonder they all liked Ashley. Sharon had even laughed that some of the male waiters made more in tips than the ladies did. This was certainly something to look in to, and Mathers, without betraying a trust, had tried dropping the hint to Tony.

'Maybe I'll pop over to the men's club tonight to see what Ashley has got planned. Will you be going over there later?' said Jake. He wanted to speak to Ashley privately; this was business.

$\wp\diamond\wp$

Jake opened the door to the entertainment room and was surprised to see that it was busy. The strippers had a full audience. When he'd passed the other lounges he'd seen some of the older men sitting in the comfortable wingback chairs, with their brandies and cigars; some were even asleep. He hadn't expected more of them to be in the entertainment room than in the lounges. It was proving to be a money-spinner.

Jake looked around the room. It was dimly lit, with only the bright spotlights focused on the dancers on the stage and a couple of lamps above the bar. He spied Ashley standing amongst the men, laughing and joking. It seemed he was doing Tony's job and playing host, and these men were lapping it up. There were a lot of men there, the number seeming to far outweigh the members' list.

Jake caught Ashley's eye and discreetly beckoned him over. He saw Ashley look up and then excuse himself. 'Jake, love,' he said, as he reached him, 'it's nice to have the pleasure of your company.'

'Come with me, Ashley, I need a quiet word.' Jake walked away to a private room he knew Mathers used as a staffroom. He entered, waited for Ashley to follow him in, then shut the door behind them. Ashley could tell by the look on Jake's face this was not the time for silly jokes.

'Who are all those people?' said Jake. 'Not all of them are members.'

Ashley sat down; he too was serious. 'Members have always been allowed to bring a guest with them; didn't Mathers tell you that?'

Jake shook his head. He was a little perturbed. He hadn't known that members could have guests and he wondered if Tony did. 'Sharon tells me you've had a lot of interest in your men's night.'

Ashley nodded. 'Yes, there has been a lot of interest. I knew there would be, I told you so, didn't I?'

'You did, but why, Ashley? Why are these old fuddy-duddies so interested in seeing men dance around half-naked? They don't strike me as men who would even approve of that kind of thing. So, go on then, enlighten me.'

Ashley let out a deep sigh. 'Jake, Jake, Jake, where do I begin? Some of these men are ancient, I admit. In their day, people still went to prison for liking men, so they hide it, get married, have kids and do all the usual things that respectable men do, but sometimes they need to be themselves. That's where this exclusive club comes in. There's a code of silence, here. As they say, "what happens in Paris, stays in Paris". What did you think the rooms upstairs were for? Yes, some of the men get put to bed when they are too pissed to go home, but others use it to be themselves, and indulge their natural urges.' He looked at Jake and cocked his head to one side, as though explaining to a child.

'You're telling me, some of those old guys – stockbrokers, police chiefs and government officials – use this as a knocking shop for gay guys.'

'Ouch! Jake, that wasn't nice.' Ashley looked offended. 'Does it matter what job you do, or who you are? Didn't you always fancy women when you were a penniless guy? Just because you're loaded now doesn't make a difference, does it?'

Jake nodded, Ashley had a point, and he was being unfair. He was just shocked. This place seemed so strait-laced, he couldn't believe it. 'Does Mathers know any of this?'

'Oh, yes, Jake, Mathers knows everything. Nothing goes on here that he doesn't know about. Before you ask, he's not gay.'

'Mathers lets all this go on and doesn't bat an eyelid. Is that what you're saying?'

'Jake, come into the real world. Some of those guys out there went to famous public schools, and believe me, from what I have heard, that kind of thing is common practice, there. Mathers has been butler at some of the grandest houses going, and I was once his under-butler.

'You have to be discreet. You see everything and say nothing. Stuff like this is all old hat to Mathers, he's seen it all before.'

Jake was gobsmacked; this was new territory for him. He didn't know a lot about public schools or what supposedly went on inside of them, but Ashley and Mathers seemed to, and now so would Tony. Maybe this was just another reason why they didn't want Tony hanging around. He brought attention with him, people always wanted to know what he was doing and who with. These men didn't want attention; they paid for privacy.

'Where do you come in, Ashley? Do you turn tricks for this lot?' Jake sounded harsh, and he knew it, but he wanted some truth.

Looking him directly in the eye, without his usual flamboyant smile, Ashley looked his age, possibly older. 'I've done my bit in the past, Mr Sinclair, I don't deny it, but these days I'm more of a go-between.' His tone was serious and he was even using Jake's surname, and giving him the respect he deserved as his boss.

'You mean you're a pimp. Tell me, Ashley, just a couple of last things. These guys who entertain, are they all above the age of consent? And is Ralph Gold a closet gay guy?'

Ashley put his hands to his mouth shocked. 'Oh, God, yes! There are no schoolboys involved, or anything nasty like that. Seriously, Jake, they're all grown men, and it's their choice. Ralph Gold, no, you hardly ever see him in here. It's more of a status thing that he is a member. Honest.' Ashley held up his hand, as though swearing on the Bible.

'Very well; keep it that way. You know I'll have to discuss this with Tony, don't you. I'm not sure what his attitude will be. Thank you for your honesty.' With that, he walked out of the room, leaving Ashley behind.

∾◊∿

Jake felt he had to speak to Tony as soon as possible about what he'd just learned. It was crazy; Tony wouldn't want to be associated with anything like that. He wouldn't want the newspapers thinking he liked men, for God's sake.

Jake went back to the club. Sharon was in the office with the accountant, going through the night's takings.

'Did you know that fancy men's club is some kind of gay knocking shop, Sharon?' he said.

Sharon looked up; she showed no sign of shock, and then she looked down again. 'Yes, I did. What of it?'

This was a night full of surprises. Jake was dumbfounded, everyone seemed to know all about this except himself and Tony. 'Is that all you have to say about it?'

Sharon looked up, took off her glasses and held them in her hand, 'Why is it, Jake, that no one ever questions men looking at strippers or picking up prostitutes? Don't be a bigot. I thought you were better than that. Did you know that some of our most glamorous strippers are lesbians?'

Jake nodded; yes, he did know that. Some of the

strippers were heartily sick of hearing the same old chat up lines, sick of the way the punters wanted to maul them or pick them up, even though they had no interest in men. They danced and teased them for the money and to pay their bills and the punters never thought anything of it when they went home with their best friend, who just so happened to be their girlfriend.

'I'm not a bigot, you know that. Live and let live, that's my attitude, I'm just shocked that that Mathers guy, with all his pompous ways, lets all that go on. That's all.'

'Well, Jake, love, it seems he's more broad-minded than you, doesn't it?' With that, Sharon carried on with her work.

The accountant looked up at Jake. 'Why do you care so much what goes on in there? It's making a lot of money, that's business.'

Jake felt he was going mad. No one seemed to care, only he thought it was crazy. Tony had tried all this time to make sure that the strip club was respectable and didn't get a bad reputation, and yet now he'd learned the men's club was everything Tony had tried to avoid.

Jake left Sharon and the accountant to their sums and walked back into the club. He needed a stiff drink. Worse still, he was the one that would have to tell Tony.

ℰᴥ◊ℭℛ

The next morning, after a sleepless night, Jake went to Tony's apartment at the club. It was weird; Tony only ever did his female entertaining at the nightclub, he never took women to the casino apartment. He watched as Tony went through his usual ritual of getting rid of the woman he had spent the night with. Jake was surprised that it wasn't Roxy.

Tony kissed the woman quickly on the lips and shut the door behind her. Jake had to grin to himself; who said romance was dead! Still, those women knew there was no future in anything with Tony, what they did was entirely their choice. Then it struck him that was exactly what Ashley had said last night. These gay guys were consenting adults and it was their choice.

'What happened with Roxy? I thought you were going to spend the night with her.'

Tony poured two mugs of coffee and smiled. 'I did, for an hour or two, and then Tracey telephoned me for a chat. You know I'm never one to miss a golden opportunity.'

'You randy old sod, one day that thing of yours will go on strike or drop off, believe me.'

'Just not last night, eh, Jake. Right, what is it? It's early, you knew I was entertaining, and yet you're here with that look on your face that spells trouble.' Tony was dressed in his white towelling bathrobe. He sat at the breakfast bar and took a sip of his coffee, waiting for Jake to speak.

'I wanted to tell you last night, but you were busy,' Jake said, then he took a deep breath and started to fill Tony in on everything he had discussed with Ashley. Tony sat drinking his coffee and never spoke, he just watched Jake's distressed face as he explained what the men's club was known for. 'What do you think, Tony?' he said, when he'd finished.

Tony put his mug down, picked up the coffee pot and poured himself a refill, then offered some to Jake. 'I knew there was something. Ashley was far too quick off the trigger asking to host male striptease nights. Remember, I've been in prison, Jake, I do know that kind of stuff goes on.'

'So, you're okay with it.' Jake's nerves were frazzled. He had been worried all night, expecting Tony to fly off the handle and close the club.

'Well, not okay, exactly, but that's life. Those guys are paying a lot of money for their membership and their guests are buying drinks, and hoping to get on Mathers' reserve listings. He'll keep everything in order, I trust him. Money is money, and they are paying well for the privilege. Also, a bird in the hand is worth two in the bush. These men may not accept me or my lifestyle, but they'll come around if they think I know their little secrets. Blackmail is an ugly word, but very useful in business.' Tony smiled and raised his mug.

He walked away and went to the bathroom to shower.

Jake sat back on the sofa and rested his head; he let out a deep sigh. So that was Tony's angle. The members were going to accept Tony one way or another. He had it all worked out. Tony was right, of course, Ashley had been a little too quick to suggest his entertainment ideas. Why hadn't he seen it?

৪০◊ଫ

When Tony was ready, they got in the car and John pulled away.

'Where are we going?' said Jake.

'We're going to see Angus,' said Tony.

Reports of how Angus was running things in the south of London were good. Angus was loyal and did as he was told. He was also under the threat of his wife, which still made them both laugh.

'What do we need to check up on him for? He's doing okay, isn't he?' Again, Jake was at a loss, wondering what Tony had up his sleeve.

'I need him to do us a favour.'

'What sort of favour?'

'Things are too quiet, Jake, we need to stir up a little trouble in the pubs, shake them up a little, and then we'll rush in and save the day, and they'll all be grateful they're paying us for protection.'

'So, what are you going to do? Get him to barge in, causing all kinds of trouble?'

'Not him, some of the old mob under his charge. Just a few fights and maybe some threats, and we earn our money, so to speak.'

Jake couldn't understand why Tony needed to upset the equilibrium. Why did he want to cause trouble, when everything was running smoothly? It was like he enjoyed the excitement of trouble and hated routine boredom. He needed another project, and yet there wasn't one.

Walking into the old pub that Marlon had used as his

office seemed strange. Under Angus's wife's orders, the whole place was clean and tidy. It certainly didn't look like some old drug den. Inside the pub, they could clearly hear Angus's voice, that strong Scottish accent bellowing down the corridors.

'Everything okay, Angus?' asked Tony. There were two men in front of Angus, and he was giving them a piece of his mind.

'Och, aye, boss, it's you. Come in, laddies, sit down.' He looked at the two men standing before him, and then back at Tony and Jake. 'Nothing I can't handle.'

Tony and Jake both forgave Angus's tone and lack of respect. To him, that was a friendly welcome and he meant no disrespect. Angus waved his arm and indicated that the two men were to leave the room, and then stood at the door and watched them walk down the stairs.

'How are you settling in, Angus? Is everything okay?' Tony wanted to know what that argument was all about, but he didn't want to undermine Angus.

'Settled in just fine. The wife's happy and off my back, I hardly recognize her these days, she hasn't nagged at me half as much as she used to. The kids are okay, as well.' It suddenly dawned on Angus what Tony really wanted to know. 'Oh, right,' he said. 'Some of them are not quite used to me, yet, they still think they're working for that black mob boss. Well, it's up to me to show them they're not. They want to do their own thing, and collect the money in their own time, when they finally fall out of bed. No, it's not the way things are going to be run around here. You had us all on a strict routine, Mr Lambrianu, we all had our daily rotas worked out, and that's what I have to teach those numbskulls.'

Tony nodded and smiled at Angus; he had made a good choice here. Angus wasn't used to thinking for himself, he was all brawn and no brains, but what he was doing was copying how Tony ran things. 'You can fire them, if you think they're not up to the job, you know.'

'It won't come to that, Mr Lambrianu, they just need putting in their place and a good battering now and again, and they'll soon come around.' Angus was sure about that; he wasn't going to let anyone steal his thunder.

'Well, Angus, we need to stir up a little trouble in the East End. Possibly some threats and a little chaos, nothing too serious, just enough to let people remember why they pay us the amounts they do.' Tony looked at Jake, they both waited for this to work its way into Angus's brain. Jake had said he reminded him of his favourite comedian, Billy Connolly, only without the brains.

'Why, Mr Lambrianu? Everything's going okay, here, I have things under control. Granted, I've had to go around to some of those guys' houses and pull them out of bed, but they are all getting the hang of things.' Angus looked worried. He had done his best, all the money had been collected on time and it was all the correct amounts, and he had even gone around collecting himself to introduce himself to the publicans in South London.

'Calm down, Angus.' Tony's smooth, velvety voice seemed to put Angus at his ease. 'This is nothing to do with you, you're doing a good job, but we have to keep reminding these people we rely on for our wages who they are dealing with.' That seemed to do the trick, now Angus understood.

'What do you want me to do, Mr Lambrianu? Just tell me when and where, and I'll see that chaos is caused.' Angus banged his fist on the table, and nodded his head.

Tony was thinking; he wasn't sure what to do yet, but he wanted everyone to be ready to act when he did.

'Firstly, Angus, I want you to get some of the laziest guys you have. Let's not fire them, let's use them. I presume Marlon's men are still sniffing drugs and think they can get away with it, like they used to do with him; that's why they're still in bed at midday, they're sleeping it off. Are there any of them you trust, have you made a friend?'

'Aye, I have that, Mr Lambrianu. Big Jamaican lad named Neville, hard as nails, likes the money and the ladies.

Always on time, he is.'

'Good. When the time comes to put my plans into action, I want the old South London mob doing this dirty work, not any of our men that you brought with you. That would make it look too obvious that I'm involved. The east fighting the east? No, you and your friend Neville are to await my plans. Not a word now, I'll let you know the details soon.' Tony stood up to leave.

'Mr Lambrianu, sir.' Angus looked almost too embarrassed to ask. He flashed a fleeting glance at Jake, in the hope of some back up. 'This trouble you want causing, it's not going to end up with me back inside, is it?' Angus wasn't afraid of prison, but he had done more than his fair share of life behind bars. Now he was settling down and had a good life, he didn't want to return to that, although he realised that he worked for Tony, and if he wanted to carry on doing so, he would have to carry out his orders.

'Good God, no Angus. That is certainly not my plan. A few of your lazy troublemakers might get a hard time, but rest assured, definitely not you.' With that Tony and Jake left.

છ◊ભ

Back at the club, Sharon had organized bacon sandwiches all around. It was much appreciated by the bouncers. They were treated like human beings, not just gorillas in suits.

'I'll have one of those,' shouted Jake to the delivery driver, who had a cardboard box piled high with individually wrapped bacon sandwiches.

'Sharon,' said Tony, while drinking his coffee and eating his sandwich, 'when is this male strip night Ashley has organized?' He was intrigued; a plan had formed in his head. Now was the time to strike, while the iron was hot.

Sharon burst out laughing. 'Why? Have you had enough of the girls, already? Are you thinking of going and seeing how the other half live?'

'I am, actually, and so is Jake.'

Jake nearly choked on his sandwich and spilt his coffee in the process.

'You're not bloody serious, Tony, I don't want to go and see a bunch of male strippers with their dicks hanging out.' Jake was still trying to control his cough, after nearly choking on his sandwich. He couldn't believe his ears; Tony had some crazy plans at times, but this was the worst. 'Don't you think it might ruin your reputation as a ladies' man? Ha, ha, got you there, haven't I?'

'Why would it? Who knows about it, but the members? And, from what you tell me, they don't exactly shout about their inner fantasies. No, we have to go to put our stamp of approval on it, and to let them know they haven't pulled the wool over our eyes. Our approval of them is their mild acceptance of us. They may not like us, but they're not going to cross us.' He looked at Sharon and grinned. 'Besides, we'll get to see the amazing Ashley in action. Your wife's new bezzie mate.'

'The pair of you may well laugh at my friendship with my new "bezzie mate" but, believe me, he is a mine of information. Also, he thinks I already know about some stuff, so he talks freely about it.'

Jake frowned and looked across at her. 'What can he possibly think you already know? What information can he share?'

Tony and Jake sat waiting for Sharon's next instalment. She obviously had something to tell them, but she was going to tease them a little first.

'Mmmm, let me see. Such as, Mathers used to be Don Carlos's trusted wingman and butler. Oh, yes, Mr Butter-Wouldn't-Melt-In-My-Mouth knows everything.' Sharon smiled at them both. She could see this intriguing piece of information had captured their interest. They both looked shocked.

'And Ashley was footman and then under-butler. He, too, knows how the world works. So, don't judge a book by the cover, boys, eh? Mathers was put in charge of that club to be the eyes and ears, watching over those aging politicians with their secrets. Blackmail, Tony, just like you prepare for with the cameras in the VIP booths, here at the club. How else does Ralph Gold, otherwise known as "the untouchable", have all those politicians and judges licking his arse? Borrowing money off him to fight their campaigns? They owe him everything. He is one clever bastard, I'll grant you that, and he doesn't get his hands dirty.'

Sharon had definitely given them something to think about. 'So, Mathers is a gangster? Well, he scares the shit out of me.' Jake laughed.

'They're watching us and schooling us, Jake, and sometimes they're even helping us. Maybe, just maybe, we might get a foot in the door with Ralph Gold and the big boys after all,' Tony said, nodding his head.

'Can't wait for that,' said Jake.

'Why do you think Mathers is grooming you?' said Sharon.

'By the way,' said Tony, his mind returning to the plan he had in mind, 'on the subject of cameras, I want a small camera installing above the bed in each of those rooms, upstairs at the club.' Tony looked at Sharon and wagged his finger. 'And even your precious Ashley is not to know about that, do you hear me?' Tony was serious; what he had in mind was only for the people that needed to know.

'Oh, God, Tony.' Sharon looked horrified. 'What have you got in mind, now?' She looked at Jake; he, too, was open-mouthed. 'Don't you get enough material from the VIP booths, here at the club?'

Tony had an evil smug expression on his face. He crossed his legs, put his hands behind his head, and sat back in his chair. 'If we should ever need important help, those recordings would give us something to barter with. Why waste a good opportunity?'

Sharon opened her mouth to protest, but he continued.

'They might talk in front of Mathers, but they wouldn't

say anything in front of us, and Mathers won't share what he learns with us. If everything went wrong tomorrow, those posh members would pretend they didn't even know us. They would wash their hands of us, even though we know their little secrets. This way, they can't forget us. Should we ever need the kind of intervention they could offer, well, all's fair in love and war, eh?'

'That's proper blackmail. You could go to prison for that,' said Sharon.

'True, but do you think those guys, with their skeletons in the cupboard, are really going to report us to the police? I don't think so.' Tony gave a smug grin.

'How are you going to get them installed without anyone knowing?' said Jake. 'That Mathers guy knows everything. God, he probably knows the last time I farted!' Jake was both shocked and surprised at Tony's suggestion, although he knew Tony hadn't liked being snubbed, and now he had an angle on their weaknesses, he was going to use it to show them who was boss.

'Electricians, sorting out the wiring. No big deal, workmen have already been there, and you, Sharon, the good and trusted friend of both of them, are going to be on hand.'

'You've got it all worked out haven't you.' Sharon didn't sound at all pleased. 'You're an evil bastard, at times, Tony, you really are. So, I'm to keep them both busy, while you're installing your porn cameras, am I?'

'Tell her, Jake.' Tony looked at Jake for approval. 'I don't care who you're friends with, Sharon, it's always been us three.'

Jake nodded. 'He's right, Sharon. It might never be needed, like the stuff we get from the VIP booths, but it's insurance, should these guys ever start revoking gaming or club licences because something is not to their liking. I see that now. At the moment it's all goodwill and their little whims are being pandered to, but what about us when the shine wears off? Do it, Sharon, for all of us.'

Even she had to admit there was some sense in it. If the going ever did get tough, they would drop the three of them like hot coals. 'Okay. You sort out your workmen. I presume they'll be people you know, who are discreet?'

Tony nodded. 'All in hand, nothing for you to worry about. Just be there, drink coffee and laugh and joke with them both, as always. By the way, does Mathers ever laugh?' Tony was now trying to raise the mood. He knew it was an underhand thing to do, but he had to think of himself. He wanted no ill-feeling, but the club members thought they had the upper hand, and were laughing at this gangland boss who thought he had his finger on the pulse. Now it was time for him to show them he did, and he knew everything.

'There is one more thing,' said Sharon. She looked uncomfortable, and her eyes darted around the room. She had something on her mind, and was contemplating whether to say it. 'Oh, well, here goes. Our friendly accountant is on the members' list, and he'll be at the "Fun Night", as Ashley is calling it. Well, you two, have you ever seen him with a woman?'

Silence filled the room; they all looked at each other. Sharon was biting her bottom lip. She felt she had betrayed a trust. She had only mentioned it because Tony was insisting on going.

Tony spoke first. 'Fair point, Sharon, I've never known him be with a woman, but then, you surprise me that he actually takes that calculator out of his hand.' He was surprised. Bloody hell, Sharon seemed to know everything that went on in that club.

'I'm only telling you because I didn't want it to come as too much of a shock when you see him there. I'll be telling him that you're going, too. Also, I don't want him falling prey to your little recording plans; he's one of us. We've all worked together for a very long time.'

'You're right, Sharon. Jake and I are not homophobic, you know that. A lot of the people we know swing that way, and it doesn't bother me, it's how people treat me, that's what I'm interested in.'

'What, Tony? And you're smarting a bit, because those well-to-do guys haven't fallen at your feet, like all those women in the club, and worship the ground you walk on? Hurt your ego, has it, Tony? Grow up.' Sharon looked at him, disgusted.

His face went red, he was now beginning to get angry. His temper was rising, not only because Sharon had shouted at him, but also because of the fact that she was probably right. Apart from everything else, he didn't like the way some of those men snubbed him.

'I am grown up, Sharon, that's why I'm taking out this extra insurance. They don't care about me, or you, or even Jake. They shake hands with you both and they talk to you, but mark my words, if the shit ever hit the fan, they would be the first to denounce you to save their own skins. I'm just protecting our own interests. As for the accountant, thanks for telling me. I couldn't hurt him even if I wanted to, though. Don't forget, he also works for Ralph Gold and Don Carlos. He has powerful friends who could ruin me in minutes.'

They all agreed to disagree. Whatever happened, they were all in it together, as they always had been. 'The accountant's safe, Sharon. As you say he's one of us. Hell, he's never judged me and my wicked ways.' They all started to smile at each other again. It eased the tension.

꧁◈꧂

Tony got changed and went to the casino. It was doing exceptionally well. Tony and Jake were the front men, and they owned it, but Graham and the accountant, who seemed like a member of the family now, had everything running smoothly.

Tony liked looking around at his empire. It was large, beautiful and all his. It was his crowning glory. It was full most nights and the turnover was even better than predicted.

He was taking lessons from Graham about working in the casino. He knew how to play poker and had often sat in on a private game and had a good evening.

This was a whole new ball game – learning all the roulette rules, how to deal cards properly, and most of all, the mathematics side of it all. The croupiers were regularly put through their paces to make sure they were able to add up quickly, to shout out bets. Tony enjoyed it, and Graham was a good teacher. What was the point in owning something you didn't know how to run? He wanted to learn about his new venture from the bottom up. This was a real challenge.

14

A FUN NIGHT

Ashley's male fun night was upon them, and Tony wanted to look his best. Jake was still moaning about having to go with him, but he'd agreed to it.

Sharon had told the accountant that Tony and Jake would be attending the night, and that she had told Jake he was a member and was possibly going along himself.

'What did they say when you told them, Sharon?' The accountant, as always was straight-faced and never showed any sign of emotion, although Sharon could see he felt embarrassed.

'They didn't care, although they appreciated being told; it saved all that awkwardness on the night, didn't it. Don't be ashamed of who or what you are.' Sharon leaned over and kissed his forehead.

The club seemed to be a real mixed bag. A few of the members, who were obviously straight, sat in one of the lounges discussing the day's business, while ogling the scantily clad waitresses in their satin costumes. Down the hallway, it was a whole different ball game. On opening the entertainment room door, they saw that it was buzzing. The atmosphere was relaxed, and the members were laughing, smoking their cigars and drinking their large brandies.

There was a drag artist on the stage, telling the usual dirty jokes and making innuendos. It all seemed like a fun night, indeed. Ashley was wandering around, talking to the men who were there and laughing with them. He really was the consummate host.

Although there were men at the bar talking business, they were still in the room enjoying the music and the atmosphere. Tony took Jake by the elbow and steered him towards the bar. He could already see the puzzled looks on the members' faces. They were obviously wondering why Tony was there; they hadn't expected him to be. Suddenly the atmosphere seemed to change, and they were on their guard. Now it was Tony's turn to put them at their ease.

Tony and Jake picked up their drinks, and Tony smiled at the men there. He shook some hands, and laughed at the drag artist's jokes. It was corny but it was funny, even he had to admit that.

'Are you having a good evening?' Tony said to some of the members, who seemed to be making all kinds of excuses about being in the room. They'd just popped in to see what was going on. They didn't know it was a male night. Every excuse under the sun was used. Some even put down their drinks, and said they were going home. It was time for Tony to think fast; maybe this had been a mistake. None of these men wanted him there, they all felt threatened by his presence.

'Come on, guys, have another drink. The drag artist isn't that bad, and the real entertainment will start soon.' Tony was smiling and laughing and even incorporated Ashley to help him out.

'Come on, boys, Mr Tony is here for some fun entertainment, aren't you, love?' Ashley looked at Tony. He hoped he wasn't going too far, but he had to save the day.

Jake was startled and rooted to the spot. It was blatantly obvious what these guys were thinking. It was now fleetingly crossing their mind that Tony was of the same ilk, or at least bisexual.

Tony started laughing and talking in Italian for them, and becoming the joking gentlemen. He breathed a sigh of relief when they decided to stay, and then the first male stripper was introduced.

Tony stood, watched and applauded. Some of the men were cheering and shouting to the strippers. Tony nudged Jake in the ribs with his elbow. Jake started clapping and getting into the swing of things – in for a penny, eh?

The relaxed atmosphere seemed to return, the male strippers were now walking around the crowd pouring oil on themselves and rubbing it in, and coaxing some of the members to rub it into their chests for them. Tony nearly choked when one walked up to where he was standing with Jake. Now was the biggest test of all. Fortunately for him the stripper picked Jake and danced around him provocatively. After breathing a sigh of relief to himself, Tony had to stifle a laugh at the stunned look on Jake's face.

This was asking too much; Jake couldn't do it. He really did not want to rub oil into this young man's chest. The accountant had seen them and, like a gift from God, he walked swiftly over to them and took the lead. He rubbed his hand across the man's chest and then put a twenty-pound note into the thong he was wearing.

Jake had paled; thank God the accountant had come to save the day. Would Tony have done it? Or would he have dined out on it for the rest of their lives, telling Sharon all about how Jake had been frozen to the spot?

The members started to mingle and take their seats at the tables. They were throwing money on to the stage, and letting the strippers sit on their knee. It was like a surreal world, although Tony and Jake had seen a version of this many times.

At the strip club, scantily clad women sat on the punters' knees hoping to get a decent tip. This was exactly the same, except it was scantily clad men. Eventually, after making the acquaintance of some of the people that had once snubbed him, Tony decided it was time to leave them to it.

'Don't you ever put me in that fucking position again, do you hear me?' Jake was shouting at him as they got into the car. 'I can't believe you were going to let that guy grope me in front of all of those people.' Jake was blowing off steam, and it was his chance to rant and rave, for once.

Tony was laughing. 'I thought you were enjoying yourself, Jake.' He was teasing him. Poor Jake, he had nearly fainted.

'No, I bloody well wasn't, and what about you? That old bald-headed guy said you were quite pretty and had lovely blonde hair. He wants you to stamp his card, mate. They all think you're that way inclined, now, you know that, don't you? You, and possibly me?' Jake was horrified.

'Who the hell cares what they think? I don't, that's for sure. Besides, I am quite pretty.' Tony slapped Jake's arm and burst out laughing. It had been a real eye-opener and once Jake had got over the shocking experience he actually started to laugh.

'I feel really inadequate now, though, after seeing that guy who came on with the python around his neck. My God, Tony, his dick nearly hung around his knees. How am I supposed to compare with that?'

'It's not the size, Jake, but then again, I wouldn't know. I didn't feel inadequate, I've got testimonials from a lot of women who come back for more.'

Laughter filled the back of the car as Tony was telling John, his driver, about the evening's events and Jake's most embarrassing moment. Even John burst out laughing, while trying to keep his eye on the road.

'Don't you breathe a bloody word of this, do you hear me?' Jake was jokingly threatening John.

No sooner had they got to the club, where Sharon was, than Tony told the tale again – he couldn't help himself. 'Jake pulled, Sharon, he's got a new friend.' Tony was still laughing at Jake's expense, but it was all in good fun.

'You're wrong, Tony. Now, let's see.' She drummed her fingers on her chin and smiled at them both. 'That stripper thought my Jake was some stud, and you're a "quite pretty blonde Italian". Jake never has to see that stripper again, but you. You are being chatted up by one of your members! So, let's see, you attend gay night, your gay accountant is there and you two are always together. Doesn't look good from where I'm standing.'

Sharon watched the smile slide from Tony's face. His jaw dropped and he looked at her.

'Hey, Sharon, you don't think they think that I'm, well, up for it, do you?'

'Definitely, Tony, and it's not the first time you've been called pretty, is it now.' Sharon was enjoying her moment winding Tony up. 'You started this, maybe you had a hidden agenda.' She burst out laughing, and saw him take a sigh of relief. Tony swept his hair back, and gave her a cold stare.

'Thank God that's a secret men's club, Tony, that's all I can say. I'm never, ever going back to one of those nights again.' Jake was emphatic, he'd seen more than enough.

'We won't have to, Jake, our work is done. We've accepted them and their secrets, and they are in two minds about us.' Tony picked up his whisky and downed it in one. What a night it had been.

∞◊℃

The next morning, while they were all checking the cash register receipts from the night before, the accountant was filling them in on all the happenings.

According to him, all had gone well after they had left, and yes, people were asking questions about Tony and Jake. There seemed to be lot of interest in their activities. The accountant had said nothing, but by saying nothing to these men it seemed he had said an awful lot. The accountant found it quite funny. He seemed pleased that his own secret was out, and he could be himself with his friends.

A lot of the members had invited guests or friends to the special night, which is why it had been so busy. Afterwards, some of the men had simply walked into the lounge area, sat in the comfortable chairs, carried on drinking their whisky or brandy and smoking cigars, and started discussing business with their friends.

Looking at the accounts for the evening, they saw they had made a fortune.

'It seems our time at the men's club is over, Jake. It's in good hands, and we're not needed. The only time I'll go back there is when I'm needed to do business. The cameras are in place, which gives us our insurance, and even you,' Tony pointed at the accountant, 'can also, now, be our eyes and ears.'

'Don't forget,' said Jake, 'Sharon's there a lot, as well, her and Ashley are as thick as thieves. She also organizes the female dancers, like she does here at the club. So, as you say, everything seems to be in order.' Jake seemed relieved that he didn't have to go back, which made Tony and the accountant chuckle to themselves even more.

'It's a fair point, Tony,' said the accountant. 'It ran with a profit before, and now you have added more to it, more profit will come. I'll keep an eye on things, discreetly, of course, if that's what you want. Leave them with the mystery about you two.' He looked at Jake and watched him squirm again.

Jake had a stupid thought, but he had to ask. 'Here, don't you find it weird kissing a bloke with a beard?'

Tony and the accountant glanced at each other, and smiled. Jake had obviously given this a lot of thought.

Tony had his shirt sleeves rolled up, and was looking relaxed in the early morning. 'I tell you what, Jake,' he said, with a smug, satisfied grin on his face, 'why don't you tell us? After all, Sharon goes and has her moustache bleached and waxed, and I've heard her say she shaves or waxes her legs.' With that he burst out laughing and slapped Jake on the back.

15

A WOMAN SCORNED

As the weeks rolled on, Tony and Jake's bank accounts flourished. Tony had spent day after day at the casino, and Graham reckoned he was becoming his number one pupil. Tony was pleased with his own efforts; he was a quick learner when something took his interest. His casino was the jewel in the crown of his business empire.

Tony had been invited to a theatre premiere, as the leading lady wanted him there on her opening night. He walked along the red carpet and the photographers, as always, lapped it up.

He liked the clothes he was wearing these days. He always felt he had dressed stylishly, but shopping with Mathers had opened up a whole new world for him. He had tuxedos, white dinner jackets and double-breasted grey suits that shone like silk. Mathers had not just chosen white shirts for Tony, but had gone for pink and dark purple, too, all with ties that matched both the shirt and the suit and, of course, the silk handkerchief in his breast pocket.

Each time Tony had shown interest in a tie, Mathers had coughed, moved on to the next rack, and chosen something from there. He had chosen well, taking Tony's colouring into consideration, and the fact that he had playboy status.

Mathers had also insisted he learn how to tie a bow tie, not use one with a clip at the back Tonight, Tony stood before the cameras in his black tuxedo, with his hair swept back. He felt and looked good.

Denise, the actress he had been seeing lately, seemed to quickly claim Tony as her own property. She hung on his arm at the bar and gave out evil stares to all the other women who smiled at him.

Denise was small and blonde. Sharon had nicknamed her the 'poison dwarf', because of her diminutive stature – she stood just over five feet tall – and the fact she was forever talking down to people, or causing an argument. Tony had liked her, at first; she was funny, when she had a mind to be, and she was okay in bed. He had thought she was an independent woman with her own career who just wanted a bit of fun, but he had been wrong. She clearly had delusions of grandeur. She saw herself as Mrs Lambrianu.

One morning, while Denise was taking a shower before leaving for the theatre, Tony decided he'd had enough. He glanced over to make sure the bathroom door was closed and then telephoned one of his regular girlfriends to see if she fancied meeting him at the club for a drink.

He had been his usual charming self, laughing and chatting to the woman on the other end of the line, not realising that while he was on the telephone, walking from one room to another, putting on the coffee and picking up his newspapers, Denise had opened the bathroom door. She was about to walk through to the kitchen when she heard Tony's voice, and she realised he wasn't talking to her because he didn't know she was out of the bathroom.

She heard Tony flattering some woman and telling her how much he had missed her and was looking forward to seeing her. After the arrangements had been made for the evening, Tony put the telephone down and went into the kitchen to pour some coffee.

Denise came out of the bathroom in her bathrobe, rubbing her hair with a towel. 'Will you be coming to the theatre tonight, Tony, or shall I meet you here?' she asked. She poured herself some coffee while waiting for his answer.

'Not tonight, Denise, I've got some business to attend to. Another night, okay.'

Denise stared at him, full of hate. Business to attend to, indeed. She had heard him making arrangements to see another woman. How could he!

She remained calm and gave Tony a kiss before she left. He was glad to see the back of her. She was beginning to get too involved. He took a drink of his coffee and looked at the clock to check the time. Jake would be here, soon, and they would go through the day's activities and discuss any problems that needed their attention.

Suddenly there was a knock at his door. Jake had his own key, unless he was just being tactful, because he knew Denise had stayed over. Tony went and opened the door and was surprised to see Denise standing there.

'Hi, Tony, love, I've left my watch in the bathroom. I'll just go and get it, back in a moment.' She disappeared for a few minutes and then emerged all smiles. 'Got it, darling, have a good day.' With that, she left.

Tony had just kept on reading his newspaper, and let her carry on with what she was doing. The more he looked at her, the more he realised he must have had his beer goggles on when they met. For some reason he just didn't fancy her anymore. Maybe it was her clingy attitude. Whatever, she was out.

Tony finished his coffee and then went for a shower, aiming to get ready before Jake arrived. He was washing his hair and soaping himself down when suddenly he noticed the water was blue! He looked at his hands and saw they were blue, as well. 'Oh, my God,' he muttered. He looked up at the showerhead and saw it was pouring out blue water. He quickly jumped out of the shower and turned it off. He looked into the bathroom mirror. Disaster! His hair and body were dyed blue. He took a towel and started rubbing at his hair. He was panicking, wondering what on earth had happened. Even his fingernails were stained blue.

Jake let himself into the apartment and heard the commotion coming from the bathroom. It wasn't the usual noises he heard from Tony's apartment – all he could hear was Tony screaming and swearing – and so he decided to investigate. Jake swung open the bathroom door and his jaw dropped when he saw Tony standing naked, skin tinged blue, blue water dripping onto the bathroom floor. What was more, his hair was blue, too! Tony's blonde pride and joy now looked like a pensioner's blue rinse.

'What the hell has happened to you?' Jake couldn't help but laugh, but he could see Tony wasn't amused. The air was as blue as his hair.

'The bloody water's coming out blue. Get a plumber around here, now. Someone is for the high jump. Jesus, what am I going to do about this?' Tony ran his hands through his hair.

'Blue?' Jake was confused, he had never heard of water coming out of pipes blue before. A rusty red from the pipes, maybe, but blue?

'Let me see.' Jake pushed Tony out of the way and looked at the showerhead. It was all stained blue, and so were the tiles around the shower. Jake ignored Tony stomping around and shouting and just let him get on with it. He was running the taps in the kitchen and they were running clear.

Jake unscrewed the showerhead and discovered blue ink had been put inside it. Bloody hell, this had been done on purpose.

'Tony, I've found it. I've found the source of your blue water. Quick, come here.' Still holding the showerhead, Jake waited for Tony to come charging in. He looked even worse; not only was his skin tinted blue, his hair was blue and his face was now flushed red with anger.

'You look like an extra out of that *Braveheart* movie.' Jake laughed. 'Either that or a Smurf.'

'Shut up and show me, will you? What have you found?' Tony was in no mood for laughing, maybe another time, but definitely not now.

'Someone has put blue ink in the showerhead. This was done on purpose. See?' Jake showed Tony the showerhead and the ink.

'That bitch, Denise, I bet it was her. She had her shower and left, then came back supposedly for her watch. She said she had left it in the bathroom. Yes, this is definitely her doing.'

Now Jake was confused. 'Why would she do that, when she's already window shopping for engagement rings? What have you done, Tony?' Jake paused and waited. This was not the way to get a ring on your finger, so what had compelled her to do it?

'I don't know.' Tony looked innocently at Jake. 'Maybe she's taken the hint and knows I've had enough of her. The bitch!'

'No, there's more to it than that. If she thought you were losing interest, she would have upped her game a bit. She would only do this to anger you. Come on, Tony, what have you said or done.'

Tony shook his head, and drops of blue ink flew out of his wet hair and on to the bathroom wall. 'I've done nothing,' he insisted. Then a thought crossed his mind. Surely not. 'I was on the telephone to that woman, Ami, earlier, asking her to come around here for a drink and stuff.' He looked at Jake. 'But Denise was in the bathroom, the door was shut.'

'Not all the time, it wasn't, Tony; she's heard you. Don't ask me how, but she has. Evil, vindictive cow. You've got that boxing charity night for the police, tonight. Oh, my God, you really are one of the boys in blue.' Jake couldn't help but laugh. Sharon was right to call Denise the poison dwarf, because this was over the top. But then again, why was Tony ringing other women when one was still in his apartment? God, would he never learn.

'What am I going to do? For God's sake, stop laughing and bloody help me. Do something, now.'

'I'll get Sharon, she'll know what to do. Women have calamities all the time when they're having their hair dyed, there must be some way to sort it out.'

'Sharon! You're going to give her the satisfaction of seeing me like this?' Tony started to stomp around again. He went into the kitchen and put his head under the cold tap to try and rinse more of the ink out. The floor was covered in puddles. It looked like there had been a flood.

Jake rang down to the main bar, where he knew Sharon would be, and asked her to come up.

'Put a robe on or something, will you? Cover up your bare arse before Sharon comes up. Especially that blue dick of yours, that really is a sight for sore eyes.' Again, Jake tried to stifle his laughter.

Jake opened the door to Sharon. 'What's the emergency? What's going on?' She walked into the apartment and noticed the floor was wet. Tony was nowhere to be seen. 'What's happened here, has there been a flood?' Sharon was looking around and then from behind her she heard a noise and turned.

Tony was walking out of his bedroom, with pale blue hair. His skin, no matter how he had rinsed it, still had a faint blue tinge. Sharon burst out laughing. She couldn't help herself, it was the funniest thing she had seen in years.

'If that's all you're going to do, you can piss off now.' Tony was angry and grumpy. He was tying the belt of his robe around him, and giving her the evil glare.

'What happened?' Sharon looked at Jake for an answer.

He threw his hands up in the air. 'We think it might have something to do with that Denise. Blue ink has been put into the showerhead. Tony got into the shower after she had gone this morning and, well, see for yourself.' Jake pointed at Tony.

'Okay, I get that, it's an old trick. I've heard of worse, but why did she do it?'

'Because she heard him ringing that model, Ami, and making a date. How do we sort his hair out, Sharon?' said Jake.

Sharon turned to Tony. 'Be grateful that's all it was, at least that will come out and it's not permanent. You bloody fool, you know she's a bit nutty. Why would you ring another woman when you have one in your apartment? Couldn't you wait five more minutes? You know, sometimes I think you deserve everything you get.'

Tony sat on a stool at the breakfast bar. Although angry, he looked like a sulky child. He ran his hands through his hair and saw the blue ink stain his hands. They both thought he was going to burst into tears.

Sharon took pity on him. 'It'll be okay, Tony, it's not as bad as it looks. I know a mobile hairdresser; she'll come and sort it out. In the meantime, we need to clean the showerhead. Bring it here and I'll put it in the dishwasher. And let's get this place cleaned up. Bloody hell, you leave a lot more mess behind you than blue stain!'

Jake went to get the showerhead. Sharon fetched some towels from the airing cupboard to put on the floor to soak up the puddles of water. Within half an hour, the dishwasher was on, the floors were mopped and Sharon had made some fresh coffee.

There was a knock at the door, and Sharon opened it to the hairdresser.

'Hi, Christine, come on in. I don't need to tell you what the problem is, you can see for yourself.' Sharon pointed at Tony. His once white towelling robe was now stained with ink, from where he had been clearing up, and along the collar from his hair. He looked a mess.

'What have you used?' The hairdresser was trying to sound professional, because Sharon had already told her it was a very delicate subject.

'"Used",' said Tony. He stuck his hand in his hair, which was now drying and looking even more blue. He held up strands of it so that it stuck up in the air. 'Do you think I planned to look like this, or something? I haven't "used" anything. Some crazy bitch has done this to me!' Tony started ranting on again about how Denise was a bitch and women couldn't be trusted.

'I've known worse,' said Christine. 'One angry wife put tomato puree into a showerhead, that was some stubborn red stains, believe me, and then there was the man whose wife put onion puree in the shower, so he looked okay, but everyone avoided him because of the smell.' Christine went on to tell them more horror stories. Tony and Jake listened, horrified, as Christine and Sharon discussed it in such a matter of fact way. Women – they were crazy!

Two and a half hours later, after constant washing, hair dye stripper, and even more rinsing, Tony was done. Christine finished off with a quick trim to get rid of the dry ends. There was still a very faint tint in his hair, but she had done as much as she could for now and things were looking much better. Tony was almost back to normal. Christine stood back and looked at him.

'You can barely see any blue, now, and only then if you look hard. Most people won't spot anything different about you. Of course, we could always bleach it, but not today; we've only just stripped the colour out of it.'

'You've done a great job, thanks; it will wear out though, yes?' Tony looked in the mirror. Most of it had gone, although his ego and vanity still hurt.

Christine assured him it would. 'Another couple of washes and you'll be back to normal. Do you want me to come back tomorrow or the day after and give it a conditioning treatment?'

Tony took her hand and kissed the back of it. 'That would be lovely, Christine. Thank you.' Tony gave her his best smile; in all of his anger he hadn't noticed what a pretty young woman she was.

'You're wasting your time, Tony,' Sharon said, with a bored expression. She rolled her eyes up to the ceiling then looked at Christine. 'Sorry, Chris, he can't help it. Please come back when you're free, tomorrow or the day after. And be sure to say hello to Michelle, your wife, from me.' Sharon emphasized the word 'wife', letting Tony know that Christine was a very happily married lesbian, who wasn't interested in him.

Tony blushed and reached for his wallet. 'Sorry, Christine. Here, take this for all your trouble and coming around here so promptly. Thanks.' Tony handed Christine a couple of fifty-pound notes. She initially refused such a huge amount, but he insisted she take it, not only for her hard work, but because he had made a fool of himself. 'See you soon. Thanks again.'

Sharon showed Christine to the door. 'Phew!' she said, when she came back. 'Thank goodness that's all over with. Well, Tony, you're more or less sorted out, but what about Denise?'

'Apart from strangling her with my bare hands, I am going to let the whole world know it was her who made me look like this and she did it because I dumped her!'

'Nice to know you're taking it on the chin and have learnt a valuable lesson in life. There's nothing worse than a woman scorned, and let's be honest, if the newspapers get a hold of this, women all over London will cheer, because you've had your comeuppance.'

'Are you still going to this charity night, tonight, then, and then seeing that Ami, as planned?' Jake handed Tony a whisky; he felt he deserved one.

'I am, Jake, I won't let her stop me. That's why she's done it, thinking she can force me to stay in tonight. Well, I'm not. I won't have any woman dictate to me.'

'So, what happens when you show Ami your blue-tinted pubic hair?'

Jake and Sharon burst out laughing. 'Christine!' they

both shouted together, 'you're needed again and bring your hair dye.'

Tony opened the front of his robe and looked down. He was going to have to sit in the bath for a very long time.

𝕭 ◊ 𝕮𝕽

There was a full-size boxing ring set up in the main club area, ready for the police charity boxing night. Police stations far and wide competed against each other, not only for a cup, but also for charity.

Many officers, from constables to detectives, all trained hard in the gymnasium in preparation for the annual event. It was good competition for each police station, and it was a great event enjoyed by all. Tony had agreed to host it in his club, and the boxing ring had been delivered and set up.

Although the evening was for charity, it created good relations between himself and the police. Tony's day might have been a calamity, but he was determined to make sure the night was successful.

The police had sold tickets for the event, and this year, all the proceeds were going to children's charities. This made it even more popular with the journalists. The newspapers all covered the event because the public loved to read feel-good stories.

Celebrities from all walks of life that were involved in children's charities felt a responsibility to pop along to the club to give it their support, even if they didn't stay for the boxing. This was another golden opportunity for Tony to introduce his club and himself to newcomers. A lot of the celebrities who were regulars at the nightclub also wished to attend and make charitable donations. There was plenty for the paparazzi to point their cameras at.

The main thing was that, since Tony had closed the club for the night to host the event, and had also made his own charitable donation – all in the aid of a good cause – his club would be in the newspapers again. Publicity was publicity, after all. Plus, knowing how the police force liked to relax and have a drink, his bar takings would go through the roof.

The police boxers turned up early to get ready for the night's events. They used the strippers' changing rooms, which made them all laugh and put them in good spirits. Each one had trained hard, and was determined to beat their opponent for the reputation of their station.

Superintendents and commissioners walked up the roped-off red carpet that Tony had laid down for them. It was all very over the top, and seemed more like a major movie premiere, but Tony had pulled out all of the stops. The superintendents turned up in their best uniforms, with all their shiny buttons and stripes. With their wives in awe at their side, they posed for their photos to be taken by the newspaper photographers, and then gave small interviews about why they were having this charity night for children.

Of course, in doing so, they all thanked Lambrianu's nightclub for the hospitality. Crowds were turning up, and the atmosphere inside was electric.

Tony had given his usual doormen and bouncers the night off to do as they pleased. He thought it was pointless them being there. After all, who would be stupid enough to cause trouble in a club full of police?

As Tony had predicted, the bar staff were run off their feet and the waitresses were running around taking orders and clearing tables. The usual strippers had been given the night off, but Tony had co-opted some of them to act as ring girls. They were to walk around in the boxing ring, between rounds, holding up a sign with the number of the next round on it. This all added a little glamour to the proceedings. Sharon thought that maybe, after the boxing was over and the wives had gone home, a few of the men might like to see the pole dancers, as a little light entertainment.

Tony stood outside the club on the red carpet, welcoming the hierarchy of the police and their wives, and shaking their hands. He was smiling and being free with his compliments about how beautiful the wives looked, even though some were in their sixties, and possibly more. He was full of his usual charm; it was then that the journalists started to shout to him.

'What's happened to your hair, Tony?'

'What's with the blue rinse, Tony?'

They were all shouting to him and taking photos. Lights from the cameras were flashing from either side of him.

He had thought the photographers would notice – they always scrutinised him so closely, and the lights from their cameras also helped show off the faint blue tint. It was time for him to put on his cheeky smile and front it out.

He walked over to one of the journalists at the front, and started to smile and laugh. He ran his hand through his hair and nodded at them. 'Boys,' he shouted to the paparazzi, 'take a tip from me. Never turn your back on a woman scorned.' Now he had got their interest, he waited. He was determined to pay Denise back for her trickery and the only way to do it was by letting the newspapers know what she had done. He wasn't going to give her name, but they all knew who he had been involved with lately, and it didn't take much adding up.

The newspapers either loved or hated him; one day he was that gangland boss, another he was Tony Lambrianu, club owner and playboy. Tonight, he was the latter, and he could use that to his advantage.

'Come on, Tony,' someone shouted, 'tell us what happened.'

'Well, fellas, where do I start? Never get on the phone and make a date with a woman when a leading lady of the theatre is still in your house having her early morning shower, supposedly out of earshot.' He laughed and waited. The journalists were writing as quickly as possible. They were all looking at each other and laughing, this was a great story. Even though Tony had not mentioned Denise by name, they all knew who the 'leading lady of the theatre' was.

Tony felt now was the time to do his own kiss and tell

story. This would make Denise squirm when she read it. *This will make the public talk about her, alright*, he thought, *but they won't be talking about her acting skills.*

'Having dumped her, fellas, after a boring night, she decided to put ink in the showerhead. As you can see, I didn't notice till after my shower.' He burst out laughing and ran his hands through his hair again. He enjoyed telling the press that he had already dumped her, he knew this would make her look bitter and spiteful. Her reviews for this evening's performance would contain all of this, he was sure of it.

'Who did you dump her for, Tony? Anyone we know?' Again, they were shouting to him. They wanted to know who had already replaced Denise.

'Well, no names mentioned, fellas, but I am meeting a very gorgeous glamour model at the end of the evening.' That was the term usually applied to topless models, who were known for their very large breast implants. Either that, or God had been very generous.

They were beautiful sought-after women, whom men fantasied about and women envied. Tonight, Denise would be at the top of the list. She would envy all the publicity the new love in Tony's life was getting, and she had fantasied about being part of his empire and becoming Mrs Lambrianu. Her embarrassment and stupidity outweighed his. He had a little blue hair, and his notorious womanising ways were even more established.

He was the cheeky playboy who had been caught out. She was vindictive and bitter. More to the point, she was yesterday's news. Instead of her acting skills, everyone would be talking about how petty she had been. Surely, going out with Tony Lambrianu meant you knew what you were in for. He was not known for his monogamous ways.

Tony wished them all a good night, waved at them and walked through the doors of the club to host the night's entertainment. It was then that he spotted Ralph Gold and his wife, Julie. They were standing with the local mayor, who had come in all his finery for the evening's proceedings. The newspapers had made him pose and shake hands with Tony and the police superintendents.

Ralph Gold looked over and saw Tony; for a few seconds they looked at each other, then Ralph Gold nodded his head in recognition. That was it. Tony was desperate to get into the inner circle of Ralph Gold's friends. That really was his big dream. Ralph Gold was into everything, but he was untouchable because of the people he knew and was friends with.

Tony made his way over to Jake. 'Have you seen who is here?' Tony nodded his head in Ralph Gold's direction.

Jake nodded. 'I saw him earlier. Has he said hello yet?'

Tony shook his head. 'No, he just nodded at me.'

'By the way, nice one with the press and that Denise. She'll never live it down, believe me, that will crucify her career. Once everyone knows she's bad news and made a public fool of herself, she's history.' Jake smiled at Tony. He was impressed by the way that Tony had smiled and laughed at himself. Suddenly there was a tap on Tony's shoulder.

Ralph Gold stood there. 'Well done, Tony.' He nodded towards Tony's hair. 'Nicely saved in front of the newspapers. Well done, son, you're learning.' With that, he started to walk away.

'Mr Gold, can I have a word, if you have a moment?' Tony was impatient but respectful. Maybe now was the time to ask for a meeting; after all, Ralph Gold had approached him and Jake.

'Not now, son, it's a charity night and we're here to have fun. Business is for other times, not in front of a room full of police and their wives.'

Tony could have kicked himself. He watched as Ralph Gold turned and walked back to his wife and the crowd sitting near the front of the boxing ring. How could he have thought that Ralph Gold would talk business here, amongst this lot? And he'd made a point of calling Tony 'son', just to keep him in his place.

Suddenly, there was a huge roar and a burst of applause. He turned towards the boxing ring to see the master of ceremonies, with his microphone, waiting for the crowd to quieten down a little. When they did, he introduced the two boxers in opposite corners of the ring. Men were cheering and applauding. Everyone was in high spirits. Money was changing hands as they were taking bets against each other.

Tony turned to Jake. 'God, Jake, I'm a real prat at times. I'm standing here with blue hair, surrounded by most of the Metropolitan police, and I ask Ralph Gold for a meeting. Shit!'

'Don't beat yourself up about it. Here, have a drink and forget it.' Jake handed him a glass. 'He knows you want to meet him and, when the time is right, you will. Come on, let's go and watch the fighting.' He headed towards the boxing ring.

The air was filled with cigar smoke, beautiful women walked around the boxing ring holding up numbered signs displaying how many rounds the boxers had fought and the referee, who was from the local boxing club, was in charge of the situation.

As Tony heaved a deep sigh, he caught sight of himself in the mirrored wall. He smiled at his appearance. Bloody hell, what a sight for sore eyes. It had been an eventful day, to say the least. Maybe Jake was right, maybe it was time to join in with the fun and have a few drinks – and, of course, Ami would be popping around later on.

The evening was eventually coming to an end. Sharon was sick of the ring girls moaning. The glamour had gone out of their status, and instead they were complaining about trying to keep their balance in high-heeled shoes, while walking around a boxing ring spattered with sweat, water and sputum. It was like a skating rink.

When one of the boxers had been knocked out, someone had poured water on his head and face to bring him around, then someone picked up a brush and swept it all to one side. All of this was going to take some cleaning up in the morning.

On leaving, Ralph Gold made a point of walking up to Tony. 'Next year, son,' he said, 'I should have a free appointment by then. I'll put it in the diary.' Then he walked to the exit with his arm around his very drunk wife.

※◇◎

Next morning, Tony came down from his apartment at the club a little worse for wear. Although he had decided to have some fun and make a night of it, he hadn't realised how much he'd overdone it until he woke up with a banging head.

Wearing a pair of black tracksuit bottoms and a T-shirt, he wandered into the club. Jake was standing at the bar having a coffee with Sharon, while she was working out the strippers' rotas for the week.

'Well, rise and shine, Tony. How are you feeling?' Jake said. He reckoned he could see how Tony was feeling – his face was pale and those wide blue eyes were now slits. He was unshaven and his hair hadn't been combed. Jake grinned. 'Pretty rough, I'm guessing.'

'Do I look as bad as I feel?' Tony walked towards them. Thankfully, Sharon was on hand to pour him some coffee, then she rummaged in her handbag for some painkillers.

'Here,' she said, 'keep the whole strip. I reckon you'll need them.'

'Did that Ami turn up last night, then?' Jake waited for an answer as Tony picked up his coffee mug from the bar, walked to a nearby table and sat down at it. He was nursing his head in his hands. Jake joined him.

'Yes, she did, mate. Don't worry, my reputation is intact. No problems there. It was an outstanding performance, even if I do say so myself.' He attempted a smile, then picked up his coffee and then took a gulp.

Jake turned to Sharon and saw her grin. She was holding her usual clipboard and gave them both one of her glances.

All these years on and they were both still like naughty schoolboys.

'What did she say about the blue bits?' said Jake, smiling; he lowered his head a little so he could see Tony's face.

'No idea, mate, everything was in blackout mode. Which, in your language, means I kept the lights off.'

That made Jake smile.

Tony rubbed his face took another sip of his coffee. 'Aaah, that's better. Did you hear Ralph Gold say he would make us an appointment in his diary?' The spark suddenly came back in Tony's eyes.

'Yes, in a bloody year's time. What's he doing for the rest of this year, for Christ's sake?' Jake thought it was useless. A year from now, and he was going to put it in his diary. Yeah, right.

'He's testing us, Jake. He has been all this time, and it seems we must have cleared some of his hurdles or he wouldn't have even mentioned it. A year's not too long, it gives us time to plan and get it right.' Tony took another drink of his coffee and gave Jake the thumbs up.

'Have you thought anymore about Angus and that other little plan of yours, or are you going to leave everything as it is?'

'Not now, Jake.' Tony picked his mug up and started walking away. 'Let me have a shower and then I'll tell you all about my master plan.'

'Master plan, indeed,' said Sharon, still writing on her clipboard. 'What he means is, he'll think about it in the shower, and then he'll tell you his cockeyed scheme. Why do you always go along with it, Jake?' Sharon seemed exasperated; Jake always fell in line when it came to Tony's plans.

Jake stood up, his face now serious. 'I love you, Sharon, but don't forget how you live, and where. How many credit cards and accounts you have at some of the best shops in London. All that is down to his cockeyed plans, as you put it, that he comes up with in the shower. On top of that, he may not be my blood, but he's my big brother, and he's always looked after me.'

Sharon pouted and looked apologetic. Jake was right. Most of the way they lived was down to Tony. He had done all the planning and took most of the chances. He had put his life on the line many times.

'Sorry, Jake, it's just that we don't need to keep striving for more, we have everything anyone could possibly want already. Why does Tony always reach for the stars when the moon will do?' She raised her hand and stroked Jake's face. She knew Jake was very protective of Tony, he always had been and he wouldn't hear a word said against him.

'That's okay, love.' He smiled at her, and took hold of her hand and kissed her palm. 'It's just that Tony feels this is the time when we need to keep our eye on the ball. All the other bosses, whom I may say didn't have half as much as we do, stopped worrying about their business deals. They felt they had done enough and that was how it all started to go wrong. It's easy getting to the top, Sharon, the trick is staying there.'

Sharon nodded, she could see Jake's point, but over recent months they seemed to have worked themselves into the ground, sorting out the clubs and the casino. 'Why don't you and Tony go on holiday for a few days? Get away from it all, you deserve it. Ashley and Mathers are looking after the men's club and so, may I add, am I. Graham is more than capable of looking after the casino, and of course the accountant is there to look after us all.'

'Wouldn't you like to come away with me? Just us, some sun, sand and time for ourselves. We haven't had a lot of that, lately.'

Jake's eyes were full of love for Sharon, they always were. She had been patient, in fact very patient, especially lately, taking a back seat while he sorted out the business with Tony. She was a good woman and an even better wife.

'Go and see Miriam in Italy. Tony hasn't been there for a long time. You and I will go away soon, just us, together.

I'll look forward to it.' She leaned forward and kissed him, and suddenly they were kissing passionately. This moment was the most intimate they had been in a long time. Tony didn't care about intimacies, he enjoyed playing the field. Easy come, easy go.

Sharon started undoing the buttons on her blouse. 'Come and help me check something out in the office. I hear there's a large chesterfield sofa in there.' She walked around to Jake's side of the bar and took his hand. It wasn't perfect making love on a sofa in the office, but at least it was making love.

ᔓ◊ᔓ

Sharon emerged from the office an hour later and walked back out into the club. She headed for the ladies' bathroom to freshen up. As she looked down the corridor, she saw Tony, now well-groomed and dressed in one of the fancy suits Mathers had advised him to buy, talking to the accountant at one of the tables. Jake walked over to join them.

'Well, Jake, what have you been doing?' Tony burst out laughing and gave him a cheeky wink. 'That's my boy.' Tony slapped Jake on the back, and watched him blush. 'Why are you blushing, for goodness sake? Sharon is your wife. I presume you have sex every now and again.' Again, he thought it was funny.

Finally, he saw the broad grin appear on Jake's face. Trying to change the subject to a much cleaner one, he said, 'Sharon thinks it might be a good time for us to have a break, take a few days holiday. It's been a gruelling couple of months. What do you think? We could visit Miriam.'

More serious now, Tony nodded. 'Maybe, but we have things to do first, I'll think about it.'

It was the accountant who clinched the deal. 'If you're going to go away for a break, now might be the time to do it. You're going to be busy, with one thing and another,

145

sorting out your business plans for Ralph. Everything is up and running now; when are you going to get the chance again?'

'Maybe you're right,' Tony said. He hated the idea of leaving his empire and possibly being too far away to sort it out, should anything go wrong. He had been away before to see Miriam, and to visit other countries, but there was a lot more at stake now. It wasn't just the club and the security firm. It was the casino and the men's club. Angus was in charge of the South London mob, and he was doing a good job, but what if …?

'You think about it, Tony,' Jake said, although he feared it was useless. He knew Tony didn't want to turn his back and leave all of this. It was like taking a blanket from a baby. He liked being in the midst of it, knowing every twist and turn.

Tony's mind was working. 'Maybe you're right,' he said. 'I suppose we do both deserve a break. Okay, we'll sort it, Jake, and we'll go and see Grandma.' Tony called her that now, she was his family, and he had grown to love her.

The heat was on; Tony needed to make an impact. He'd realised that Jake's idea about going away was, indeed, a good one. While he was away, he would get Angus's men to cause a little trouble in the East End, then everyone would wait with bated breath for Tony to go home and sort out their lives.

He would make sure everyone had everything in hand during his absence, and all the businesses he collected from would be able to appreciate his good work, protecting them and keeping them and their livelihoods safe. The thought of it made Tony smile. Superman to the rescue. It appealed to his vanity.

He was slowly working out a plan in his mind. A lot of the old South London mob weren't known faces. It would be so easy to get them to stir up a little trouble under Angus's guidance. Under no circumstances could they be recognized as his own men.

It was time to go back and see Angus and fill him in on his plan, after he had told Jake.

First, he wanted Christine to come around and have another go at sorting out his hair. There was no way he was going to see his grandmother looking like that. If Christine had to put a hair dye on it for now, then so be it.

ℰ◊℘

Getting into the back of his beige Rolls Royce, with the oyster finish that made it look as though it changed colours in the sunshine, made Tony feel like he had achieved something. Dressed as he was, in a double-breasted grey suit and tie, bought under Mathers guidance, made him feel like a man about town.

Now and again Tony still drove past the old haunts where he used to sleep as a child, just to remind him what he was striving for. It kept his feet firmly on the ground.

'My plan is simple, Jake; and no one is going to get hurt. Maybe a few bumps and bruises, but nothing they can't handle, and I'll see that they are well paid for it.'

Jake took a deep sigh and put his head back on the luxurious leather head rest of the car. 'Go on, then, let's have it, Tony. I've seen that brain of yours working overtime.'

'What do these pubs really not want on their doorsteps and what is it that the South London mob were famous for? Take your time.' The smug grin on his face made Jake feel sick inside.

'Drugs, that is what they don't want on their doorsteps, they cause too much trouble and that is what the South London mob were famous for.'

There, now Jake had the smug expression on his face. He was sure Tony hadn't expected him to come up with the answers so soon.

'Nice one, Jake. That's definitely one to you. We go away, like you and Sharon suggested. Thinking that we are out of the way, the South London mob, via Angus and with a little bit of gear from our old friend, Bennie – whom I hear is doing okay with his new set up – will hang around the pubs and snooker halls and do some dealing.' Tony nodded at Jake; he was beaming at his masterplan.

He continued. 'Dan, and those guys he hangs around with, are still our eyes and ears. He's always been loyal, and he's turned out okay. A few years ago, he was on a downhill slope. Now, he's got money coming in and got his act together.'

Jake was astonished. 'Dan? You've got him working the bar at the club, that's how he keeps his ear to the ground these days. And his mates, well, some of them work our doors. Why would you want to get him into trouble, selling drugs?' Jake shook his head. Tony was right, Dan and his mates had been more than useful, so why was Tony turning against them now?

'No, I like them all, and they've trusted me all this time. What I want them to do is stir up a bit of concern, a bit of worry, if you like. I want them to spread the word that they've seen dealers hanging around.'

'What? You mean you just want them to start some kind of gossip, like old women?' It was unbelievable how Tony's mind worked. Jake couldn't believe what he was hearing.

'You've got it. And then Angus gets some of the guys down there, to have a drink and make it look like they are looking the place over. With that kind of gossip, they are going to be on their toes, and so any stranger that shows his face is going to cause concern.'

'Bloody hell, Tony, that blue rinse of yours has gone to your head. Do you realise how wacky that sounds?'

Tony laughed and ran his hand through his hair. 'Worry and concern causes paranoia, Jake, and gossip makes it worse. I think I'll probably get Angus's men to throw in a fight somewhere and cause a little fear and mess. Then,' Tony spread his hands wide with an innocent look on his face, 'who are they going to call for? You and me, but we'll be away. However, out of a sense of loyalty and protection, we'll fly back and sort the problem out. What do you think?' Tony was smiling, he had it all worked out. He was waiting for Jake's response.

Jake found it unbelievable. 'Oh, yes, superhero to the rescue, I get it. Of course, this has nothing to do with the size of your ego.' Jake stared at him wide-eyed, still in disbelief.

'No, Jake, but it will remind them what they are paying for and why. We have to keep them feeling safe under our wing, that is good business.'

The car stopped outside of the casino and Tony reached for the door handle, about to get out.

'Wait! Just hold on, superhero Tony. Just how far into this holiday do you intend to be called back? Because if we're flying all the way out there for a day, we may as well go to Margate.' Jake was fed up; even going on holiday seemed to create an opportunity for Tony to do some form of business.

'For goodness sake, Jake, don't you think I've thought of that? The gossip starts a few days after we leave, a little fight starts, what, at least a day before we are due to come back. Then, when people are worried and panicking, they are told that we are doing our duty and coming home at their request. With that sort of protection, they'll be willing to pay us double.' Tony laughed at the thought of it. 'Come on, I need to see Graham, he has a training room starting up, upstairs.

'Why? There are already training rooms for croupiers, where do you think you got yours from?'

'Aaah, Jake, but these are going to be "Lambrianu trained" croupiers, the very best. That, my friend, is the difference, and if I may say so, I've done quite well under Graham's guiding hand.'

'You really have a warped brain. What do you propose? If this all goes tits up, you'll have a job to fall back on. Okay, mate, have it your way. You will, anyway.'

Jake was worried Tony was becoming a workaholic. He

lived and breathed the business. Even the female distractions he had didn't seem to distract him that much. He loved the ladies and the ladies adored him, but Tony had a heart of stone. Jake knew he felt he had been let down by women for most of his life, starting with his mother, and as much as he was a control freak, he seemed wary of them.

It was a fair point, because all he had ever met were models wanting to promote their career, or actresses from the theatre and well-known porn stars, getting on the front pages to boost their reviews. It was all a bit sad, really. It seemed everyone wanted Tony Lambrianu, and the celebrity status he had acquired. He was in the newspapers, he had been interviewed on television, talking about his clubs. Some of the male celebrities he knew and who seemed genuine had also mentioned to Tony the price of fame.

Tony went into the casino to see Graham. 'Well, if it's not my number one pupil,' Graham said, and Tony blushed at the compliment.

'How is everything?' Tony walked towards the offices. He always liked to check the receipts for the evening's takings himself, and he relied on the accountant to go through them with him.

'Everything is fine, Tony, and business is booming, which I am sure you already know. It seems no one ever goes home. Thankfully, we have a twenty-four-hour licence.'

'That table has dust on it. Get the cleaners to make this place spick and span, will you? Who is the cleaning firm that comes in?'

Graham informed him, while looking at Jake. He couldn't see any dust; well, nothing major.

'I'll sort it, give me the telephone number.' Tony took the telephone number of the cleaning company and put it in his pocket.

Graham waited to see if there was anything else Tony wanted. 'I can always have a word, if you want me to, Tony. After all, that is my job.'

'Tony,' Jake half whispered in Tony's ear. 'You're becoming obsessed. You and I seriously need to talk. Let Graham do his job, is he the manager or what?'

Jake felt Tony's shoulders relax a little and the tension reduced. He really did need to get away from it all for a while.

'You're right, Graham, it's your job. I'll leave it in your capable hands. Sorry, I said I wouldn't poke my nose in, and I won't, but if you need me, you know where I am.' Tony gave a weak smile, and saw the relief on Graham's face. 'Jake and I are going on holiday for a week or so, possibly to Italy. Are you okay with that?'

'Absolutely, Tony, and everything will be in order and here for you, when you get back.'

Even Jake thought Graham looked pleased to know that Tony was going away for a while. He was permanently hanging around, checking things. He must have driven them all crazy.

'Come on, Jake, things to do, people to see.' With that, Tony walked out of the casino, followed by Jake.

Jake turned around to look at Graham, who was still standing by the table with the 'dust' on it. He wiped it and looked at his hand. He couldn't see anything unusual. 'Sorry,' Jake mouthed to Graham, and he smiled.

'Tony, you're becoming a pain in the arse,' Jake said, when they were back in the car. 'Everyone is doing their job, they're afraid not to. You're always there, breathing down their necks. Go easy, mate, or else they'll all leave you to it. If you show them you think they're not up to the job, trust me, they'll leave. You're like a coiled spring, you're so wound up. The sooner we go away, the better.'

'You're right, Jake. You always are. I need to keep my mouth shut. I tell you what, Christmas is coming soon, I think they're all due a big fat bonus, don't you? Will that suit you and them?'

Jake nodded. 'Good idea. By the way, I'm going to get Sharon to book our trip for next week. As you say, we're not going to get away much around Christmastime. Now is the time to let them all get on with it.' He punched Tony in the arm. 'And it's time to tell Angus about that wacky plan of yours, though I'm not sure he'll understand it. We would be better off telling his wife!' That made them both laugh.

⁎

'You want that Bennie's boys hanging around your pubs and that stripper agency in town. But, why? They're nothing but trouble, Mr Lambrianu, everyone knows that.' Angus's face was going red again. The very thought that someone was going to cause trouble for Tony annoyed him. He felt he owed him a lot; his loyalty was unquestionable.

Tony smiled that smug, charming smile of his and looked at Jake. He had said he wanted to cause concern and worry to the businessmen he collected from. Angus was already upset about it, and he was in on it. He had been right; there would be some form of public outcry. Tony and Jake felt it was like explaining to a child. 'No, Angus, listen to me,' Tony said.

'God help us all.' Angus's wife was making herself busy, dusting, making tea and making it absolutely obvious she was doing her best to listen in on the conversation. She looked up at the ceiling, then hit Angus with her duster. 'You Scottish idiot, you're going to shake those people up. You're going to scare them, even I got that bit. And I'm not listening.' She looked at Tony and Jake and folded her arms, as if daring them to contradict her.

They both thought she looked scary. She had a headscarf on, and a full-length floral apron that fastened at the back. Her face was set, like stone, and looked like she had never been taught how to smile. Her tone was harsh, and the dull red lipstick she wore was smudged just in the middle of her lips, like a little rosebud. *It looks like she just bit the head off a bat*, thought Jake.

'Hello, Mrs Angus,' said Tony. His voice was weak; even he was wary of this matriarch.

'Elsie, my name is Elsie, Mr Lambrianu.' Even though she was introducing herself, she didn't sound very friendly about it. She stood there, feet apart, wielding her duster.

'Well, Elsie, as you can hear, we have business to discuss with Angus.' Tony wanted her to leave. Elsie turned on her worn slippers and left the room, muttering to herself.

Jake leaned forward to whisper in Tony's ear. 'Her name might be Elsie, but I'm wondering what everyone else calls her.' He glanced up at Tony and gave a little grin.

'Angus, I want you to make sure that Bennie's men are seen hanging around in my absence. All strangers. I want a couple of the old South London mob having a drink in the pubs, and playing snooker in the halls. Then I want some fighting to break out and a few threats to be made to the customers. Do you understand? You do all of this when I telephone you and tell you to. Okay?'

'Aye, boss. There is one man I have in mind, always borrowing money, has debts all over the place. Greasy little shit, but he isn't known by anyone. Christ, even I don't want to know him, but he comes in handy for stuff like this. His name's Luke, thinks he's some kind of ladies' man, but he's a total waster. Aye, lads, he's the one for the job.' Angus seemed pleased with himself.

Tony was curious. 'What do you mean, "stuff like this"? Who is he and what have you used him for?'

Angus looked a little sheepish, and worried. 'He sometimes does some work for Bennie and his lot. I'm not into all that, so I've used him as a kind of go-between. He's trying to get in with the lads, thinks he's a part of the team. No way, though; like I say, he owes money everywhere and so he gets a few pounds for dropping stuff off for Bennie.'

'How did you meet him? What makes you think you can trust him with this arrangement?' Tony wasn't happy; he eyed Angus up suspiciously while he waited for an explanation.

'Look, Mr Lambrianu, if you don't want to use him, that's okay, it was just a suggestion. He's in with the moneylenders, and owes them money. They give him real low-life jobs to do for them to pay off his debts. I only know this because when I still personally go to pick up your money from them, he's usually hanging around like a lap dog. They use him for the crap stuff, that's why I thought maybe we could, too. Your name wouldn't come into it. It would be that mad dog Angus stirring up trouble and needing a tough man for the job. He's an idiot and a wife-beater. I hear he would jump at the chance to prove he's a hard nut.'

'A low life like that, who no one cares about, could be just what we're looking for,' said Jake. It seemed Angus was learning fast.

'I'm not going to get our guys into trouble, Mr Lambrianu, I've been in prison with most of them. That's why an outsider like him, who thinks he's on the inside, we can all afford to lose. Your choice, you're the boss.'

Even Tony thought Angus's argument couldn't be any fairer than that; he just didn't like the idea that maybe all this power was going to Angus's head.

'I'm going to trust you on this, Angus, as long as you remember I'm your boss. Cross me and I'll slit your throat. Do you hear me?' Tony's eyes darkened and he stared at Angus with that cold chilling stare of his.

Angus was upset; he turned to Jake. 'Jake, man, help me out here.' He spread his hands out in wonder and innocence. 'It was only a wee suggestion, you know I'm not going to piss down your back and tell you it's raining. Aye, Jake, you know that.'

'Calm down, Angus. It's just that this is a delicate job, and there is no room for mistakes or careless whispers, okay?' Jake was trying to ease the situation.

Tony didn't particularly like outsiders. He had his own army that he could trust, but he had to admit, using some low-life scumbag protected his own men.

Tony nodded at Angus. 'Jake's right, you've done a good job, and it's time I trusted your judgement.' Tony held out his hand to shake Angus's.

Tony turned to leave and Jake shook Angus's hand. 'Don't worry, Angus, we'll be in touch when the time is right, okay?'

'Aye, laddie.' He shook his head. 'I didn't mean to upset him, you know. Man, he can turn as quick as a slippery eel.'

'I know, Angus.' Jake patted him on the back and started to leave.

Tony really does need a holiday, he thought to himself, *it can't come soon enough.* Although Angus's turns of phrase about slippery eels and pissing down your back might be weird, he was absolutely right; Tony could turn on you very quickly, at any time. Everyone knew that, which is how he kept all those hard prisoners in order.

'Bye, Elsie,' shouted Jake, as he walked down the stairs. Even though Angus's wife had made herself scarce he knew for a fact she would have been listening in on the conversation; she couldn't help herself. That made him laugh; now she would go upstairs and give poor old Angus a piece of her mind, for upsetting Tony.

'Did you really need to threaten him?' Jake said, when they were back in the car. 'His work has been excellent. Your money is always in full and on time, sometimes even earlier.'

'I know, Jake, but it doesn't hurt to remind people I'm watching them. Just because I'm on the other side of London doesn't mean I haven't got my eye on him. Out of sight, out of mind, eh? No, that's not how I work.'

Jake knew it was time to change the subject, this was only winding Tony up more.

'I heard through the grapevine that there's a big money poker game going on this afternoon. Do you feel lucky, Tony? I'm sure our professional card sharp, Graham, has put a few tricks up your sleeve.' He elbowed Tony in the ribs and smiled.

At last the smile appeared back on Tony's face. 'I reckon I could risk some of our hard-earnt money on the cards, it'll get me in the holiday mood.'

Jake phoned Sharon to book some flights to Italy for himself and Tony, and he also told her they would both be gone all afternoon. He said he was going to get Tony to wind down a little. Even she gave a sigh of relief, and sounded like she would be glad to have him out of the way for a while.

16

RESPECT

After a late lunch, Tony and Jake went to the poker game. It was at a closed local club they all knew and it was high stakes. The players were all businessmen who liked to take off the odd afternoon and have a little fun in their free time.

Eight of them sat around the table. The stake was a minimum of a thousand pounds a game. Jake watched as Tony shuffled the cards like a professional. He knew he wouldn't have let Graham get off with just showing him the right way to play cards, he knew Tony would also know how to cheat.

The atmosphere was tense. Tony made a point of losing a few hands of cards gracefully, and the whisky was poured. Then he started to win, and win fast, claiming that at last he was having a lucky streak. It was finally left to Tony and an estate agent, who only dealt in big properties.

Everyone else had decided the game was getting out of hand and had folded.

On the table between Tony and the estate agent was eighty thousand pounds in cash. Normally, anyone who was out of their depth would have thrown their cards in by now, but the estate agent was determined to take that money off

Tony and make him a laughing stock, as well. Tony put another ten thousand pounds down on the table, thankful that he had helped himself to a lot of money out of the safe before they went. He was determined not to back down to this man.

'Your call,' said Tony calmly, giving his friendliest smile. He could see the sweat on the man's brow. All the other men were watching intently, and not a word was spoken. It seemed like everyone was holding their breath.

'Will you take a credit note?' the man asked Tony. He was wiping beads of sweat away.

'No, I don't do credit, and if you're out of your depth, you should have folded. You shouldn't be sitting at this table with these fine gentlemen if you can't cover your bets.' Tony reached forward; if the man couldn't double his stakes the money was his. He put his hand on the huge pile of money and looked at Jake.

'Stop! Wait, I have this.' Everyone watched as the estate agent took out a set of keys with a brown label attached to them. 'It's a large mansion house by the sea, in Essex, around ten bedrooms; will you take that?'

'Easy, fellas,' said one of the other men at the table, who could see this was going too far. It had nothing to do with the cards each man was holding, it was a matter of reputation and who could hold their nerve under all this pressure. 'That house is worth a lot more than what is on the table. I know it. It used to belong to a lord or something, it must be worth a couple of million.'

'With what I'm holding in my hand,' said the estate agent with a satisfied grin, 'I won't be losing. I won't be losing anything. Will you take the keys?' He looked across the table at Tony.

'A lord, you say. Well, I haven't seen the place so I suppose I have to take your word for it, but okay, I'll accept the keys. Do you have the deeds?' The man nodded at Tony and took the deeds out of the inside pocket of his jacket.

'It's been empty a while and is up for sale; my firm's in

charge of selling it. I have all the paperwork.' The man put the deeds and the keys on the table. 'Show me your cards, Mr Lambrianu, I'm about to take your money.' The atmosphere was tense and even though the man seemed cocky, he was sweating and his hands were trembling as he waited for Tony to show his hand of cards.

Tony fanned out his cards, teasing the other men and stringing out the big moment. Finally, he displayed his cards on the table. Each man gave an intake of breath. Tony had a full house. He saw the look on the estate agent's face. He looked crushed; all he had was two pairs. The tears started to roll down his face and he was shaking. He stood up so quickly he nearly knocked the table over, then he ran to the bathroom.

'Well done, Tony.' The other men gave him a round of applause. 'You had a great hand and you held your nerve. That man was a bloody fool; how is he going to explain he has just given away a house?' They all started mumbling together about how foolish the man had been.

Eventually, he came out of the bathroom, wiping his mouth. It was blatantly obvious that he had been sick.

Tony wanted to appear friendly and decent in front of these businessmen. 'I tell you what,' he said, 'we're all friends here; how much is the house worth, seriously?' Tony waited; he saw the colour start to appear in the man's cheeks again.

'Two point five million,' the estate agent said.

'I'll take your credit note, instead, but I want all the money by this afternoon. Send it to my casino. Is that fair?' Tony looked around at the other men at the table with a questioning look.

'Bravo, Tony, that's the gentleman's way of playing the game, bravo,' said the leader of the men, who had set up the game. Each and every one of them agreed that Tony was being a good sport about things. The leader put a large Havana cigar in his mouth and drew on it, then blew a large cloud of smoke into the already hot and sweaty atmosphere.

'I don't have it! I would need a month or two at least,' the estate agent blurted out. He looked ashamed and embarrassed. His eyes were wide with horror and fear.

The leader of the poker game looked horrified and disgusted. 'Are you telling us all that you carried on gambling and placing bets with money you don't have, to prove a point?' He turned to Tony. 'I'm sorry, Tony, I would never have asked him to the table if I had known. I feel it is my debt.' He blew out more cigar smoke into the air.

'I'm sorry, I thought I had a winning hand. Sorry.' The estate agent was disgraced in front of all these men. They were washing their hands of him.

'No need for that,' said Tony. He was gritting his teeth and playing yet another kind of poker game. 'Everyone, take all your money back and let's just call it a day, shall we?' Tony gulped back his drink and stood up. 'Gentlemen, it's been a nice afternoon. Come on, Jake, time to go.'

Jake felt he was taking this very well indeed. Normally, Tony would have gone berserk by now, but he was being very calm about the situation, and it was evident all the other men felt he was being more than generous.

The leader of the poker game stood up and put his hand on Tony's shoulder. Clearly, not everything he had heard about this man was true; he seemed to be a very decent chap who was prepared to let bygones be bygones.

'Take your winnings, Tony, the house is yours. This game is my responsibility and I will sort it. As for you, sir,' the leader looked at the estate agent, 'you are not a gentleman, get out.'

Tony spoke up, his voice velvety, his demeanour calm, almost humble. 'If you are sure … it is only a game, and we are all friends and businessmen. Really, I don't mind. It's been a nice afternoon away from the toils of work.' Tony smiled genuinely at all of the men, making them appreciate his generosity and manner even more. He was being very decent and sporting about the whole sorry affair. He was portraying the British stiff upper lip and they were lapping it up.

The leader of the game picked up the house keys and the deeds, and nodded to one of the waiters to put the money into a bag. 'Here, I insist you take this, Tony, if for no other reason than that I can hold my head up in public again. I have never been so embarrassed. You won it fair and square; and after all, if you'd lost, he would have happily taken your money.' The man held out his hand to shake Tony's; he looked very apologetic.

Tony took the bag of money and the keys and deeds offered to him, then quickly said his farewells and left. He waited till he got into the car, then heaved a sigh of relief. 'Thank God that's over.'

John, the driver, drove away from the club quickly.

'Bloody hell, Tony, that was tense. I thought you would have killed him. He was going to take thousands off you, and you were going to give them all their money back. I think I've lost weight just watching. I was wetting myself,' said Jake.

'So was I, Jake.' Tony swept his hair back, then sat forward on the car seat and held his arms out straight, angled down towards the floor of the car, and half a dozen playing cards fell out of his sleeves. Jake watched them fall, amazed. He picked up the cards and looked at them.

'You don't have anything; it's a rubbish hand of cards.' Jake held them up and looked at them again. How the hell had he done it? He had been watching Tony all of the time, and so had the others.

Tony burst out laughing loudly. 'Oh, yes I do, Jake, I have eighty thousand pounds, an estate with a mansion house in Southend, by the seaside, and the respect of all those men. I don't mind saying it, though, it freaked me out when they shook my hand with all that decency and gratitude, I thought my cards would fall out! But that estate agent, snivelling little rat, he deserved what he got. He could have done that to any one of those guys, but he was desperate to prove a point and do it to me. Like you say, Jake, I always have something up my sleeve.'

Jake put his hands to his face; he couldn't believe what he was hearing, or seeing, for that matter. 'That guy is probably going to go out and shoot himself. That is the gentleman's way, isn't it? For God's sake, Tony!'

'Shoot himself? He'll be lucky.' Tony smiled, but there was little warmth in it.

'You kept calm, though, I'll grant you that.' Jake was in awe.

'I'm not a gentleman, but I've gained respect amongst that lot. Now, let's go to the seaside and see what these keys have in store for us.' Tony held up the keys and waved them in the air in front of Jake's face. He looked very pleased with himself. A house by the sea; it was an investment, and by all accounts, according to the men in that room, a damn good one. A lord's house, and he had paid nothing for it. That was the best sort of business.

🙰◊🙰

The following afternoon, Tony and Jake stood in an old derelict warehouse, looking up at a man with a noose around his neck, balancing on a rickety wooden chair.

'Jump, or I'll push the chair from under your feet anyway,' said Tony.

'Please, Mr Lambrianu, don't do this. I have a wife and family. I'm already ruined and disgraced. I've lost my job because I gave you that house. You don't have to do this.'

Tony looked up at the old dusty beam with the rope wrapped around it and shook his head. His ears were closed to the estate agent's pleadings. 'If you're not prepared to do the time, then don't do the crime. Isn't that what they say?' Tony's voice was calm and almost friendly. Standing there with his hands in the pockets of his camel coat, he looked bored.

Tears were pouring down the estate agent's face; he was trembling, but trying not to move. The old chair that stood between life and death was already wobbling underneath his feet.

'Jake, here, thinks I should give you a chance. Consider this a lesson, set the record straight, so to speak. What do you think?'

The dark, derelict warehouse hadn't been used in years. Only a small streak of sunlight shone through the tiles missing from the roof. Pigeons had made it their home and rats had made it their food source. Tony rubbed the soles of his shoes on the floor, in an attempt to get some of the pigeon shit off them. He waited.

'Yes, yes, Jake's right,' said the estate agent. His voice was as shaky as the chair he stood on. 'Give me a chance, Mr Lambrianu. I'll go to prison when they find out I gave that house away, I *will* do the time. When I get out, I can leave London and never come back. I won't say anything about this. Promise.' He sniffed. 'I'm a gambler, Mr Lambrianu, I have a problem. But you got your money and more. There's nothing they can do, the house is yours. You have the deeds and I signed it over. Please, Mr Lambrianu.' He turned his eyes to Jake. 'Jake, tell him for God's sake, please.'

The warehouse was large, but felt claustrophobic. Sweat poured down the estate agent's face and dripped off the end of his nose. That, combined with the tears, made him a pitiful sight. *He's a far cry from the clever, smug bastard who tried conning me out of money yesterday*, Tony thought to himself. He turned to look at Jake. 'Tell him what you think he should do, Jake.' He remained calm, and looked and sounded bored.

Jake stepped forward and cleared his throat before he spoke. He, too, was feeling hot and sweaty in the airless dump. 'You like to play poker with gentlemen. The elite, you might say. Well, from what I've read about gentleman disgraced in society, they kill themselves to save their families from further embarrassment. Also, it would save us a lot of explaining. We haven't beaten you up, we just bundled you into the car and brought you here. Everyone will breathe a sigh of relief that you did the decent thing.'

The man's eyes widened and he stared at Jake. He'd thought he was going to help him, give him a chance to redeem himself. This was not what he had hoped for. He knew he was doomed. The pair of them stood there, staring at him in a nonchalant way. His life meant nothing to them. The end was inevitable; his bladder gave way.

'You disgust me,' said Tony. 'You tried making me look a cunt in front of those uppity posh bastards and you were going to rob me. No, it's not enough. Look at you now, you've pissed yourself and you're shaking.' He looked at Jake. 'For fuck's sake, let's get this over with. I'm bored and hungry.' He turned his eyes back to the estate agent. 'Now, fucking jump or I'll kick the chair out from under you myself. Either way, you're dead meat. Have some pride, be a man. Come on, we'll count together. One … two …'

'Wait, no, wait. You're not going to kill me, you fucking criminals.' The estate agent had accepted his fate and felt the braver for it. It didn't matter anymore. That bored expression on their faces said it all.

He took as much air into his lungs as the tight noose around his neck allowed, then jumped from the chair, knocking it over in the process. His body started twitching and dancing in the air as he choked on his last breath then, suddenly, there was an eerie silence as his motionless body swayed back and forth.

Tony gave Jake the thumbs up and nodded, then started to walk towards the old planks of wood that had been used to board the place up. He was just about to step out into the daylight when he turned, almost knocking Jake over. He walked back to the body dangling in the air, put both his arms around the estate agent's legs and pulled them down with all his might. Hearing the beam crack, he stopped, and walked back over to Jake, wiping the dust off his hands as he went.

Jake watched and waited for Tony to join him. 'Was that

absolutely necessary? You could see he was dead.'

'He looked dead; he might have just been unconscious. Now, I know he's fucking dead for sure. Come on, Jake, I need a bacon sandwich.'

John, the driver, opened the door for them. He had stopped the estate agent and asked him for directions outside of his house, and bundled him into the car. Three people had gone in to the warehouse and only two came out. He knew what had happened.

Jake yawned, closing his eyes and stretching out his legs in the back of the car, then shook his head. 'You can be a nasty bastard sometimes, Tony. I actually think you enjoy it.'

'It's a nasty business, Jake.' Tony looked back at the warehouse and smiled to himself. That was a job well done. 'John, take us to the club.'

When they got back, Sharon told them she had booked the flights and they were due to go to Italy in two days' time. That would give them time to get their affairs in order before they left. The flight towards the warm sunshine was indeed a welcoming thought. Rosanna at the door, greeting them both, was an even nicer one.

₱◊ℛ

When they arrived, the weather was warm and the workers on the vineyard were going about their business. Sure enough, it was Rosanna who opened the door to them and she made a big fuss of them both.

'Where is Nonna?' Tony said, when they were in the house, and Rosanna had brought them a cold drink each. Although Tony called Miriam 'grandmother' now, he still like the Italian word for it; he thought it sounded friendlier.

'She is at the church, Antonias. She will be back soon.' Rosanna went and made herself busy, airing the bedrooms.

'You take the cases up, Jake, I want to go and see Miriam.'

Tony walked out into the courtyard and went to the little

church on the grounds. He saw his grandmother kneeling before the altar, praying. He waited until she had finished and then spoke. 'Grandmother, Nonna.' He held out his arms and watched her stand, turn, and walk swiftly towards him.

'Antonias, my beautiful boy, why didn't you call? I could have had things ready. Truly, God answers my prayers.' She fell into his open arms and held him tightly.

The next few days were truly relaxing: no newspapers, no hassle, that all seemed a million miles away.

17

GANGLAND WARS

Miriam enjoyed the fact that Tony would accompany her to church in the daytime. She wasn't sure if he prayed or not, but he would kneel and watch her intently as she did. This obviously meant something to him.

'I have got something for you, Antonias, here.' Miriam held out a small cloth bag. It was old and worn.

He took it from her and looked inside. It was some sort of beaded necklace with a crucifix attached. He looked up at her.

'It's a rosary. In fact, it was your father's rosary. It's yours now, and hopefully, it will always keep you safe. Your father always carried it with him. It seems strange now, or maybe just coincidence, but he left it in his room on the day he had his accident. Probably just coincidence.' Her eyes wandered off, as though she was remembering her dead son, Antonias's father.

Jake had laughed at Tony at times, asking if he was going to spend all the holiday in there confessing all of his sins. Then he would remind him that it was only a short stay and they would need a lot longer if Tony was to do that.

'I like it there, it's peaceful. There is something holy

about that place, I don't know what, and I know I've had too much to drink and I'm talking rubbish, but that place has meaning for me.'

Jake thought it was strange. Tony, who seemed to have a heart of stone at times, had a different side to him that no one saw. He liked that little church, possibly even loved it. It held a lot of family meaning for him. 'Maybe you'll get married in there, one day,' Jake joked.

Tony scoffed at the idea. 'I would never bring any of the women I know here, it's my place. Come to think of it, I wouldn't marry any of them, either.'

'You will, one day, when the right woman comes along and sweeps you off your feet.'

'Indeed, he will, Jake, you are right,' said Miriam, walking into the dining room, where they were still drinking their wine and talking. 'She's out there, Antonias, you just need to find her, and she will appear when you are not looking for her.' Miriam gave him one of her wise old smiles. Tony reached out his hand to Miriam.

'You're the only woman I'm going into church with, Nonna.' Tony was a little drunk; he could let his hair down, here. He didn't have to deal with everyone's problems, here. It was sanctuary.

'Do you think he ever will get married, Nonna?' Now Jake was drunkenly smiling at Miriam and joking, while propping himself up on one elbow.

That was the worst thing about living on a vineyard with bottles and bottles of delicious wine at your disposal. Miriam was not a drinker and was used to it, but to Jake and Tony it was like nectar.

'Oh, yes. I have asked God. He says, she will fight him all the way, and eventually fall in love with Antonias, not Tony.' With that, she wished them both goodnight and went upstairs to bed.

'What's it like, Jake, sleeping with the same woman every night? Don't you ever get bored?' Tony was swaying slightly and his eyes were glazed, but he was suddenly curious.

Jake looked at him seriously. 'There is a big difference between the sex you have with your women and making love with someone who is your friend, lover and life partner, someone you can trust implicitly. It has meaning, it's not just a release of the animal instincts.' Jake watched Tony taking it in. He knew he wouldn't remember this conversation in the morning but maybe, one day, he would understand. He hoped so.

℘ ◊ ℭ

After a week of enjoying good food in their bellies and hot sun on their backs, Tony decided it was time to get down to business. 'Now it's time to stir up a little trouble back home, Jake. Are you ready to contact Angus?'

'Sure. I'll give you your due, you've taken longer than I thought to get around to it. This place does you good. You're like a different person here.'

It was true. They had gone riding through Italy on little mopeds, and buzzed around the vineyard on them, having some fun. A thought had occurred to Tony and he had tried to brush it off, but he couldn't help it. It felt good to be home. Here was home. So was Elle, and he didn't want to betray her after everything she had done for him, but this was his true home.

Tony told Miriam that he had bought a house by the sea, although without going into any details. Jake interrupted and told her that Tony was getting in the decorators and had hired some designer to furnish it. He was leaving it all to them. After all, what did he know about a house that big?

'I thought, maybe Elle could look after things there, after all, she lives nearby.' Tony looked at his grandmother for approval.'

'That's an excellent idea, Antonias, she is a good woman and has served you well. She will look after things for you.' She realised Tony didn't want to take sides, to have to choose between his fondness for Elle and herself.

'It's a beautiful house, Nonna, enormous and with lots

of land attached to it, and out of the windows you can see the sea and the waves crashing against the beach. Maybe you'll come and visit one day.' Tony waited pensively.

'I'm an old woman for travelling, but maybe I will, one day. In the meantime, I expect lots of photos.'

She felt that was good enough for him. He had two women in his life, and each was some kind of mother figure. It was for the best that he kept them apart. That way he wouldn't feel awkward, showing either of them attention in front of the other.

Tony had already told Dan what to do while he was away, and he had apparently done his job well. Sharon had told Jake that people were on their guard, waiting for trouble. Dan had let the whispers out that while Tony was away, he suspected that the South London mob would try and cause trouble. Angus had got a few of his men that were known to the older publicans to drive erratically through the streets, hooting their horns, playing loud music and shouting abusive comments. It was nothing major or out of the ordinary, but once Dan and his friends had started up the gossip about the possibility of trouble brewing, everyone seemed nervous.

Publicans noticed that there were strangers hanging around on street corners, whispering to other men. This all awoke a cold feeling of dread in them. What was about to happen? Some of the publicans had already been to see Sharon and told her their fears. Apparently, they knew there was going to be trouble. Tony's plan was already working.

Hearing the reports from Sharon, Tony and Jake couldn't help but laugh. This was ridiculous behaviour and they were all paranoid, but yes, they would all be pleased to see Tony back at the helm. It made them feel safe.'

'So, Jake,' said Tony. He was relaxing on a sunlounger with a glass of home-grown wine. The sun was shining and the floral smell of grapes emanating from the vineyard filled the air. Jake was dozing on a lounger; business seemed a million miles away. 'Jake, are you listening to me? And don't pretend you're asleep behind those dark sunglasses. Listen to me, time for plan B.'

Jake sat up, it was no use. 'Yes, I'm listening.' He yawned and stretched, then he moved his sunglasses and placed them on the top of his head. 'What is plan B?'

'Let's see what Angus's friend, Luke, can do, shall we? I've got Bennie to make up a few little packets of cocaine. He can sell them outside of Mick's pub, and then he can start a fight in the pub or something. I don't really care about the details, just as long as people are worried and prepared to pay for our help.'

'Okay.' Jake lay down again. He wanted to soak up the sun and sleep. Rosanna's huge meals were making him tired, and what with the many bottles of different wines Miriam insisted they tried, well, he was enjoying just letting the world pass him by.

'Do you want to go clubbing tonight, Jake? I thought we could check out some of the local talent in the nightclubs. Come on, we'll go into town.' Tony knew Jake didn't want to move; he was settled in his lounger and that would be it until Rosanna shouted that their next meal was ready.

'No, I don't want to go clubbing to check out the talent, I'm a married man, for God's sake. I'll come for a drink with you, though, and if you get lucky, that's your business.'

'Done … but what if I get lucky and you're thousands of miles away from your wife, and my lady friend has a friend?' Tony teased. He knew there was no baiting Jake, but he liked winding him up, anyway.

'You'll get lucky, Tony, we both know that, and she will probably have a friend, but her friend won't be half as beautiful as my Sharon, and she won't know the way I like things done.' Jake could have kicked himself. Now he knew he had raised Tony's curiosity.

'The way you like things done, what do you mean?' Tony was laughing and he sat up on his sunlounger to look at Jake. 'Have you got some hidden agenda in the bedroom that I don't know about?'

'None of your business, I'm not discussing it with you. All I'm saying is, Sharon is the woman for me, and that is final. Let's go for your drink and come home.' Jake had never discussed his sex life with Tony; whereas Tony's sex life was an open book, what went on between himself and Sharon stayed in the bedroom.

Jake knew he had started something and that Tony wouldn't give up. He kept throwing out jibes and comments at him.

'Do you dress up, Jake? Do you like all that whips and chains stuff? Do you use toys?'

All afternoon Tony kept coming out with the weird and the wonderful, and Jake just sighed and shook his head. 'You're sick, Tony, you do know that, don't you. Some of the things you're saying, I haven't even heard of.' They were laughing and joking together like the old days when they didn't have a care in the world. This was, indeed, a much-needed break.

'Hey, do you know that Wendy I've been seeing? She likes being blindfolded and doing it. She says it heightens her other senses. Have you tried that?'

'Maybe,' said Jake, while he was getting ready to go out that evening, 'just maybe she likes to be blindfolded so that she doesn't have to look at you.' He burst out laughing and watched Tony's face fall. That definitely ended the conversation.

The club scene was good, in the centre of Italy, and the girls were certainly plentiful. Jake sat at the bar while Tony flirted with the women. Finally, he settled on one, and she wanted to take him back to her place.

'Come on, Jake,' he said, 'you're my wingman. Her apartment's only around the corner and you're coming with me.' Tony took hold of Jake's glass and put it on the bar. He then took the arm of a beautiful Italian woman with long black hair. 'This is Maria, and this is her good friend and flatmate, Susie. Girls, this is Jake.' Tony charmingly did the introductions and led them all to the exit.

A few hours later, Tony and Jake emerged from the women's apartment. Tony was still doing up the buttons on his shirt and stuffing his tie into his jacket pocket. He had a broad grin on his face as they walked away from the block of apartments.

'It's been a good night, don't you think?' Tony was smiling, and put his arm around Jake's shoulders. The cool early morning breeze was a welcome relief from the stuffiness of the apartment. They were walking along the high street towards the taxi rank.

'Not bad at all, and no, just for the record, I didn't. She seemed pretty pissed off, but after I put the television on and sat down with a mug of coffee, she took the hint – although once she had given up on me, I saw her make her way into that noisy bedroom with you. I told you, Tony, I'm a one-man woman, and Sharon is the only woman for me.'

'I know that, you idiot, I just wanted you there so they couldn't help themselves to my wallet. Like I said, you're my wingman, always will be. Come on, let's go home and get some sleep.'

∞◊രു

'Antonias! Wake up, Antonias.' Tony was fast asleep in bed and Rosanna was shaking him roughly. 'Antonias, it's late afternoon, will you wake up.'

Tony tried coming around, but he was bleary eyed. He could hear Rosanna shouting at him to wake up, and her rough shaking of his arm didn't help. He looked up at her and tried hard to focus. The sun was peering through the windows and shining in his eyes. He held his hand up to block it.

'What time is it?' Tony was hungover and tired. What was all the panic?

'It's nearly five, you must get up. I'm going to wake Jake. Don't go back to sleep.' Rosanna ran across the landing, shouting Jake's name, and looking backwards to see if Tony had got up yet.

173

Jake had heard the noise. He was sitting up on the edge of his bed with his head in his hands when she rapped on the door then hurried in.

After Tony and Jake had got back, in the early hours of the morning, they had drunk another couple of bottles of wine. Big mistake!

Jake held up his hand to stop Rosanna shouting. 'I know, I heard, Rosanna, what's the big panic?' Jake was trying to make sense of what she was saying, but she was speaking so fast and in Italian, he was having trouble.

'It is Sharon, she is on the telephone. She said she will wait because she needs to speak to you now, it's important, there has been some sort of trouble. She is waiting for you both.'

Once Jake heard Sharon's name, he seemed to sober up. He looked up at Rosanna. 'What's wrong? Is she okay?' He stood up; he was only wearing his boxer shorts, but went down to the telephone on the landing anyway.

'Sharon, what's wrong, are you okay?' Jake was rubbing his head and blinking, trying to get his eyes to stay open.

'It's not me, Jake, I'm fine, but you have to come back now, the pair of you. You said you were only going to start an argument and a couple of fights, but it's been mayhem. There was an acid attack, they tried to throw it in someone's face, but they missed and hit his arm and back. Come home now.'

Jake continued to listen; he looked up and saw Tony emerging from his bedroom, and he told Sharon they would catch the first flight back to England. Tony could see Jake was serious and he sobered up quickly.

'We're going home today, Tony. I'll fill you in as we pack. It doesn't sound good, though. It seems plan B has gone wrong.' Jake filled Tony in on all the details he knew. He could see Tony was fuming and when Tony picked up the telephone and rang Angus, his temper flew down the line.

Poor Angus wasn't able to get a word in, Tony was shouting and screaming at him. Jake was already on the telephone booking a flight back. He had told Rosanna, although she already knew that there was an emergency at home and they had to leave. She was helping them pack their things.

'Stop pacing, Tony. Well, for now, anyway. Let's go and say goodbye to your grandmother. Let us leave on a high note. The rest we can sort out in a few hours. Go, Tony, and thank her for letting us both have the run of her house. I'll come along in a few minutes.' Jake was giving Tony time alone with Miriam to say goodbye.

Tony hugged and kissed Miriam and painted on a charming smile, although inside he was seething. Jake followed behind and hugged her. Once all the farewells were over, they were on the way to the airport. Tony couldn't get home quick enough.

'What the bloody hell has happened, Jake? How does someone get told to start a fight and instead launch an acid attack? Who would do that?' Tony already knew the answer to that, it had been Luke, the very man Angus had suggested using. He should have trusted his own instincts and put a stop to it.

'Tony, ease up. How the hell would Angus know that this idiot would do something like that? Let's just get back and find out what happened properly.' Jake knew this was futile, Tony was angry and he wasn't going to stop going on about it, until they got home.

John, Tony's driver, was waiting for them at the airport when they arrived.

In less than half a day they were both back at the club, having a drink with Sharon, while she filled them in on the details.

'Where do I start?' Sharon took a big deep breath. 'It seems all was going to plan, a few dealers were hanging around but, as instructed, there was nothing heavy. To be fair, Angus had it all under control. It was mayhem, but controlled mayhem. Then this Luke guy went into one of the pubs and punched one of the strippers. Can you believe that? Obviously, a fight broke out when a few of the guys there stepped in to help her out.'

Jake could see Tony's face turning red with anger. He looked like a kettle about to boil. He was about to speak when Jake put a hand up to stop him. 'Carry on, Sharon, what happened?'

'Can you believe it, one of our own bouncers, Joe, stepped in to pull this Luke guy away, and he pulled out a canister from under his coat, took the top off and threw it at him. Liquid flew out everywhere. Thankfully, when the bouncer saw him put his hand under his coat, he half turned away. He must have thought he had a knife or a gun, or something. The liquid was acid, Tony. This Luke guy threw acid at him. It went down his back and his arm, where he tried to shield himself. The publican threw the contents of the ice bucket on Joe and pulled his shirt off to stop it from sticking to his flesh, and thank God he acted so quickly.' Sharon looked concerned, even a little scared. 'What are we going to do, Jake?'

'Was anyone else hurt?' Tony was in command now and he wanted to know everything.

Sharon sighed. 'Well, the stripper will be off work for a couple of weeks with her black eyes, I suppose, but it's mainly the bouncer, Joe. Everyone is shit scared, Tony, and they want you to put them at their ease. After all, this is what you wanted, isn't it? Superheroes, Tony and Jake, what would we do without you both. Well, the hospital wouldn't be full up, that's for sure. All this to keep people paying you both protection money. Jesus Christ. This is people's lives you're playing with!' Sharon walked away from the table and went to the ladies' room. Anything to stop her arguing with them both. She had said more than enough.

Jake watched her leave. What could he say? He had agreed to this and gone along with Tony's idea, although, to be fair, there weren't supposed to be any casualties.

'Now, we go and see Angus. And you tell Sharon to stop spitting her dummy out, will you, Jake? She's your wife; sort her out.' Tony stood up and went to the car. He was in no mood for Sharon's sarcasm. He was angry, and wanted some answers.

Jake ran towards the car; there was no way he was going to let Tony meet Angus alone, not in this mood.

This time there was no preliminary chit chat. Tony went straight upstairs to Angus's apartment, walked directly towards him and threw his fist into his face. Angus was knocked backwards and fell on to the floor. Tony took out his gun and pointed it at him. 'You stupid bastard! I give you one job to do and you can't get that right. Get up, so I can hit you again. I'd blow your brains out if I thought you had any.'

Tony walked forward to where Angus lay on the floor and shoved the gun in his mouth. He was angry, his eyes had gone that awful dark blue that meant his mean streak was well and truly to the surface, Jekyll and Hyde style.

'Stop it, Tony.' Jake pushed his body in between Tony and Angus. He knew if Tony started hitting him, he wouldn't stop, would possibly even shoot him. 'Everybody, take a breath. Angus, come on, get up, man.'

Angus wiped the blood off his mouth. He started to stand, although his legs were weak and he was visibly shaking. All the while he was watching Tony, waiting for him to leap at him again. Tony's breathing was heavy and his face was set like stone.

Jake pulled out a chair for Angus to sit down on. 'What happened, Angus? Why did that Luke guy hit the stripper? Why would he do that?'

Angus sat down and Tony lunged forward. Again, Jake pulled Tony by the arm away from Angus. Fighting amongst themselves wasn't getting them anywhere.

'Please, Mr Lambrianu, Jake, I'm sorry. That wee lassie was walking past Luke with her collection mug, and she asked him if he wanted to give her a tip for her dance, apparently. That was when the bloody fool said yes and fisted her in the face. I told you he was a wife-beater, but I didn't expect this.'

Angus burst into tears. 'That young bouncer lad, Joe, he stepped in and that bloody Luke threw acid at him. It burned his body. He's a right mess, in the hospital. On the other hand, boss, no police were involved because it was considered more gang wars than anything else, and apart from the wee lassie stripper, no civilians were hurt or maimed. Also,' Angus was trying to get Tony and Jake to see the bigger picture, 'it seems you achieved what you wanted. Everyone is running scared.' Angus wiped away his tears.

'Where is this Luke, now, Angus? What have you done to him, is he alive?' asked Jake.

'I got some of the big Jamaican lads to give him a good beating up. Believe me, he's going to be in hospital a lot longer than Joe.' Angus seemed pleased with himself.

Tony started to calm down; he knew this was all of his own doing, and maybe some good would come out of it. As Angus said, there were no civilians involved and yet the local businessmen had well and truly been scared to death by this acid attack. After all, it could have been them or, even worse, their children.

'Angus, it's too soon now, but you said before that this Luke guy owes money everywhere?' Tony said.

Angus nodded.

'Buy his debts. Give it a long while, maybe a year, and we'll kill him. There's too much attention around at the moment, if he suddenly gets killed now, it's too obvious.' The time to even the score with this guy would come, but the dust had to settle first. The beating would be enough for now.

'I'm sorry, boss, I didn't mean Joe no harm.' Angus looked apologetic and scared. He looked towards Jake, and mouthed, 'Thank you.' He knew Tony had a reputation for being a crazy, mad bastard and many had been the time he had seen him lose his temper, but he had never been on the receiving end of it, like this, before. Angus was worried – what if he lost his home and job? What would Elsie say? Tears began to fall down his face again and he wiped them away quickly.

'That's it for now, Angus, if I decide to let you keep your job and home, I'll inform you. Buy those debts and keep your eye on that man's whereabouts. I don't want him out of sight.' Tony kicked a chair out of the way and stormed out.

Once outside, Tony hit the roof of the car with his hand. 'Damn it, Jake, can't anyone do a simple job anymore? Right, first things first, get Joe moved to a private hospital. Does he have a wife or family? If so, see that they are okay, financially. Get Sharon to call a meeting with the publicans and tell them we're back and it's all in hand. Tell that Angus we no longer need Bennie sniffing around with his dealers, but tell him to thank him for his co-operation.' Tony was mentally adding up all the things he needed to do. 'Can you think of anything I've missed?'

Jake shook his head. He knocked on the glass window between the back seat of the Rolls Royce and the driver's seat. 'John, take us to the hospital to see Joe, will you? We're going there first.'

Jake looked at Tony and saw him nod at him.

'We need to go and see him, Tony, he works for us and we caused this. Let's see what damage has been done. In the meantime, we'll set up a meeting and get Dan to start spreading the word that the South London mob have been well and truly put in their place and scared off. Then we find out who this stripper is and make sure she gets some sort of compensation – sick pay, if you like.'

Tony knew he was lucky to have Jake. He was the voice of reason.

They went to the hospital to see Joe. He was in the burns unit. His skin had blistered badly; he lay on his stomach and the whole of his torso was bandaged. Fortunately, his head and face hadn't been touched. Joe was full of morphine to stop the pain, but he acknowledged Tony and Jake.

'We're going to have you taken to a private clinic, Joe, and I promise you, this will get sorted. The person who did this will pay for it, I assure you. Obviously, you will remain on full pay while you recover.'

'Thanks,' he said.

'Have you told the police anything about it?' Tony was curious. Although Angus assured them that the police weren't involved, he thought that the hospital would have to inform them, especially about an acid attack.

'I told them I don't know who it was. It was just some random punter picking a fight with one of the strippers, I stepped in and, well, this.' Joe looked down at his bandaged body. 'They said they would look into it, but they don't have any leads or anything. The guy ran out of the door before anyone could stop him.'

'Do you know who it was, Joe?'

'No, boss, never seen him before, not one of the regulars.' Joe winced in pain. His breathing was laboured.

Tony and Jake looked at one another. Joe had no idea who Luke was and so, even if he had felt bitter about being in so much pain, he still couldn't tell the police anything and drag Tony, Jake or Angus into it. Angus had done a very good job, after all.

In a way, it had gone even better than Tony planned. A fight had broken out with a stripper? Well, she wasn't going to say anything, was she, and let her family and friends know what she did for a living.

This outsider, who was now beaten to a pulp and would be out of the way for some time, was seemingly unknown to everyone. Tony and Jake had been out of the country. Now Tony was back and would have the dealers removed from the streets and calm would be restored. Angus, Tony had to admit, had been right. They had achieved what they set out to accomplish.

ઝરૅ

Sharon had organized the meeting with the local businessmen and invited them all to the club for it. They were all in awe of the club, they had never been there before, and Tony felt Sharon had only decided to invite them to a meeting there to spite him.

Tony and Jake had showered and changed out of their travelling clothes into their suits. As this was a meeting, they had to look like businessmen. When they walked towards the office at the club, they could see a dozen familiar faces that they knew. Each and every one of them wanted to be heard, they were shouting questions and looking at Tony and Jake for answers.

'Mr Lambrianu, I presume you have heard what has happened.' The owner of the snooker club looked up at Tony. His face was pale and drawn.

Tony nodded. 'You don't have to fill me in on the details, gentlemen, I already know everything. As we speak, things are being sorted out, and I promise you, peace will be restored.' Tony sat down beside Jake; he felt he had already said enough.

'That South London mob were dealing near our premises, Mr Lambrianu; is that what is going to happen every time you go away?' Each one of them had a question to ask, they showed proper respect, but it was clear they were afraid.

'No, this will not happen each time I go away. As a matter of fact, I have already been to see the South London mob leader.' They all looked shocked that he had already started to sort things out. They knew he had only just got back and yet he hadn't let the grass grow; they all seemed relieved at his prompt action.

'What did he say about that guy and the acid attack? Is it going to happen again?' Tony looked across at the publican who spoke and raised one eyebrow.

'It won't happen again, I assure you. I will not go into details, gentlemen, but that is what you pay me for. Protection. While we're on that subject, I will be hiring more men to look after your properties and your families, and so I will have to increase the payments a little.'

'That's okay, Mr Lambrianu.' The group of men all nodded in unison. 'As long as you're sorting it out and we can go about our daily business without fear.' They all seemed satisfied that Tony looked confident and in charge of the situation. They all seemed satisfied that they had him to rely on in situations like this, and he had proved himself to be worth every penny they paid.

Tony waved them all off after listening to any more concerns they might have and finally went to his own apartment, with Jake and Sharon in tow. 'What a day, I'm knackered.' Tony threw himself on the sofa and kicked off his shoes. 'Did you get Dan to start spreading the word that everything is under control now?' Tony had his head laid back on the sofa and he closed his eyes.

Jake started to speak to him, but noticed that Tony had drifted off to sleep and was starting to snore. 'Come on, Sharon, let's go home,' he said. He took her hand, turned off the lamp and left. He hadn't had a moment with her since he got back.

18

LEROY

'Tony!' Jake barged into the office, took in the sight before him, then looked directly at Tony. 'I think you might want to put her down; you really need to see this.'

Tony had a half-naked woman perched on his desk, her legs wrapped firmly around him. 'For fuck's sake, Jake, haven't you ever heard of knocking? I'm not finished—' Jake's words got through to him. 'See what?' he said. It was clear from the expression on Jake's face that whatever it was, it was serious.

He separated himself from the woman and pulled his trousers up; it was obvious the moment had gone. This was pleasure; whatever Jake had come to tell him was business, and business was always the priority.

'Sweetheart, pull your dress down and leave,' said Jake. 'Leave, now.'

The young woman stood up and adjusted herself. This was not the time to argue. 'Will I see you later, Tony?' she said.

'Maybe. It depends. We'll talk later.' He kissed her on the cheek. She wasn't very happy and slammed the door behind her.

'For God's sake, doesn't that dick of yours ever sleep?'

'It doesn't have a watch on it. A speedometer, sometimes, but not a watch.' Tony smiled, swept his hair back and sat down. He was still doing up his shirt buttons. 'So, what's this thing I need to see?'

Jake beckoned him and opened the office door, then marched down the corridor to the back exit. Tony hurried after him. Jake had his serious face on. Something was definitely wrong.

Leaning on one of the dustbins to hold himself up was John, Tony's driver. He was holding a cloth to his nose, which had obviously been broken. Blood was all over his face. He was holding on to his ribs and clearly in a lot of pain. A couple of bodyguards stood next to him, looking lost.

Tony looked at the injured man, weak, swaying, trying to catch his breath while mopping the blood from his nose and the other cuts on his face; he immediately reverted to business mode. 'What the fuck happened to you?'

'I'll tell him, John, it's okay, catch your breath,' said Jake. He turned to Tony. 'Do you remember Leroy, the pimp who used to work for Marlon?' Jake saw Tony's face redden and his eyes grow darker at the mention of Leroy.

'Do you mean that bastard that emptied Marlon's safe and did a runner before we got there? Yes, I remember him. Are you telling me he did this?'

Jake nodded. 'It's a message for you.' He lit a cigarette and handed it to John, hoping that it would calm his nerves. 'That bastard has set up his own little gang, apparently over in Streatham, somewhere. Still pimping and prostitutes, but now he wants to meet us to discuss terms about sharing the south of London. This is his message. John was filling up the car with petrol when the bastards jumped out of the car and beat the shit out of him. They want to meet us at three, this afternoon.'

'Jesus Christ, it's only a week since we sorted the last lot out! Why hasn't Angus done anything about this? Get that bastard on the telephone, now. And, you two.' Tony looked at the bodyguards standing beside John. 'Stop fucking standing there like lampposts and get him inside. Get him cleaned up and get him a drink. God, do I have to think of everything!'

The two men were glad to make themselves scarce. Tony was in a foul mood. Someone was going to be on the receiving end of that temper of his and they were glad it wasn't them. They each took an arm to help support John's weight and half-dragged him inside. Tony and Jake walked behind them along the corridor to his office; they went inside while the other men headed up to Tony's apartment.

Jake called Angus. When it was obvious the call had been answered, Tony snatched the telephone out of his hand and screamed and shouted at the Scotsman. Angus was oblivious to it all. Yes, he was aware that some gang had been shooting their mouths off about Tony and Jake, but that had been in Hammersmith, somewhere.

Breathing heavily, Tony said through gritted teeth, 'They might have been in Hammersmith then, but they live in fucking Streatham. Right on your turf, Angus. Now, sort it out.' He looked at Jake, then had second thoughts. 'No, Angus, scratch that – I'll sort this out.' He slammed the telephone down and turned to Jake. 'They want to meet, you say?' he said.

Jake nodded. 'At the Two Brewers pub.'

'Okay, we'll go and meet them.'

'They'll be going mob-handed; what about us?' Jake darted a look at Tony. He could see his mind was racing and this had pushed him way over the edge. Someone was going to challenge him on his own turf. This was going to end badly.

'I don't need anybody to fight my battles. It's just you and me, Jake. That's how it's always been. I want to watch those bastards squirm myself.'

෨◊ಐ

Tony and Jake surveyed the dingy pub as they walked across the floor and up to the bar. There was a handful of men sitting at different tables, supposedly just having a drink. The landlord excused himself, something about having to change a barrel, and went down to the cellar.

'I see you got my message then, Lambrianu. Turns out it weren't that hard, bringing the rat out of its hole.' Leroy walked up to where Tony was standing at the bar. 'I want fifty-fifty of the South London mob. It was Marlon's, not yours, and I know you fucking killed him. I aren't making no deals, I'm telling you straight. You don't scare me. My boys, here, will make a mess of you and that fucking club of yours.' Leroy's Jamaican tones echoed through the pub. He was making his stance and he wanted 'his boys' to know that he wasn't scared. He took a metal baton from his coat pocket and waved it in front of Tony's face. 'Coming here on your own, white boys, to face me and my boys … how stupid can you get.' Leroy smiled, showing a row of white teeth in his black face. He turned to look at his men, who were now standing up to surround Tony and Jake.

'What the fuck is that?' Tony turned to look at Jake and then looked back at Leroy. 'I came for a fucking shoot-out and you bring a metal vibrator. You've been pimping those whores of yours for far too long, Leroy.' Tony had his hands in his coat pocket, and he raised them. He might not have gone mob-handed, but it was clear to Leroy and his mob that he had a gun in each pocket and both were now pointing at Leroy.

'I'll show you what this is, Lambrianu. Did you think we would come without being tooled up?' Leroy was trying to hold his nerve while he looked at Tony's coat pockets.

'Oh, fuck this, Leroy, I'm leaving,' Tony said. He dropped his hands. 'This is no gangland war. It's a bunch of Jamaicans with a metal rolling pin. You got some plastic guns in there from the toy shop, as well? Fuck off, I'm leaving.' Tony barged through them and walked out the door, leaving Jake standing in the circle of men.

'Left you to it, has he, Jakey, my boy?' said Leroy. 'Some good friend you got there. Well, you'll do for now; maybe that will show him we mean business.'

Jake nodded. He leaned over the bar and when he picked up a glass, they all reached for their weapons, then turned to look at each other and shrugged as they watched Jake pour himself a drink.

Jake took a sip of his drink and smacked his lips, then looked directly at Leroy. 'Tell me, Leroy, what do you get when an angry psychopath walks into a pub?' Again, Jake took a sip of his drink and watched as they turned their bemused faces to one other and shrugged. Looking over their shoulders, Jake shouted, 'Show them, Tony!'

Standing behind them was a very angry Tony Lambrianu, with a very large claw hammer in each hand. Instantly, he started waving them around and hitting the men on their heads and bodies.

'And you,' said Jake, looking at Leroy as he put on his spiked knuckledusters, 'will be very glad I brought these.' He threw a punch into Leroy's shocked face. Blood spurted out of the holes the spikes had made. Again and again, Jake punched Leroy in the face, until he collapsed onto the floor.

Tony was in the middle of the men, bringing his hammers down hard. Shouts of pain filled the room. Everyone was covered in blood. Some lay on the floor where they had fallen after Tony had hammered their kneecaps. They couldn't stand to fight back. One man jumped Tony from behind and pushed him forward. Tony crashed into one of the tables and fell to the floor on his knees, his face cut and bleeding.

Jake walked swiftly over to where Tony was kneeling and saw the man that had pushed him had a gun in his hand and was about to shoot Tony in the back. He hit the man with a bottle. 'Bastard! Is that all you lot do? Surprise people from behind? Why not look into people's faces when you kill them, you spineless bastards!' Jake carried on kicking the man until he could see he was unconscious.

Tony was panting for breath and bleeding. He rose to his feet and surveyed the room. It was covered in blood – thankfully not his own. He picked up the gun and walked over to where Leroy lay on the floor. Blood was pouring from his face. 'Now, I've got a message for you,' Tony said. He pointed the gun at Leroy's head and fired. He picked up a pint of beer, walked over to the unconscious man who had been going to shoot him in the back, and threw it into his face, to bring him back to consciousness. 'Oy, you lot, I want you to see this,' Tony shouted.

Some of the men on the floor who were still conscious, albeit holding their broken legs and howling in pain, turned their heads to see what was happening.

Tony wiped his bloody mouth then pointed at the man's hand. 'That is the hand you were going to shoot me with, right?' He didn't wait for an answer; he reached into the inside pocket of his coat and took out a machete, then crouched down and chopped the hand off with one blow. The man's piercing screams filled the room. One man found the energy to vomit on the floor. Still kneeling beside the handless man, Tony smiled. 'Don't ever fuck with me again, you lot,' he said. He stood and looked around the room at the men there. 'This is a message for you – all of you – and your friends. You did your best, but it wasn't anywhere near good enough. Nevertheless, you tried, and I applaud you for it.' He bent and picked up the severed hand lying on the floor, then held it aloft. 'In fact, gentlemen, I raise a hand to you!' He grinned and threw it in the middle of the room, amongst them. He and Jake shared a look and turned towards the door. They both knew it was time to leave. This gangland war had been nipped in the bud.

ℰℴ ◊ ℭℛ

A few months passed after Tony and Jake's holiday in Italy. Everything was back to normal. The local businessmen were pleased that, as quickly as all the trouble had started, it had been stopped. They were thankful they had Tony

188

looking after their interests, they reckoned it was worth every penny, even at the new – higher – price they were paying.

Joe, the bouncer who had suffered the awful acid attack, was back at home. He still lived with his parents, and they were grateful that their son was being looked after by Tony and Jake. He was still on full pay, and all of his hospital bills were being paid by them. He had undergone some surgery and some skin grafts, and now they just had to let the skin heal before they could do anything further. Thankfully, his face was okay, it was mainly his back, side and arm that had been affected, so it wouldn't affect his prospects.

Angus was relieved to know that he still had a job. He would make sure things wouldn't ever threaten his own livelihood again. He knew he had taken a chance with that Luke guy and, in line with Tony's instructions, he had him watched. Not long after Luke got out of hospital after being beaten up, he'd had both his legs broken. Angus was determined not to let Tony down again and, when the year was up and it was time to make Luke disappear, he would be first in line to see it happened.

19

FATAL ATTRACTION

'Tony, did you remember to order the Christmas trees?' Sharon popped her head around the office door and could see by the look on his face he had forgotten.

Tony was sitting at his desk looking through his accounts. 'I'm on it, Sharon, how many do we need again?' He looked towards Jake and shrugged.

'I told you, we need seven – two for this place, one for the men's club and four for the casino. Come on, get on with it. It's okay for you, sitting there with your pink shirt sleeves rolled up and pretending to do a bit of work, but some of us actually have real work to do. Trees, now!' With that she turned to leave, but then suddenly stopped. 'Actually, you two, forget it, I'll sort the trees out.'

'She wanted to do that all along, you know, order the trees, I mean,' Jake said to Tony.

This was the run up to the busiest time of the year. Christmas was coming and everyone wanted to party and gamble. Sharon had Christmas parties to organize and had taken on an assistant of her own to help her.

Tony pointed to a box of video tapes in the corner of the room. 'Have you seen some of the stuff on that lot?' He shook his head in disbelief.

'What are they?' Jake leaned forward and took one of the tapes out of the box. It had no name on it. He held it up and looked at Tony.

'It's some of the recordings from the men's club bedrooms. Believe me, Jake, it's more than I bargained for. There's a well-known celebrity dressed in a French maid's outfit, plus two guys having sex. It doesn't do it for me, it made my jaw drop. It's not for me to judge, but it does make me see them through different eyes. It's insurance, though. If I ever need their help, they'll move heaven and earth to provide it, not because they like me, but because of this.' Tony waved a video tape in the air.

'Oh, God, Tony, are you telling me you've been watching them? That's disgusting.' Jake squirmed.

'I had to check if there was anything on them worth saving. It wasn't the best job in the world, but it needed to be done. Anyway, there is some stuff that'll be useful, and those tapes in particular need go into the main safe for a rainy day. Mind you, I think I'll let Sharon look through them in future.'

'Not bloody likely! You can do it or, if absolutely necessary, I will, but not my Sharon.'

Tony burst out laughing. 'Jake, you are still so easy to wind up, sometimes you make me feel like a wicked teenager again. Of course I'll do it, some of it is quite funny, actually. Something for when we're both pissed and fed up and need a good laugh.'

'I'm going to see Elle today, are you coming? It's been a while. While we're there we can see how that mansion of yours is coming along.' Jake was referring to the house Tony had won in a poker game.

'Good idea. Count me in.'

Elle was helping oversee the decorating, if you could call it that. Tony had just told the decorators to paint the rooms in magnolia and the designers to choose whatever furniture they thought best. Apart from that, he had claimed one room as a study and the main bedroom as his own, if he were to ever stay over. That was about as far as his interest in the house went.

ℰᗩ◊ᗺ

Elle was more than happy to see them, when they landed on her doorstep. Although they spoke regularly, it was nice to have a proper catch up. Tony and Jake enjoyed telling her all their plans for the clubs, now Christmas was looming.

'How is the house coming on, Elle? Everything okay, no problems?' said Jake.

'No, none at all, it's all pretty straightforward. I really like the chandeliers they bought, though. Did you know they have to hang them from the joists? I suppose it's because they're so heavy – you wouldn't want one of those to come crashing down.' This was a whole new world to Elle, who was used to her little bungalow.

Tony held out a notebook. 'Elle, I know you're busy, but this is a list of everyone that works for us, plus a few of the publicans. I don't suppose you could write all the Christmas cards, could you?' Tony had a sheepish grin on his face. He knew Elle would say yes and that she had probably missed being involved so much. This was his way of giving her something to do. He reckoned her life must be quiet these days with just Minnie for company.

Elle beamed. 'Of course I will, Tony, love. Do you need presents buying for any of them, as well?' Elle took out her pen, turned to a new page in the notebook and started to make a list.

Tony didn't want to just give Mathers the usual Christmas bonus; he felt he and Ashley deserved a gift, as well, though he didn't know what to get them. He felt Graham should be on his Christmas present list, too. He had taught Tony the casino life well, and had managed the casino excellently while he was learning. He would let Sharon do some investigating; she could find out what they liked.

The list seemed to get longer and longer. Tony decided

192

it would be best to throw a giant party at the club for the strippers and the pole dancers. The bouncers and the drivers would also be invited to it and would get a cash bonus for all of their hard work.

'Dear me, Tony, you're in your mid-thirties and this is the first time you have actually made a Christmas list. Does it just pass you by, love?' Elle put her hand on top of Tony's. She still felt motherly towards him. He was a hard worker, striving to prove himself to himself. She thought that, no matter how he dressed or what he owned, every time he looked into a mirror, he still saw that young boy dressed in hand-me-downs.

He had never been fond of Christmas. It seemed to her, he just worked all the way through it, sorting the club and watching everyone else having a good time.

'Christmas is a money-spinner for me, Elle, busiest time of the year. That's all I focus on. Mind you, I look forward to having Christmas dinner with you. I'll be here like a shot, this year – that's if you'll have me, of course.' He smiled at Elle; whatever happened, he made a point of having Christmas dinner with her.

'Of course I will, you know that.' She smiled, grateful that he had brought the subject up. She hadn't wanted to ask or put pressure on them to make them feel they had to go for Christmas dinner. They were grown up now, and had their own plans. 'What about you, Jake, will you and Sharon be coming?'

Jake nodded. 'Oh, God, yes. I can't put up with her family's cooking, not at Christmas. We'll be here, no fear.' The thought of Sharon or any member of her family cooking Christmas dinner sent shivers down Jake's spine.

The next few weeks seemed to go quickly. The Christmas trees were all up and decorated, and each place had a differently coloured theme. The trees inside the casino were nearly twelve-foot high and decorated in black and gold, plus there were two small ones outside of the main doors to give it that festive feel.

The men's club had a traditional pine tree in the reception area, which Mathers took charge of. It looked like something out of the Victorian age. Ashley had had to remind Sharon that he wanted one for the entertainments room. He seemed to use that as his own little club. That one was much more outlandish!

The trees at the club were black and pink, and all in all they looked splendid and very festive. Neon lights had been put up outside, wishing everyone a merry Christmas. All that helped put everyone in the Christmas spirit and they wanted to dance the night away to the same old Christmas songs everyone loved. Sharon had even put the pole dancers in red leotards trimmed with white fur.

A lot of trouble had gone into promoting Christmas, and now they were going to sit back and watch the profits roll in.

෮◊ඏ

'Where are you off to?' asked Tony. He put his coffee mug down and rubbed his eyes. He had been looking at figures all day and his eyes were bleary. He reached over for his enormous ledger diary and flicked through the pages. 'We have nothing in the diary.'

'I've got to do a bit of shopping later, then I have to go to Sharon's sister's party this evening,' Jake said. 'Grim, I know, but that's married life. I'll see you in the morning.' He put his jacket on.

'That's later; where are you going now?'

'I'm just going for a chat with a publican, nothing to bother you with and no heavy stuff. Just a chat, that's all,' said Jake. The man's protection payment was short; Jake wanted to go and find out why.

'A chat? Who with, Jake, what's wrong?'

Tony listened as Jake explained that the problem had been brought to his attention by one of the collectors. This particular publican was someone they had known for a long while and he had always paid up, in full and on time. Jake wanted to find out what was wrong now, and why he couldn't pay, preferably without Tony interfering.

'I'll go,' said Tony. 'You have to go to the party with Sharon. Let's face it, Jake, you can't arrive late or let her go on her own, she'll have your guts for garters. She doesn't ask much. I'll go and see if he is having money problems. Anyway, I haven't seen him for a while and I don't want him forgetting me, now, do I?'

Jake opened his mouth to protest, but Tony was having none of it.

'No, I insist, Jake. I'll go, and you can have an evening with Sharon and her family's buffet. Personally, I think I've got the better deal.' He started laughing.

Jake didn't know whether to laugh or cry. Tony was right. If he got delayed in any way and turned up late Sharon would go berserk. He didn't relish the idea of the family party. They really were the worst nights, and the most boring, but he was married and that meant compromise, didn't it? He emphasized to Tony that he wasn't to lose his temper and start throwing his fists about.

'He's a bit short on his money, that's all, but I did also hear he's throwing a massive Christmas party tonight. If he's that short of money to miss his full payments, how can he afford to host a party? That's the only reason why I'm going. No hard stuff, eh?'

Tony looked up to better see Jake's worried face. 'No hard stuff, Jake, I promise. Party, eh? Well, as you say, let's see how he is robbing Peter to pay Paul, shall we?' Tony made the sign of the cross on his chest and smiled.

It was true, this particular publican had always been good as gold and never missed a payment. Time to pay him a visit in the flesh and remind him who was boss. Tony hadn't been around the East End a lot of late, what with one thing and another. Now was not the time to let things slip.

Jake left to collect Sharon, who wanted to do a bit of shopping and to buy a new dress for the evening. She seemed pleased that Jake was making the effort and taking time out for her and her family.

Tony carried on with his paperwork. When he heard the club getting into full swing, he checked his watch. It was time to get washed and shaved and check out this publican's party.

⚜

Tony looked out of the car window as John drove him through the streets to the pub. He saw people all dressed up, wandering around; some were holding their drinks and having a cigarette outside, others were just arriving and already looked the worse for wear.

'Just follow the music, John, that racket is where we need to be.' The music was blaring out of the pub door each time someone opened it. Tony sat in the car looking at the little side street the pub was in. it was dark and icy and he could see the two-up two-down houses with their Christmas decorations and lights flashing in the windows. It all seemed a million miles away from the West End. It had been a long time since he had been down this neck of the woods – years, in fact. Now, his collectors looked after all the stripper pubs in the area.

His thoughts drifted back to Joe; he had been one of the bouncers who looked after these East End pubs. Hopefully he was on the mend, although he would be scarred for life.

John pulled the car around the back of the pub, where the delivery drivers dropped off the barrels of beer. Tony's car was far too obvious, and if spotted, would give the publican the opportunity to run for it, if he felt he had to.

'Will this do, boss?' asked John, half turning to look into the back. He parked up and turned off the headlights. 'Some party … are you sure you want to go in alone? It looks like a real rathole.'

'I'll be fine, John, but thanks. I used to do some collecting around this area, you know, back in the day. It almost feels like a trip down memory lane. You're right,

196

though, it is a rathole.' Tony laughed; he waited for John to get out of the car and open the door for him.

As soon as Tony stepped out of the vehicle, the icy wind hit him and he shuddered, then he fastened up his long camel coat and put his hands in the pockets. 'This won't take too long, I'll be back in a bit.'

'Remember to wipe your feet on the way out!' John got back into the warm car and settled down to wait.

Tony walked through the back entrance, where the publican had set up some sort of cheap beer garden in his back yard. He had put up a few hanging baskets, full of plants that were now dead, and there were some wooden tables with benches. Real class.

To give the man his due, he had tried decorating it with some Christmas lights to give it that seasonal feel. The overly full ashtrays didn't help, though. Some people came out, laughing and joking and obviously very drunk, sat themselves down on the benches and lit cigarettes.

Tony walked past them and opened the back door. It led into the rear of the pub, near a quiet corner that in the past was known as the snug room. This was where some of the older men would gather to read their papers or play some pool, while getting away from the noise.

Tony stood at the side of the bar and looked around at the place. He felt a little disgusted when he realised his shoes were nearly sticking to the worn carpet. It was then that the publican, dressed in a Santa suit and hat, but not wearing a long white beard, came around the side to see if anyone needed serving.

Tony thought the shocked look on his face was a picture, and watched as the happy smile slid from his features.

'Mr Lambrianu, what brings you here?' Tony could see he was nervous and, remembering Jake's words, put him at his ease.

'Mine's a whisky, if you're offering?' Tony was tempted to rest his elbows on the bar, but seeing the dirty bar towels and the puddles of alcohol, he decided against it.

'Sure, Mr Lambrianu.' The publican picked up a glass and made a point of polishing it with one of his bar towels, to impress Tony. He turned around and filled the glass with some whisky from the optic.

The publican was mid-forties; his father had owned the pub before him. He was slightly balding on top, with designer stubble and a smile on his face. He was a pleasant guy, and by all accounts got on with the money collectors okay and paid them regularly.

'Quite a crowd you have tonight. How come you don't have any strippers on?'

The publican put the drink on the bar and gave a deep sigh. He rubbed his chin and looked at Tony. 'I know why you're here, Mr Lambrianu, but I didn't think it would merit a visit from the boss. The truth is, every year all the local stripper pubs in the area take turns to host a Christmas party for the stripper agency and the strippers. Some of the usual punters and other publicans come, as well. It's a free bar, which is why it is so packed out. People do love a freebie, don't they.' The publican was fidgeting with his hands and looking down. 'The problem is, Mr Lambrianu, this year it's my turn to host it and I couldn't afford to both fund the party and make my full payment, so there it is. I've always been straight with you and you know my payments are always on time, it's just a bit short this month.'

Tony watched the nervous publican as he was talking. He noticed that, as much as he was aiming to look Tony in the eye, he was looking everywhere but. He looked quite comical, wearing his Father Christmas hat, and suit to match. With his blushes and embarrassment, his face almost looked as red as his suit.

In the far corner was an old piano that hadn't been played in years and on top of it was a small Christmas tree, over decorated with tinsel and baubles. This place was really scraping the bottom of the barrel, considering it was one of the best and most popular pubs around.

Tony smiled to himself; as grubby as this place was, he

remembered being a young man and thinking pubs like this seemed like the hottest places in town. He had enjoyed cutting his teeth in these pubs, enjoying and experiencing everything they had to offer. It had been good fun, but only now did he realise that Mr Mathers had worked his magic, and along with the clothes and the money, he had become a bit of a snob.

People in their Christmas outfits had tinsel in their hair and around their necks, some of it stolen from the pub's Christmas tree. Although it was a sight for sore eyes, the pub had a friendly party atmosphere. Everyone seemed to be having a good time, firing party poppers and streamers in the air.

'Did you say the stripper agent was here?' Tony didn't comment on what the publican had said, he thought he would let him sweat it out a little first.

'Yes, Mr Lambrianu, sir, the agent is over there in that corner.' He pointed, and Tony saw a man and a woman he recognized.

'Shout them over for me, would you?'

Without any kind of discretion, the publican shouted over the bar, 'Oy! Oy, you two, over here.' He beckoned to them and waited for them to stand, then walked round to the side of the bar where Tony was and waited for them to come over to him.

The man was slurring his words, but the woman stood up straight and took off her paper hat when she saw Tony. 'Mr Lambrianu, how nice to see you. I didn't know you were coming to the party.' She gave Tony her best smile, but seeing that he didn't return one, straightened her face.

'I believe you owe me some money; it's just as well I did turn up, isn't it.' Tony knew he was being unreasonable, because their protection money wasn't due for two days.

'Mr Lambrianu,' she stammered, 'I don't carry that kind of cash around with me. Anyway, it's not due yet. It's in the safe for when your collectors come, I assure you.' She stuck her nose in the air, as though trying to prove a point.

'I don't mean that; what I mean is you,' he pointed a finger at her, 'expecting him,' he pointed at the publican, 'to short change me,' this time the finger pointed back at Tony, 'so that you can have a free bar for all this lot.' Tony half turned and waved his hand in the air, in a gesture that took in the room full of people.

'Everyone takes a turn, Mr Lambrianu, not just the pubs. We hold a party for all of the publicans and the strippers, too, and it's also a free bar.' Again, although not raising her voice, she made it stern enough to make her point. She seemed quite put out by his interrogation and alcohol was making her feel brave.

Tony nodded; he had proved his point by being there and reminding her his money was due. He knew all the pubs had this goodwill yearly party, it came as no great surprise, but while he was there he thought he would just shake things up a bit. It was actually making him laugh inside, but he kept it to himself.

He picked up his drink and turned his back on her. This was his way of dismissing her, and she waited a couple of minutes and then walked away, no doubt telling the other agent what she thought of him. Although he wanted some kind of friendliness between them, he didn't want familiarity. This, he felt, was when they would start asking favours about paying their dues.

The publican had disappeared while Tony was talking to the agent. He popped back up as Tony took another sip of his drink. 'Here, Mr Lambrianu, let me top up that drink for you,' he said. The publican took his glass, turned to the optic and refilled it. 'Here, please take this.' He put five hundred pounds down on the bar. 'I promise I'll settle the rest I owe you in a couple of days, if that's okay. You can see how I'm fixed.' The publican looked apologetic.

Tony didn't reach out to take the money. He just left it there between them. 'Is that with or without interest?'

'Whatever you say, Mr Lambrianu. I don't want any trouble, not tonight when everyone's having a good time for

Christmas. If you want the interest, then you know I'll pay it.'

'As it's Christmas, just pay the rest, without interest, when you can. Okay?' Tony picked up the money; he was going to put it in his jacket pocket, but noticed the bottom notes were wet, from the bar top, and so decided to put it in his coat pocket instead.

The publican beamed a broad grin. 'Thank you, Mr Lambrianu, you're a gentleman. Here, have another one.' Again, he took Tony's glass and refilled it. The telephone was ringing through the back room. 'Excuse me, Mr Lambrianu, I'll have to get that. I'll be back in a minute.'

Tony picked up his drink and surveyed the room; obviously, there were more women there than men, after all, it was a strippers' party. They would have come with their partners or friends, even the odd well-paying punter.

The room was hazy with cigarette smoke, which was allowed, considering it was a private party, and no one would be offended or tell the authorities they were breaking the law. He looked at all the different shapes and sizes of the women. Some looked as rough as old boots and probably reminded some of the younger punters of their old dinner ladies. Some were overweight, which is one thing he would never allow in his club. On the whole, they weren't a bad-looking bunch of women. All of them were a bit rough around the edges, but there were some that were okay. Maybe that was the appeal, they were all such oddballs. Maybe his own strippers were too uniform.

Tony was always mentally doing business, and now he had an idea. He would run it past Sharon first, but he thought they could maybe have a different sort of night at the club, full of this rough lot. After all, the same well-to-do gentlemen that went to his club would almost certainly come in here for a little variety. It could be some sort of novelty night.

People were dancing and singing along to the music and bumping into each other, laughing and joking, but it was all in the name of fun. Tony took another gulp of his drink and his eyes stopped roving.

In the far corner was a young woman. She had long, dark wavy hair that cascaded down her back. She was sitting with a Jamaican woman and what appeared to be the woman's husband. Tony thought the young woman looked totally out of place. She looked awkward and embarrassed.

It was obvious she wasn't in the party mood or particularly enjoying herself. Tony could see she was managing a half-hearted smile as she spoke to the people that passed by the table and chatted with the Jamaican woman and her husband. Tony looked around, wondering who she was with. He was curious.

His eyes searched and scanned across the bar to look at the customers waiting to be served, wondering if maybe one of them might be her husband. His head turned again to the young woman; he watched her take a sip from her glass of wine. She was looking around the room at everyone, again with a smile fixed on her face as though trying to pretend she was having a great time. Still, he saw no one sit beside her that suggested she was with a husband or a partner.

Her large dark eyes – the very windows to her soul – seemed to take up most of her face, and they held a warmth that in other circumstances would be welcoming and loving. Tonight, though, they were her giveaway. She didn't want to be there and that was blatantly obvious, so why was she? Maybe she was the plus one of one of the strippers and hadn't realised how common the party would be.

Tony was mesmerized by her, but he didn't want to make it obvious and so he stepped back a bit further behind one of the columns that held the pub up. He took another sip of his drink and continued watching; it made him feel like a peeping tom, but he couldn't help himself. He was contemplating asking the publican who she was, but didn't want to look stupid in front of him.

After all, he was supposed to be a heartless womanizer, with glamorous women throwing themselves at his feet, and here he was watching some woman in her twenties in the most run-down pub in the East End!

Suddenly, he saw her stand up. Tony was hypnotized by her, he wanted to see where she was going, or rather who she was going to. It seemed strange to him, because the volume of the music seemed to get lower, as if it were background music. People's shouts and glad tidings seemed to dim and all the noise blended together. All he was aware of was this young, slim, almost petite, woman walking towards the bar.

Tony didn't know why, but he moved forward to the spot she was walking towards. He stayed a foot or so behind her, still waiting for someone to come up and claim her, but they didn't. He waited to see what she ordered from the bar; that would be a big giveaway. If she was getting a round of drinks in there would be four glasses, one each for her Jamaican friend and her husband, one for herself and one for whoever she was with.

There was one solitary glass of wine put on the bar in front of her. Tony didn't know why, but he felt compelled to step closer as he watched her pick up the stemmed wine glass. She exchanged a few words with the barmaid and half turned to leave. Just then, someone dancing wildly to Slade's 'Merry Xmas Everybody' crashed into the woman and shoved her aside. She was knocked off-balance and most of the wine from her glass spilt over Tony's coat sleeve.

The poor woman looked horrified, but then she looked up directly into Tony's eyes. For a few seconds that seemed like an eternity, they stared at each other. Not a word was spoken.

Then, she said, 'Sorry.' She looked embarrassed and was blushing. She put her glass on the bar and brushed wine from his sleeve. 'I'll get a bar towel.'

Tony smiled at her. 'Don't worry about it, no harm done,' he said.

'I'm so sorry, I couldn't help it, I was bumped. Are you sure I can't get you something to wipe your arm?' Again, she was blushing, but she was still looking at him intently. She seemed modest and shy, so what the hell was she doing in a place like this?

'Why don't you have a drink with me? That'll make up for it.' Tony didn't take his eyes off her face.

The barmaid had seen what happened and went to get another glass of wine for the woman and a fresh whisky for Tony. 'Here you are,' she said, as she put them down on the bar top next to them.

Tony handed the new glass of wine to the woman, who was still gushing her apologies and blushing profusely. She showed no recognition of who he was. That was most unusual, because most people knew him, if not personally, then from the stories in the magazines or newspapers.

People either watched their tongues in front of him or told him what a pleasure it was to meet him. This woman said nothing of the sort.

The woman put the wine glass to her lips. Tony noticed they were full and well-shaped, and formed a perfect Cupid's bow. He felt his stomach churning, and a deep stirring inside. The more he looked at her, the more he wanted her. He didn't want to break the magic by speaking; he had never felt like this before. No woman, especially one that didn't know who he was and wasn't draped over him, particularly took his attention, but this awkward-looking shy, embarrassed woman did.

He put his hand to the bottom of her wine glass and tipped it towards her lips, so that she took a sip, and smiled at her. He knew he said something but wasn't sure what. They were just looking at each other. It was a feeling he couldn't comprehend, and he still waited to see if anyone would come up to the bar and claim her as their wife or partner. Thankfully, no one did.

She raised her long dark lashes, lifted her head and looked him squarely in the face. When she smiled, her whole face lit up. She was truly beautiful. Tony smiled back, displaying a perfect row of white teeth in his suntanned face.

He was mesmerised.

He saw her put her glass down and she mumbled something to excuse herself from the bar. He smiled again as he saw the blush return to her cheeks. Then she started to walk away, and for the first time in his life Tony didn't know how to stop a woman from leaving him. Usually he had the opposite problem – he couldn't get rid of them!

He watched her walk away, back towards her friend who still sat at the table with her husband. His mind was in turmoil. In different circumstances, he would have simply given his most charming smile, introduced himself and whisked them off to the club, but he had a strange feeling that approach wouldn't work.

Tony ran his hands through his hair and looked around at the drunken crowd to see if anyone was watching him. He felt slightly embarrassed, awkward, even. Suddenly the silence was broken.

'Do you want another one in there, Mr Lambrianu?' Tony looked towards the bar to see the publican reaching out for his glass.

He was tempted to ask the publican who his mystery woman was, but didn't want to look overly eager and start gossip flying around.

'No, thank you, I'm just leaving.' Although Tony was speaking to the publican he was still glancing across at the woman. He saw she had stopped at the table where her friends were, and the Jamaican woman had beckoned her closer and put her mouth to her ear so that she could be heard above the music.

Tony's heart sank; the mystery and the magic were gone, and he knew that now. It was quite obvious to him that the Jamaican woman would be telling her who he was, and possibly encouraging her to come back and have another drink with him.

'Are you okay, Francesca? You look all flushed,' said Candy. Her husband was shooting off party poppers from their table. She looked at her friend quizzically, she knew she hadn't been eager to come along tonight, but for the sake of future bookings she had no choice; she had to come to keep the publicans and the agency happy.

The young woman put her mouth near Candy's ear. 'I'm fine, I'm just a bit hot, that's all. I'm going outside to get some air.' She gave a weak smile to her friend.

'What's wrong, honey? Have you had more than two glasses of wine or something?' Candy turned to her husband and started to laugh. 'She can't drink, you know, she's a real lightweight.' She turned back to her friend. 'Do you want me to come with you, Francesca?' Candy half stood up. She didn't really want to lose her seat at the table, but felt she should go out of loyalty and friendship.

'No, I'll be back in a few minutes, it's just so hot and smoky in here, I need some air.' With that, Francesca started to walk away towards the back doors leading to the beer garden.

Tony had continued watching her and was surprised when neither she nor her friend had pointed his way, or even given an indication they were talking about him. He saw that she was walking towards the beer garden, and impulsively, he pushed his way through the crowd and started to follow her.

When he got outside, he saw her standing with her back to him. He looked up at the sky; on this icy night it was clear. The stars twinkled and the large moon seemed even bigger and brighter than usual. He looked back at the woman. She'd turned to see who was there, and her eyes were fixed on Tony.

Again, they just gazed at each other in silence, then before either of them knew it, they were in each other's arms, kissing ardently. Although the crisp night air sent a shudder through him, Tony felt his whole being tremble, wrapped in this woman's arms, holding on to her tightly, the way she was clinging on to him.

He was kissing her neck while his hands roamed over her slim body. She had her arms around his neck and her hands in his mane of blonde hair. He felt himself dance her backwards towards the pub wall and in moments, without thought or conscience, they were making love.

It was very passionate and very heated, he felt the woman's body tremble and tense up, and then he felt her relax and her breathing slowed down.

It had been a crazy head-spinning moment, and slowly, he began to loosen his grip on her legs from where he had hoisted her up against the wall and she had wrapped them around him. They were both trying to catch their breath.

He looked down at her and her eyes opened, but instead of love or passion, he saw she looked horrified! She held her hands up to her face and muttered something, which indicated she was ashamed of what had just happened between them and regretted it instantly.

She pulled down her dress and pushed past him, then fled, fast as a bolt of lightning.

'Wait!' Tony shouted. He moved forward, and nearly tripped over his trousers, which were still halfway down his legs. As he was trying to steady himself, he banged his leg on one of the wooden benches. Some people were now opening the back doors to come into the beer garden. He dressed himself quickly and, with his foot, pushed the condom packet near the guttering.

He went out of the back gates. He saw John, his driver, parked outside, but the street was empty – there was no sign of the woman. He banged on the car window.

'Did you see that woman that just came out? Where did she go?' Tony was almost shouting at John. While waiting for an answer he was still looking around at the street for any sign of her.

'What woman, boss? I just saw one come out and get into a cab, is that the one you mean?' John hadn't really been taking any notice, he had been dozing off in the front seat waiting for Tony to come out.

'Yes, where did she go, do you know?' Tony knew it was a stupid question, after all, if she had jumped into a taxi, how the hell would John know where she was going? John just shrugged his shoulders and sat upright. He lowered the car window even more.

'Is there something wrong, boss? What's happened?' John thought there must have been a fight or something. Tony looked flushed and agitated; he ran his hand through his hair and gave a deep sigh.

'No, John, nothing's wrong, time to go.' He opened the car door and got into the back seat, still looking out of the windows for any sign of her. He realised he had to compose himself in front of John and sat back in his seat. 'Take me to the club, will you? No, wait a minute, take me to the casino.'

Tony went straight up to his apartment at the casino; he wanted to be alone to gather his thoughts. He couldn't fathom out what had just happened, it had all been so quick and so surreal.

ဆဝ◊ର

Next morning, Jake went to see him at the casino. 'Hey, how come you spent the night here? I've just been to the club, I thought you'd be there.' Jake was bright and breezy and was waiting for the report of what had happened when Tony saw the publican last night.

Jake poured two mugs of coffee, and placed one in front of Tony. The more he asked him about what had happened on the previous evening, the shadier Tony was about it. He knew he shouldn't have let Tony go. He reckoned he must have threatened the publican and it had all gone wrong.

'Okay, Tony, what did you do and what hospital is he in? For God's sake, he was only a bit short on his money. So, tell me, what happened?' Jake sat opposite him, waiting for the worst. He noticed Tony's serious yet sheepish face; he wasn't laughing or joking about how he had scared the publican.

Tony stood up and reached for his overcoat and took the money the publican had given him out of his pocket.

'Here.' He threw it on the coffee table between them. 'I told him to leave the rest and just make sure he paid up properly next month.'

Jake was now concerned; the solemn tone in Tony's voice was unusual, not what he had expected at all. 'Are you okay, Tony? Come on, mate, what's happened?'

Jake sat back in his chair and listened intently as Tony first told him about his meeting with the publican, and then he paused and seemed to blush a little. With a shy smile on his face, he told Jake about his encounter with the woman in the beer garden.

Jake laughed. 'Oh, well, not a totally wasted evening, then. Sounds better than mine at Sharon's sister's place. Maybe I should have gone, after all, maybe I would have had some passion in that shithole of a so-called beer garden.' He shook his head. 'Let's be honest, Tony, it's the back delivery area, with a few tables in it. So, what's the problem? You look weird.'

Tony took a gulp of his coffee. 'I want you to do me a favour, Jake. I want you to find out who she is, and if she's okay. I didn't get a chance to, I fell over my trousers and banged my knees on one of those wooden benches.' With that, Tony smiled; it was the first proper smile Jake had seen all morning.

Jake nodded. 'Yes, okay, shouldn't be too hard. A pub full of strippers, they are bound to all know each other. What was her name?' Jake waited and then saw Tony shrug his shoulders.

'I don't know, we never introduced ourselves. In fact, we never spoke, not while we were … you know.' Tony looked down at the floor; he felt embarrassed admitting this to Jake. He saw Jake raise his eyebrows and smile; he obviously thought this was amusing.

'Okay, next question, what was she wearing? Who was she with?'

Again, he saw Tony shrug his shoulders.' I can't remember what she was wearing. No, I do, it was a dress, and she was sitting with a Jamaican woman and her husband.' Tony seemed pleased that he recollected this information.

Jake held his hands open wide. 'Is that it? She had long dark hair, wore a dress and was sat with a Jamaican woman. That is, until she decided to have sex with you in that old back yard. That's not a lot to go on. I'll ask around, although it seems pointless.' Jake suddenly turned serious. 'You did use protection, didn't you? After all, she sounds a bit easy to me. How many other people hasn't she spoken to in the beer garden with her knickers down?'

'Don't say that about her! It wasn't like that. I just want to know if she's okay, she seemed like a frightened rabbit caught in the headlights when she ran off. I just want to make sure she got home okay, that's all.' Tony seemed angry at Jake's suggestion that the woman had been 'easy', he put his mug down and started to walk towards the bathroom.

Jake watched him go; he would try and find out who this mystery woman was, but even he knew it was futile. They would all have been drunk, why would they notice anyone having a bit of hanky-panky, outside? Then it struck him. Oh no, he wouldn't have to go searching for her, she would come to them. This encounter was going to be another 'kiss and tell' story for the newspapers! 'My night of passion with Tony Lambrianu'; Jake could just see the headlines now.

Jake stood up, straightened his leather jacket and walked towards the closed bathroom door. He could hear the shower was running, but shouted through anyway, 'I'm going to go and see that publican before he opens, see you later.'

John, Tony's driver, was outside polishing the car. Jake walked up to him. 'Hi, John,' he said, 'I've got to pop to that pub you went to last night with Tony. Any chance of a lift?' Jake had his own car around the corner, but he wanted to go with John in case he could shed any light on the previous evening's events.

'Did Tony seem okay last night when he left the pub?'

Jake tried skirting around the subject as best as he could. 'I hear there was some misunderstanding with a woman or something?' He knew it sounded vague but he wanted to get to the bottom of it.

'Well, between you and me, Jake, he seemed a bit flustered when he got back to the car. He did ask if I had seen a woman, which I had briefly, but I didn't pay much attention to her. There were loads of people milling around, shouting to each other.'

At last, Jake thought to himself, he had a lead. If John recognized what she was wearing or even knew her, that would be a start, and maybe he could stop her spreading gossip about Tony and making herself a small fortune while doing it.

'Would you recognize her again? Did you notice what she was wearing?' Jake waited with bated breath.

'No. All I saw was some woman running out of the dark, she hailed a cab and jumped in the back of it. I never took any notice until Tony came out asking about her. Why? Is it important?'

Jake shook his head.

He had the same conversation with the publican, and it all came to a dead end. Apparently, Tony was at the bar one minute, having a drink, then he declined another one and just disappeared. The publican did go out of his way to remind Jake what Tony had said about the payments.

'It's okay, I already know that. It just seems he thought he knew this woman, but couldn't remember where from. He thought maybe you would know who she was, considering she was at your party.'

The publican was still slightly hungover, having got into the party mood, himself. 'I'm sure there are lots of lovely ladies Mr Lambrianu can't remember, but none of these old slags, Jake. They are not in his league.' He winked at Jake and laughed.

Considering the mood Tony was in this morning, and the fact that he had already snapped at Jake for calling the woman 'easy', he was glad he wasn't there when the publican called her an old slag. He seemed to vaguely know the Jamaican woman he mentioned.

'That would possibly be Candy. Nice woman, the guys all like her, but she was with a lot of people and has a lot of friends.'

Jake decided to call it a day; all this probing was causing suspicion. He decided another way to tackle the problem would be to check the daily newspapers to see if Tony was on the front page. There was nothing. Again, it was a dead end. He would wait a few more days; maybe they hadn't had time to do anything about it yet.

Three days later, Jake went into Tony's office, threw a bunch of magazines on his desk and sat down. 'There is no "kiss and tell" story about you, Tony. Your Cinderella didn't even leave a shoe for us to track her down with. No one seems to know who she is or where she's from. Forget it, mate. I haven't heard of a woman being hurt or anything in the area, so I presume she got home okay and that's that.'

Tony glanced up at him, as though trying to remember what he had asked him to do. 'Oh, yes,' he said, 'I'd forgotten about her. You're sure there is nothing in the news about it?'

Jake shook his head.

'Well, that's good, anyway. As you say, it's over now.'

Jake thought it was strange that Tony didn't seem disappointed there was no lead on 'Cinderella'. Maybe he was just relieved that it hadn't become common knowledge. Who knew? Who would ever know?

ॐ◊ॐ

Christmas, as hoped for, brought the cash rolling in, as the club hosted its many Christmas parties. Companies hired the place to put on Christmas parties for the men, who enjoyed all the fun the club had to offer, especially the strippers. At the weekends, there were the usual nightclub events, where everyone came out to dance the night away, all in the name of Christmas.

The casino, with all of its glamour, beckoned in people from all walks of life, hoping to have a good time and win some money. Graham had given Tony a good saying to remember: 'It doesn't matter who wins what, always remember, the casino always wins.' That was true enough, because even when they did win, they would bet it all again, trying to win more.

Although in the beginning the security firm they had set up was intended to be a front for the protection racket, it had taken off and was doing very well in its own right, and at Christmas it seemed to thrive. Everyone wanted their special event to have some security doorman on hand, to help out if needed.

Ashley had a special Christmas fun night planned at the men's club, to which Tony and Jake were both invited. They had sent their apologies and declined, but whatever it was, they knew it would be a money-spinner.

Tony and Jake were in the office at the club, each dressed in a designer Italian suit, Tony in grey and Jake in black. They sat back in their wingback leather chairs and toasted each other. This was going to be the best Christmas ever. All of their hard work over the last year was paying off.

'To us, Jake.' Tony held his glass up, and bowed his head as a form of acknowledgement for all of Jake's hard work and standing by him when things got tough. Jake did likewise.

'I wonder what next year will bring, Tony? In a year from now, when we are sat in this very spot, toasting each other as we are now, I wonder what it will be about.' Jake seemed to be daydreaming.

'For God's sake Jake, let's get this one done and out of the way with, first, shall we?' Tony said. He smiled at his friend, who seemed to be in a world of his own.

Sharon came running into the office; she had a cloth bag full of money, which she had taken out of the cash registers before they burst. She took in the sight before her, Tony and Jake lounging in their chairs, each with a glass of whisky in his hand.

'Are you two sure you're not working too hard?' she said, sarcastically. 'Put this in the safe, will you? It's mayhem out there, but at least we're getting rid of all that cheap champagne at top prices. They are so drunk they don't know the difference.' She half chuckled to herself.

'I've come in here to get out of the way,' said Jake. 'If I hear the same Christmas song again, I think I'll scream. It seems to me they are played every year, without fail, and in every pub or club you go in, but people still don't know the bloody words!' He was indignant, he sat and folded his arms.

Sharon looked at Tony, who was starting to dial in the combination on the safe so he could put the money away. 'So, what's your excuse?' she said, with a smirk on her face.

'I'm helping you out, Sharon.' Tony picked up the bag of money and deposited it into the safe. 'If I wasn't here, who would you come running to with all your earnings, so that you can get back into the club and fleece them all some more? Come on, Sharon, you're worse than us … cheap champagne, more like fizzy water … you put Robin Hood to shame, except you're robbing the poor to pay the rich.' Tony picked up his glass again and raised it to her. 'Come and have a quiet drink with us. It's all about us three amigos, and how we work together.' Tony put his arm around her shoulders; she was like his sister, always there to support him and Jake.

She leaned her head on Tony's shoulder while Jake poured her a drink. Tony was right, they had all come a long way together, through the good and the bad.

'To us.' She raised her glass, and gave them each a kiss on the cheek. 'So, Tony, which one of those lucky ladies out there will be having the pleasure of your company tonight, then?' Again, she gave him a mischievous smile.

Tony burst out laughing. 'All of them; after all, it's Christmas, and I want to spread my Christmas wishes around.' They all creased up laughing; Tony would never change.

'By the way, Sharon, business now. You know I went to the East End last week to one of the stripper pubs.'

Sharon took a sip of her drink, nodded her head and sat down.

'Well, this is going to sound a little jumbled up, but some of them weren't bad looking, and I thought maybe you could give some of them a look over. Maybe we could use some fresh faces.' Tony stopped and waited. He had agreed a long time ago that this was Sharon's side of things and he wouldn't interfere, and he never had, but he thought this was worth mentioning.

'You have a point; the men have seen all of these girls dozens of times, maybe a little variety wouldn't go amiss. I bet it's all the same punters, anyway.' She took a drink. 'We could hold an audition day. Let me think about it, Tony, I'll have a word with the local agencies and ask them about their A list girls. Let me work on it.' Sharon finished her drink, put down the glass and left the office, to walk back into the mayhem of the nightclub.

'You still trying to find your Cinderella, Tony? I mean, since when did you want to hold auditions for any of those girls?' said Jake. He put his feet up on the leather pouffe and waited for an answer.

'Who? Oh, you mean that woman. No, that's long gone. Ancient history, now, but I did have a look around while I was at the party. Some of the women were as rough as the roads, but some were okay, and with a little bit of Sharon's magic, well … you never know, do you?'

'I've been thinking about that woman, Tony. I genuinely don't think she knew who you were; either that, or she's married and if she did some story for the newspapers, it would be a great risk to her marriage, and possibly her family. I'd say you've got away with it.'

'Married?' Tony had already discounted that. 'I told you, she wasn't with anyone.'

'He might not have been at the party. Was she wearing a wedding ring?'

Tony shrugged.

'Me and Sharon are not joined at the hip, even though we're married, but yes, she wears a ring. Mind you, you weren't looking at that woman's hands, were you?'

Tony shook his head. He reached over and poured them both another drink. Jake had a point. He hadn't thought of looking at her hand to see if she had been wearing a wedding ring. Why had that never occurred to him? He downed his drink in one. 'Come on, Jake, let's go and see what's going on in the club, and furthermore, who is waiting for me.'

They both straightened themselves up, switched off the office light and walked into the noisy club. Lights were flashing, the floor was lit up and the DJ was doing his very best to get them all in the Christmas mood. Tony looked across at the bar; Sharon was standing at the side of it, organizing the staff, as usual, and Jake was walking towards her. Then Tony caught sight of Roxy at the bar. He swept his hair back, straightened his tie and walked up to her and her group of pals. After all, it was a fun party night and what better way was there to spend it than with beautiful women, champagne and friends.

≲∘≳

Tony walked downstairs the following morning; he hadn't showered or shaved yet and his hair was ruffled. He had left Roxy in bed and come down early because he wanted to see the aftermath of the night before. Whatever happened in his personal life, his businesses came first. Women would come and go, but he would make sure that his business empire would last forever.

The cleaners were in, filling their rubbish bags and vacuuming, which didn't help his hangover.

'Morning, Mr Lambrianu,' said Lydia, the old cleaner, who had her nose into everything. She wore an old floral headscarf wrapped firmly around her head, flattening her hair so much that Tony wondered if she actually had any. The tabard she wore was at least three sizes too big for her and she wandered around with her polish in one hand and her duster in the other.

Tony nodded at her. She was an old gossip, he knew that, and he was waiting for the usual barrage of questions she asked. She was a good worker and always on time, in that way, he had no complaints, but God, she was nosy!

'Nearly Christmas, Mr Lambrianu, very expensive time of the year for us common folk, trying to make ends meet. I bet you don't have those worries, do you?' Her high-pitched voice and her harsh rubbing of the tables nearby annoyed him.

'Go away, Lydia, go and polish somewhere else.' He gave her a glare and reached up and scratched his head. She carried on rambling about Christmas being the most expensive time of the year. Finally, it dawned on him and he realised what she was getting at. She was hinting about her Christmas bonus, or rather, wanting to know if there was going to be one.

Now it was Tony's turn to annoy her. 'It is an expensive time, Lydia, which is why I need to earn and keep all the money I can.' Tony looked down at the floor, he could hear her giving out deep over-the-top sighs, but thankfully the vacuuming drowned out most of her moaning and hint-dropping.

Jake walked through the doors and saved the day. 'Morning, Lydia, my love,' he said, and he bent forward and gave her a kiss on the cheek. She blushed and gave him a coy smile, then muttered something about not telling her husband of thirty years. 'You're up early, Tony, has Roxy gone already?'

Tony stood up. 'She's about to leave, Jake, just as soon as I get her up and out of bed. We have things to do.' He thought it was time to put Lydia out of her misery and then maybe she might stop polishing the same table and actually do some work. 'Oh, and I did get the hint, Lydia,' he said, 'and there will be a little extra in your wages, to help you through Christmas. There might even be enough for a new duster.'

'Ooh, Mr Lambrianu, that will be very much appreciated, thank you very much.'

'Come on, let's leave them to it and get some coffee.' Tony started to walk up the stairs to his apartment. 'Nosy old cow,' he muttered to Jake, who was following him upstairs. 'You're no better, encouraging her with your flattery and your kisses.'

'My God, we are grumpy this morning. What's wrong? Did Roxy say you were losing your touch?

Tony snorted.

'Also, I like Lydia. You're right, of course, she's an old gossip, but that workshy husband of hers hasn't done a day's graft in years because of his bad back, or so he tells her. I tell you what, though, if you need to know anything, Lydia is the one to ask.' Jake was laughing as he walked into the apartment, then he stopped. 'Bloody hell, Tony, I thought the party was downstairs.' Jake surveyed the room; clothes were discarded everywhere, there were silver champagne buckets, now filled with water as the ice had melted, corks had been popped and empty bottles were strewn around.

'How many are here?' asked Jake, looking around.

Tony just shrugged. 'Not sure, I never counted.' He yawned and ran his hands through his hair. 'Still, it's check out time, now.' This was Tony's usual procedure the morning after. All of his charm and flattery deserted him, now it was back to business.

Jake started making the coffee. He could hear Tony shouting into the bedrooms to get everyone up and everyone out. He carried on making himself busy as he watched a dishevelled Tony, in his bathrobe, doing nothing short of throwing three women out of his apartment.

As always, Roxy was the last to leave. She knew Tony well enough now not to argue about it.

Jake poured coffee into two mugs, then looked over at

her. She was wearing last night's clothes and her once perfect make-up was smudged. Her long flowing blonde hair had been quickly combed, but still looked tangled. Suddenly her sequined minidress looked tacky.

'I thought I might come back to the club tonight, if you fancy a drink love,' she said.

'Doubt it Roxy, I'll be at the casino tonight. And don't call me love, my name is Tony.'

Tony was fed up, already; he knew she was waiting for an invite, but his mind was on the day ahead of him. She'd served her purpose and he wanted her to leave. Jake felt for her; it was painful to watch, at times.

In a way, she was his most regular girlfriend and so Jake presumed she would end up with Tony all to herself, one day. She was playing the waiting game, letting him get all of his other women out of his system before he chose her, above the rest.

'Okay, well I'll see you soon, then.' Roxy hung on to Tony's every word.

Tony nodded and gave her a weak smile, then walked her to the door and closed it sharply behind her. That done, he breathed a sigh of relief. 'It's hard being a bachelor and having to get rid of the women in the morning, Jake, all they want to do is hang around.'

Jake felt sorry for the women in Tony's life. One minute they had all the flattery and attention they could want and the next minute they had nothing.

'I'm going for a shower.' Tony picked up his mug and walked towards the bathroom.' I tell you what, though, if you've got nothing better to do for the moment, you can start tidying this place up a bit.'

Jake looked around the apartment; it had been one hell of a party, there was no way he was going to clean up after Tony and his guests. Then a thought occurred to him; just to annoy Tony even more, he would ask Lydia to go up there and give it a spring clean, after they had left. That way she could nosy around to her heart's content.

Eventually, Tony emerged from the bathroom. Jake was reading the paper and drinking more coffee. 'Anything in particular we have to do today?' asked Jake.

'Not really. I want to go and see Angus, give him and Elsie their bonus face-to-face. He's done some good work lately, maybe me shouting at him worked out for the best.' Tony had never apologized to Angus about shoving a gun in his mouth and he never would. He was hoping that his Christmas bonus might just do it for him.

'Whatever you say. Everyone else's bonuses are already sorted, even the strippers. Sharon took care of all that. By the way, I thought I would ask Lydia to pop up here to clean up your harem; that'll definitely give her something to gossip about.'

Tony rolled his eyes. 'If gossip was an Olympic sport, she'd have a string of gold medals.'

'It amazes me how she gets away with it. Everyone who works for you has to sign a confidentiality contract and be police checked, so how did Lydia get the job?' Jake looked up innocently.

'Your Sharon, listening to her sob stories, that's how,' he said, then he burst out laughing. 'Christ, her wig'll fall off when she sees this lot. She'll have enough material for a month!'

20

FESTIVITIES

C hristmas came and went in a blur. The accounts showed that it had been a profitable one.

On Christmas day itself, they were all relieved to be able to forget things for a while and go to Elle's for dinner. She had laid out the fatted calf. Everything looked splendid.

Christmas at Elle's gave them all a chance to unwind for the day. The clubs weren't open until the evening, and Mathers had even suggested that the men's club not open at all, because most of their members would be at home with their families. It was a fair point; many of the members worked in the City, and as the big offices and stock exchange were closed, there was no need for them to come into town.

It was business as usual for the casino and the club, although there were no strippers or pole dancers on at the club – it was party night only. A lot of their customers would be a young crowd and it would be a noisy, profitable one. They had spent their dutiful few hours with their families on Christmas day and the evening was their chance to escape.

The next main event would be New Year's Eve. It seemed everyone felt that Christmas was for the children and New Year was for the adults. Tony personally didn't see the difference, as he had never been in that position it didn't mean anything to him.

'What did you end up getting Mathers for Christmas, Elle?' asked Jake. He knew Tony had wanted to get him something special but he hadn't heard what it was.

'Well, that one was a little strange, I grant you,' said Elle. She paused, waiting for them to look up at her. 'He hinted that he liked the look of those walnut walking sticks that are exclusively made with whatever handle you choose, to make him look more distinguished. Mathers like the silver handled one, and so that was the order I put in for him. Of course, it won't be ready for another couple of months, yet; as I say, they are all made exclusively for each customer, but he is satisfied with that.' Elle waited; she knew there would be a few comments about this, as she herself had questioned it.

'He hasn't got a limp; why does he need a walking stick?' Jake was looking around at everyone, amazed.

'Because, you moron, it's a status symbol,' said Sharon. 'A fancy cane like that confers prestige.' Sharon began explaining about how British gentlemen of his years often had a walking stick. You didn't just have one because you had a limp. It was tradition. 'Anyway, Mathers probably fought in the army and beat them all single-handed, God knows, he has everybody else under control.'

'Sounds crazy to me, but if that's what he wanted, I suppose, it's up to him.' Jake pushed his drumstick into his mouth, bit a chunk off and started chewing, ignoring the fact that Sharon was watching him intently.

'That's because, Jake Sinclair, you have no bloody class.' She yanked the drumstick from his hand and put it on the plate. 'Look at you. Will you take a breath before you take another bite? It looks like you haven't been fed in years.' Sharon looked apologetically at the others.

Tony reached across and picked up Jake's drumstick. 'Well, I definitely haven't got any class, either,' he said, and he stuffed it into his mouth as far as he could, nearly gagging on it as he was laughing and trying hard not to choke.

They were all laughing now. It felt good to be able to let their hair down after all of their hard work. Nothing had changed, as far as Elle was concerned. It had been the four of them for years and, apart from the distance, which made it harder for them to see each other as often, everything was exactly as it had always been.

'Well,' said Sharon, 'Ashley decided on us both going on a spa weekend for his Christmas present. That will be nice, won't it, Elle? I'm looking forward to it, but it's not a special present for him, so I got him a designer leather wallet, as well.'

'You never bought me a designer wallet, and you haven't suggested a weekend away with me,' Jake said, his mouth full of delicious food. 'You'll have a weekend away with another man, but not with your husband?'

'Where could I take you that table manners like that would be acceptable?' said Sharon.

Tony and Elle laughed and watched as Jake and Sharon bantered their way through her weekend away with Ashley.

'You have got to be the most easy-going guy I know, Jake, letting your wife go on a dirty weekend with another man.' Tony winked at Elle. He knew he was stirring things, but he enjoyed it.

'It's not another man, Tony, it's Ashley, and she never told me about it.' Jake pouted, and then gave a big smile. It would sound comical to anyone that overheard them, especially people that hadn't met Ashley. Jake was letting his wife go to a spa weekend with another man. Now, that was what the gossips loved!

Tony picked up his wine glass and took a sip. 'Ah, yes, Jake, but you have the lovely Lydia eyeing you up. I saw you give her a kiss the other morning. I bet you didn't tell Sharon about that.'

Everyone was enjoying themselves and laughing, the food was plentiful, the wine flowed and the banter between them was electric.

Tony didn't tell any of them that he had bought Miriam a vintage Bible. The pages were like tissue paper, and it dated back to the eighteenth century. It had cost a fortune, but he knew she would appreciate it. He had bought Rosanna some earrings. She liked big, dangly ones and so he had got the biggest pair he could find and sent them to her.

Elle never wanted anything for herself. She wanted Tony and Jake to keep their money and always said she didn't need anything. They had argued that was the whole point of Christmas – everyone got something they didn't want or need, didn't they? In the end they had decided to upgrade Elle's car and then she couldn't complain about it being a waste of money. It was something practical.

Tony had actually gone out himself and bought Jake's present. It was nothing big or expensive, they had everything they needed. Jake still loved his superhero comics that he used to read when he was a boy, growing up at Elle's. Of course, this was a private piece of information that no one else knew. After all, it wouldn't set a good example, gangland boss reads comic books!

Tony had bought him a whole bunch of them and wrapped them up. Jake was still his little brother, in Tony's eyes. Possibly, considering what they had been through together, they were closer than brothers.

Sharon had bought her own present from Tony. He had thought it funny, one year, to buy her a load of cookery books and had even enlisted her on a cookery course. She had taken it all with good grace, but from then on, she vowed to buy her own gifts and charge them to him. It was usually perfume or make-up, Tony never knew.

None of the presents mattered; what did matter was that they all had each other, and no matter what life threw at them, they could get through it as long as they did.

They all spread out in the lounge after dinner. Jake was still finding more space for Elle's homemade mince pies. Elle was amazed. 'I'm surprised you don't weigh twenty stone,' she said. 'How come you are so slim, Jake, with all that eating you do?'

Elle liked the old movies and always said that Jake reminded her of the movie star, Tony Curtis, with his black hair and boyish grin.

'I have a fast metabolism, Elle, it burns up all the fat.' Jake reached out for another mince pie.

'Well, don't ask him how he burns up his fat, randy bugger,' said Sharon, and pointed at Tony. She had her feet up and had loosened her waistband.

Elle shook her head and laughed. 'Believe me, Sharon, I won't. I've seen all of the magazines, full of Tony's lovely ladies and what they say about him.'

Tony was lounging on the sofa with a cocky grin on his face, listening to them all mock him about his reputation. His vanity soared when they mocked him like this and so did his ego. As much as he cringed at times when the newspapers were full of weird and wonderful stories about him, he liked it, too.

All in all, they had a great day. A real family day, which is what it was all about – not expensive presents. This was Christmas. Spending it with people who loved and trusted each other was worth more than gold.

All too soon, it was time to go, and Elle was already filling small Tupperware boxes with mince pies and other Christmas snacks she had baked for Jake. He was always hungry.

On the way home, as always, Tony stopped at Trafalgar Square. The Salvation Army band was there playing their Christmas carols. Tony always stopped by and gave a donation. He would look around at the crowds of people standing watching the band and clapping. It was like he could see himself, as a child, standing in that crowd. His mind wandered and was full of memories, most of them bad. He got back in the car beside Jake and Sharon and told John, his driver, to drive on.

Even though John pulled away, Tony still stared out of the car windows, watching the people listening to the band in the darkness of the city with only the street lights illuminating them. Jake looked at him; he was never sure, but there were times like now and in recent years he could have sworn he saw tears in Tony's eyes, but he never said a word and neither did Sharon.

When they got to the club, there were people queuing outside, waiting to go in. Tony's Rolls Royce parked at the kerb, and the light from the famous neon sign bearing his name bathed the car in a pink glow.

'Tonight, Jake,' Tony said, wrapping his coat around him, 'we wear our tuxedos. Let's go and change.' Tony waved to the crowds, who were shouting to him, then walked into the club, where the party was in full swing.

Later, Tony stood at the far corner of the bar, having drinks with a few of the celebrities he knew who were doing daytime pantomime at the theatres. He was playing host and everyone was lapping it up, as usual.

Then he left and went on to the casino to see how things were there. Graham, as always, had everything under control. The casino was busy and, yet again, people were shaking Tony's hand and wishing him a merry Christmas.

This was how things were for the Christmas holidays, smiling and shaking hands. Playing host and buying champagne. It was good, but it was tiring.

Tony and Jake had been to see Angus and had given him a huge bonus for all of his hard work. He had been a good choice as leader of the South London mob, and now everything was back under control. Jake had apologized for Tony's earlier outburst and it seemed all Angus wanted to do was forget it, too.

Joe, who had suffered the acid attack, was now back home. He would still have more hospital appointments to come, but he was on the mend.

Then the New Year was upon them and thankfully, for the time being, that would signal the end of the party season. Everything could return to normal.

Roxy had been to the club once or twice and she had even come with one of her gentlemen friends. He was a much older man, flattered by her attentions. She was showing off a diamond necklace that he had bought her and hanging on to his arm and laughing at his jokes. It was obvious she was trying to make Tony jealous, but it didn't. Instead, Tony walked over and shook hands with Roxy and her companion. He ordered them champagne and then purposely left her there sitting on a bar stool, watching him leave.

21

A GOLDEN OPPORTUNITY

January carried on as cold as December had been.

The accountant was back from Italy, which is where he had spent Christmas, and was sitting in the far corner of the office, sorting out the two sets of books he kept. There were the club accounts, all ready for the audit and tax inspection, and then there were the money laundering books, which few people ever saw.

None of the three amigos could understand why, now everything was set up and he could send any of the accountants that worked for him to the club to keep on top of things, he insisted on taking care of things himself. He seemed to enjoy life there with the three of them. Perhaps it was because they had all worked together for years and he was accepted for himself. They even supposed he enjoyed being in the thick of things – there was always some gossip to enjoy or a problem to deal with. Probably, from his point of view, not only was it interesting, but he was on the inside looking out.

They were all in the office, having their usual early morning meeting. Sharon was checking the diary for future parties that had to be arranged.

'I've been thinking, Tony,' she said. 'Your idea about

bringing in some fresh blood from the East End Striptease Agencies isn't such a bad idea. I've been doing some research and Ashley has been undercover as a punter, going into these pubs, checking out the girls.'

That made Jake and Tony laugh; they nearly choked on their coffees. 'You have had Ashley, of all people, checking out female strippers?' said Jake. Again, they laughed.

'Who better to look at a load of naked women than a man who is not interested in women? His opinion is unbiased and true.' Sharon looked at them both; yet again, she had got the better of them. She had thought the idea was interesting when Tony had suggested it, and then she had let it ferment in her brain. She had talked it over with Ashley and he agreed but, before wasting any time on auditions, he felt it would be best if he went and had a look, first.

'Well, what did Ashley, the great womanizer, tell you?' asked Tony. He was still laughing at the thought of Ashley being surrounded by all that female flesh. It was a wonder he didn't pass out.

Sharon sat back in a leather wingback chair and crossed her legs. She was always immaculately dressed and usually wore a black suit, either trousers or a skirt. It looked effective, with her blonde hair, and gave her that management appearance that was required. 'He told me,' she said, 'that you weren't a bad judge, Tony. Granted, he said some were as rough as a badger's bum, but there were a handful worth considering. I'm going to set up some auditions, possibly for a Sunday; that way, no one has to take the day off.'

Sharon picked up her clipboard with the daily rotas on, blew a kiss to them all and left.

🙐◇🙒

Over the next month Sharon and Ashley made themselves busy ringing around local striptease agencies and asking about which would be the best girls. This usually meant anyone without any stretch marks, preferably under thirty, unless they had one of those young faces, and definitely slim – nothing over a size fourteen, maximum, and that was pushing it. Large tattoos were not acceptable; the odd rose on the ankle or backside was passable, but that was about it.

They let the agencies put the word out; that alone would create some gossip and the word would spread. Lambrianu's open audition day became the talk of the town.

Some of the regular punters that went in to see the strippers asked if they could be there, and as much as Tony wanted to say 'yes', and charge them for this novel event, Sharon put her foot firmly down.

'They'll see them in good time, Tony. They probably know half of them and we neither want our arms twisting into taking on someone they know by doing them a favour nor do we need them poking their noses in and turning it into a free-for-all. If they know them and want to see them, then they can go to the East End and watch them.' Sharon was defiant. 'If they get taken on here, they'll be seen when they have learned a choreographed routine and are dressed the way we like our girls dressed.' She also thought some of the girls might feel a little intimidated and nervous enough, coming into a club like theirs, without some celebrity audience watching them. That would come later.

'We can check them out, though, can't we, Sharon? Surely you want a real man's opinion?' asked Jake. He, himself, was curious. He had never been in those pubs in years and wondered what would be turning up through those famous doors.

'You two, if necessary, can watch from the monitors in your office. I'll come back in when they've done their routines and we'll go through it together. Is that fair?'

Tony and Jake nodded. They felt like naughty schoolboys being scolded by the head teacher. It all sounded like a bit of fun to them, but to Sharon it was anything but. She was taking it all very seriously.

The time and date was set and, as Sharon had suggested,

it was to be a Sunday. That way, no one would lose out on their day's work.

Tony, Jake, the accountant and even Ashley had been sent off to the office to watch the proceedings on the monitors, there. Their faces dropped as the doors opened and, one by one, the strippers walked in.

They were a real mixed bunch. Some had tried making themselves look younger, by plastering on even heavier make-up than usual, and some hadn't even bothered to have the roots done on their bleached hair.

'Bloody hell,' said Jake, voicing everyone's opinion, 'it looks more like Crufts dog show. They are horrible, no wonder you're gay.' He grinned at the accountant and Ashley, who took it all in good fun and smiled back at him.

Tony was now secretly pleased that Sharon had put her foot down and made this a closed audition. The last thing he wanted to be was a laughing stock, letting all his regulars see this bunch of misfits.

'Are you sure, Ashley, that you said to the agencies that you wanted their best girls and not just the ones they wanted to get rid of?' Tony watched the monitors, there were girls from all walks of life. Some hadn't even bothered to iron the clothes they were wearing. It was a disaster.

Tony spoke into a microphone that went straight through to the earpiece Sharon was wearing. 'Give them all their cab fares home, and say thank you for coming.' He had seen enough. Here they were, being given a chance, and they weren't prepared to take it. He even saw one put her chewing gum underneath one of his tables. Again, he spoke into his microphone and told Sharon to get her and her chewing gum out of there.

He looked up to the monitor and saw Sharon coming towards the office. She threw open the door and stood there, hand on hip. 'Let's not forget, Tony, that this was your idea in the first place. Now, this is only a few girls, so far, and it's going to be a long afternoon. I don't need you in my ear all of the time.' With that, she walked out.

'Thanks,' said Jake,' now you've managed to piss her off. She's going to nag me all evening because of you.' Jake folded his arms and continued looking up at the monitors.

Sharon had already got her assistant to give some of the women their cab fares home. Even she could see they were not suitable. Their mannerisms were enough to put her off. Some of them were pure divas. They had the reputation of being the best girls at some dead-end pubs and they had got used to this status. It almost felt to Sharon that they thought they were doing her a favour by turning up.

One by one, Sharon let them go through their routines. Some, she stopped halfway through, as what they did was either far too explicit or just plain boring. Some didn't smile, others just walked up and down, without any rhythm. They seemed oblivious to the music that was playing, they were on autopilot.

More strippers came through the doors and Sharon was slightly relieved that they looked a little younger and they had made an effort; although some were overdressed, that was better than not caring. She had her assistant show them all to the dressing rooms to change, and waited. Each one had a number; she had done this so that Tony and Jake could easily remember which ones they thought were suitable.

At last there were a few who showed promise, and who, with a little polish, could do well. They were good-looking and their figures seemed okay. It was difficult, because some were pretty but overweight and some were slender but not pretty. One by one, Sharon got her assistant to hand out cab fares.

What had originally been about a hundred girls was quickly whittled down to approximately thirty. Each, in turn, did their routine and gave it their best, given the fact they were nervous and in unknown territory. This was a far cry from what they were used to.

'You do realise we've wasted the afternoon,' said Tony. He looked bored and his neck ached from looking up at the monitors. 'How many more are there to go?'

'Only four,' said Jake, 'we may as well see it through. I don't think it's been wasted, some of it has been funny, and I also see why we're so busy. Men come in to see pretty women, not their old dinner ladies.' He nudged Ashley in the ribs. He could see Tony wasn't happy and was trying to make light of it.

'Well, you can watch them; I'm going to the bathroom. Enough is enough, as far as I'm concerned.' Tony got up and walked down the corridor to the bathroom. Once in there he washed his face with cold water and stretched his neck. What would have been most men's fantasies, watching naked women all day, had been a nightmare for him and the others.

By the time he got back, Sharon was seeing the last of them out. He looked up at the monitors and saw the doorman locking the doors behind them.

Sharon came into the office. 'Well, guys, these are my choices.' She read off some numbers, accompanied by names, and waited for a response.

Ashley was the first to speak up. 'Personally, I liked the Jamaican one and her friend,' he said. 'The last two. Although I didn't think her friend ... what was her name again?'

'Francesca,' said Sharon. She looked down at her clipboard to make sure she had the right one. 'Candy is the Jamaican. Men like the black girls, we all know that they are popular.'

'Yes, well, that Francesca, I didn't think she was going to bother doing her audition, but she's definitely pretty and her boobs pointed upwards, unlike some of the others.' He shook his head. 'Cow's udders and fried eggs. You'd think they'd do something about it.'

'Yes, to be fair,' Jake said, 'it seems Sharon saved the best until last, Tony. Do you want to rewind the monitors and have a look? They weren't bad at all.' He looked up at Sharon; he didn't want to sound too enthusiastic.

'No, don't bother, I've seen more than enough.' Tony poured them all a well-earned drink. The others continued discussing the women. Tony finished his drink and left them to it – it was Sharon's project and he'd had enough of it.

Sharon had given a few of them jobs, and to start with they were doing the graveyard shift. There weren't a lot of people there, but they were paid decent wages. A lot of the regular strippers and pole dancers also got the added bonus of tips. The men would beckon the strippers towards the end of the stage and pop a twenty or a fifty pound note down their cleavage or in their stocking top. As long as it was a quick exchange and no fondling, Sharon let it go.

Mainly, when Sharon was there, the men would leave their tips on the side of the stage, like naughty schoolboys, waiting for Sharon's frosty glare. The tips were not only a welcome extra, but boosted the women's confidence and made them feel popular and sexy.

   ✦   

Peace and quiet reigned and the months rolled by. Each and every one of Tony's clubs was thriving. The money was rolling in, profits were being made and life was on the up. So why was Jake so concerned about Tony?

'Oh, God. No, Jake, love, please don't tell me things are too quiet and he needs to start another war or something to create a little excitement.' Sharon was in the office with Jake, while he was having his usual bacon sandwich and coffee. Sharon was looking through the stock sheets of champagne, and working out her next order.

'No, I don't think so, Sharon, but you know he gets a bit restless at times, and I guess this is just one of those times.'

'Why?' said Sharon. 'He's a man with everything. Women fall at his feet, he's handsome …' Sharon saw the look on Jake's face. 'He's not my type, of course. What I mean is, he's rich, successful, feared and loved; what more could anyone want?' Sharon heaved a deep sigh; it seemed ridiculous to her.

'Well, he's still hankering after that meeting with Ralph Gold and, to be fair, this year has whizzed by and we've heard nothing, yet. We'll just have to wait and see if he does have a slot in his diary, maybe that is what is on Tony's mind.'

'So, it's up to you to convince Tony that this is the calm before the storm, and he should enjoy the break before all the new challenges he's desperate for are put before him.' Sharon gave Jake a kiss on the cheek and left. Jake picked up his coffee mug and took the last gulp. Maybe Sharon was right. Time to recharge the batteries. Tony hadn't had a holiday since their trip to Italy, last year. All he had done was work.

Even Jake and Sharon had been away; they'd needed some time together. It felt like his marriage was a little strained, these days. Apart from Sharon working at the clubs and going out with Ashley, he felt another man's name kept popping up in conversation, and whenever Sharon did the banking, she seemed to come back smiling. He didn't want to say anything; after the fuss he'd made about Ashley, he thought he might just be being paranoid.

In one way, Sharon was right. Tony and Jake had reached the top of their game. They were well-established, successful and wealthy. But, while Jake was worried about Tony, he also felt a pang of his own, deep inside. What was missing in both of their lives?

Christmas was looming again; it seemed like only yesterday the Christmas trees were being ordered for all of the clubs, and arrangements were being made for the staff bonuses and parties.

Elle was taking on the role of dealing with the Christmas card lists and main presents, while organizing her own festive Christmas lunch for Tony, Jake and Sharon.

Every now and again, she went to Tony's large mansion house. The house had CCTV monitors and lots of alarmed security installed, but Elle still thought there was nothing like the personal touch, and so would call in now and again just to check things over. She knew it was a waste of time, because nothing had changed, but she still felt like a part of Tony's support network.

The decorators had done an excellent job, and the designers had filled it with beautiful furniture and ornaments. It was a dream home. The only problem was that Tony didn't live in it. She felt it was a waste, really, but from his point of view, she supposed it was a good investment.

He had stayed there maybe five times during the year. He had created a study and filled it with old account books and personal documents, and had then bolted it and put a padlock on it. Only Elle knew that, inside that study of his, was the blue folder from the social services, containing information about his childhood. She presumed he wanted that kind of information miles away from anyone. This was the other side of Tony Lambrianu. This was Antonias, the man the newspapers and the starlets never saw.

So, the house was decorated and furnished but all the furniture was covered in dust sheets; the place was just waiting for life to be breathed into it.

Elle had been surprised that he hadn't used it as a weekend getaway or a large party palace for his lady friends, but no. No woman apart from herself and Sharon ever set foot in the place. When Roxy had found out about his house, she naturally assumed she would be invited to go and see it, probably hoping and crossing her fingers that Tony had at last had come to his senses and decided he loved her. This would be their home, and this was his way of telling her, she was sure.

The worst part of all this was Tony showing preference to another 'love'; his favourite at the moment seemed to be the lovely Linda. She was a well-known model, who took Tony to all the right parties to meet all of the right people. She also felt she was in the running to become Mrs Lambrianu. Linda was showcasing him to her friends; the only problem with that was now Tony had been introduced to these love-struck models, he was also sleeping with most of them!

He knew Roxy used cocaine and he never questioned her about it. He knew a lot of the other models used similar drugs, like speed, to keep their weight down. It speeded up their metabolism and helped them get through the twelve-, sometimes fourteen-hour days, sitting in front of a camera and changing costumes. It seemed obvious to Elle that these women were nothing more than Tony's playthings, and definitely not the sort of woman he would settle down with.

She was surprised one afternoon when he had turned up at her bungalow, out of the blue. During their catch-up he had mentioned a woman he had met at a party, last Christmas. His tone was different, and he seemed remorseful about not knowing who she was. Then, suddenly, he had snapped out of it and left. She felt he had needed to get it off his chest and needed to speak to 'mum', or someone closely related to that word.

ॐ◊ॐ

'Will you two be showing your faces at the party tonight?' said Sharon. 'These dancers do work for you, you know, maybe you should put in an appearance.'

Tonight was the club's Christmas party for the strippers. None of them had ever met Tony; he had always given the revue nights a wide berth. He concentrated more on the casino in the early part of the week, but was still the host of the weekend party nights at the club.

'Why do you need me there? You're in charge. You're their boss, Sharon,' said Tony. It was becoming the busiest time of the year again and if last year was anything to go by, it was going to be hectic.

'Because, you poor tired old men, I'm their boss but they work at Lambrianu's.' Sharon was adamant they should attend. If nothing else, it was good manners.

Tony wasn't keen. The thought of smiling and standing around his employees didn't exactly excite him, even though he could see Sharon's point. He looked at Jake. 'What do you think? Shall we make the effort and show our faces?'

'We could have one drink, Tony; wish them all merry Christmas, then leave. That way, they'll have all met the man behind the myth.'

That was it settled, then, and Sharon seemed content with that. She went off to check the arrangements for the party.

'I have to go, boss,' said Jake.

'Anywhere interesting?'

'I have a meeting with a jeweller for Sharon's Christmas present. I'm hoping this will pacify her so I don't have to go to another one of her sister's parties. God, I remember last year; it was painful and my digestive system suffered for days.'

Tony laughed. 'Price of love, eh?'

Jake rolled his eyes. 'I'll be back in half an hour or so.'

Tony watched Jake leave, and then something occurred to him. The last time Jake had to go to Sharon's sister's party was the night he had gone to Stan's pub to collect some money. Was it really a year since then? A smile crossed his face, 'Cinderella', that's what Jake had called his mystery woman from the beer garden. He found himself thinking back to that night and wondering what she was doing now.

He wondered if she had ever thought about him; there had never been any kind of feedback from that night, so maybe Jake was right. She didn't know who he was or she was married.

Tony frowned, maybe she was married and he had been a bit of drunken fun. He knew how that felt; he had done it many times himself. It felt different being on the other end of things, for a change.

Christmas, although people looked forward to it and scrimped and saved all year around to make it a day to remember, seemed like a sad, lonely time, as well; maybe that was why people made such an effort.

Tony picked up his pen and continued making his lists

for how much cheap champagne he would need to substitute for the good stuff. People were always drunk at Christmas and after a couple of bottles never realised what they were drinking. They were so thirsty from all that dancing they seemed to pick up their glasses and swill back whatever was in them.

After a while he put his pen down again and poured himself a whisky. As he nursed his drink, his thoughts wandered back to last year and his encounter with the beautiful stranger in the beer garden. For the first time in a long time, he had felt like a man. He wasn't famous Tony Lambrianu. He was just some random guy with a woman who wanted him, just him. Not for who or what he was, but just for being a man who had taken her fancy and with whom the chemistry was right.

Well, that was one Christmas memory to cherish. He wondered to himself if he would ever have any more to look back on as fondly.

As he pondered, the telephone rang.

He picked it up. 'Lambrianu's.'

'Tony, is that you, son? Ralph Gold. I have a free appointment in my diary. Let's talk.'

'Of course, Ralph, I'll just get my diary and make sure I'm available.' Tony's hands were shaking; he had waited so long for this call.

'I'll give you that one, son, nice try. Don't bother looking in your diary, this is a one-off opportunity. I'll send you the date, time and place of the meeting. If you turn up, you do and if not … well, you go to the back of the queue.' Ralph hung up.

Tony put the telephone down. He was still shaking, but bursting with excitement. Jeez, what a Christmas present.

Just then, Jake pushed the office door open. 'Mission accomplished,' he said. 'I guarantee my wife will love her Christmas present.'

'Never mind that,' said Tony.

Jake looked at Tony and took in the excitement on his

face. 'What's up with you? What's happened?'

'Ralph Gold has just got off the telephone. He's arranging a meeting. For fuck's sake, Jake, we've done it! We have bloody done it!' Tony was shouting at the top of his voice. Jake laughed and they hugged. This was a dream come true.

'Tonight is my lucky night. We're going to the casino.'

'What about the party? We have to show our faces there, first.' Jake was grinning broadly.

'Oh, God, yes, I forgot about that.' Tony looked deflated.

'It's your lucky night, Tony. One drink with the troops and we're gone. You never know, you might even meet a lucky lady!'

Tony nodded. 'You're right, Jake. I don't care, let's have a drink, have some fun. The next year is going to be fantastic.' Tony put his hand up to give Jake a high five. They were grinning at each other like two schoolboys. 'Mind you,' he said, 'not a word to anyone else about this meeting, not until we get all the details, just in case something goes wrong.'

'What's going to go wrong? It's fantastic news.'

'It's our fantastic news and I couldn't have done it without you, brother.'

Jake refilled Tony's glass and poured a whisky for himself. He held his glass up in salute. 'Here's to you,' he said, 'the luckiest bastard that ever lived!'

'Tony laughed and they clinked glasses. 'To us!' he said, and they each took a drink.

Jake shook his head. 'Christ, you did it. You actually pulled it off.'

'Tonight, I feel like the world is my oyster and I could rule the world. I'm Tony Lambrianu, the luckiest man alive, and tonight is my lucky night!'

ABOUT THE AUTHOR

Gillian Godden is a Northern-born medical secretary for NHS England. She spent thirty years of her life in the East End of London, hearing stories about the local striptease pubs. Now in Yorkshire, she is an avid reader who lives with her dog, Susie.

Printed in Great Britain
by Amazon